L. T. Meade, Clifford Halifax

Dr. Rumsey's patient

a very strange story

L. T. Meade, Clifford Halifax

Dr. Rumsey's patient
a very strange story

ISBN/EAN: 9783744741507

Printed in Europe, USA, Canada, Australia, Japan

Cover: Foto ©Andreas Hilbeck / pixelio.de

More available books at **www.hansebooks.com**

Dr. Rumsey's Patient

A VERY STRANGE STORY

BY

L. T. MEAD

AND

DR. HALIFAX

JOINT AUTHORS OF "STORIES FROM THE DIARY OF A DOCTOR"

———————

NEW YORK

HURST & COMPANY

PUBLISHERS

DR. RUMSEY'S PATIENT.

CHAPTER I.

Two young men in flannels were standing outside the door of the Red Doe in the picturesque village of Grandcourt. The village contained one long and straggling street. The village inn was covered with ivy, wistaria, flowering jessamine, monthly roses, and many other creepers. The flowers twined round old-fashioned windows, and nodded to the guests when they awoke in the morning and breathed perfume upon them as they retired to bed at night. In short, the Inn was an ideal one, and had from time immemorial found favor with reading parties, fishermen, and others who wanted to combine country air and the pursuit of health with a certain form of easy amusement. The two men who now stood in the porch were undergraduates from Balliol. There was nothing in the least remarkable about their appearance— they looked like what they were, good-hearted, keen-witted young Englishmen of the day. The time was evening, and as the Inn faced due west the whole place was bathed in warm sunshine.

"This heat is tremendous and there is no air," said Everett, the younger of the students. "How can you stand that sun beating on your head, Frère? I'm for indoors."

"Right," replied Frère. "It is cool enough in the parlor."

As he spoke he took a step forward and gazed down the winding village street. There was a look of pleased expectation in his eyes. He seemed to be watching for some one. A girl appeared, walking slowly up the street. Frère's eye began to dance. Everett, who was about to go into the shady parlor, gave him a keen glance—and for some reason his eyes also grew bright with expectation.

"There's something worth looking at," he exclaimed in a laughing voice.

"What did you say?" asked Frère gruffly.

"Nothing, old man—at least nothing special. I say, doesn't Hetty look superb?"

"You've no right to call her Hetty."

Everett gave a low whistle.

"I rather fancy I have," he answered—"she gave me leave this morning."

"Impossible," said Frère. He turned pale under all his sunburn, and bit his lower lip. "Don't you find the sun very hot?" he asked.

"No, it is sinking into the west—the great heat is over. Let us go and enliven this little charmer."

"I will," said Frère suddenly. "You had better stay here where you are. It is my right," he added. "I was about to tell you so, when she came in view."

"Your right?" cried Everett; he looked disturbed.

Frere did not reply, but strode quickly down the village street. A dozen strides brought him up to Hetty's side. She was a beautiful girl, with a face and figure much above her station. Her hat was covered with wild flowers which she had picked in her walk, and coquettishly placed there. She wore a pink dress covered with rosebuds—some wild flowers were stuck into her belt. As Frere advanced to meet her, her laughing eyes were raised to his face—there was a curious mixture of timidity and audacity in their glance.

"I have a word to say to you," he accosted her in a gruff tone. "What right had you to give Everett leave to call you Hetty?"

The timidity immediately left the bright eyes, and a slight expression of anger took its place.

"Because I like to distribute my favors, Mr. Horace."

She quickened her pace as she spoke. Everett, who had been standing quite still in the porch watching the little scene, came out to meet the pair. Hetty flushed crimson when she saw him; she raised her dancing, charming dark eyes to his face, then looked again at Frere, who turned sullenly away.

"I hope, gentlemen, you have had good sport," said the rustic beauty, in her demure voice.

"Excellent," replied Everett.

They had now reached the porch, which was entwined all over with honeysuckle in full flower. A great spray of the fragrant flower nearly touched the girl's charming face. She glanced again at Frere. He would not meet her eyes. Her whole face sparkled with the feminine love of teasing.

"Why is he so jealous?" she whispered to herself. "It would be fun to punish him. I like him better than Mr. Everett, but I'll punish him."

"Shall I give you a buttonhole?" she said, looking at Everett.

"If you'll be so kind," he replied.

She raised her eyes to the honeysuckle over her head, selected a spray with extreme care, and handed it to him demurely. He asked her to place it in his buttonhole; she looked again at Frere,—he would not go away, but neither would he bring himself to glance at her. She bent her head to search in the bodice of her dress for a pin, found one, and then with a laughing glance of her eyes into Everett's handsome face, complied with his request.

The young fellow blushed with pleasure, then he glanced at Frere, and a feeling of compunction smote him—he strode abruptly into the house.

"Hetty, what do you mean by this sort of thing?" said Frere the moment they were alone.

"I mean this, Mr. Horace: I am still my own mistress."

"Great Scot! of course you are; but what do

you mean by this sort of trifling? It was only this morning that you told me you loved me. Look here, Hetty, I'm in no humor to be trifled with; I can't and won't stand it. I'll make you the best husband a girl ever had, but listen to me, I have the devil's own temper when it is roused. For God's sake don't provoke it. If you don't love me, say so, and let there be an end of it."

"I wish you wouldn't speak so loudly," said Hetty, pouting her lips and half crying. "Of course I like you; I—well, yes, I suppose I love you. I was thinking of you all the afternoon. See what I gathered for you—this bunch of heart's-ease. There's meaning in heart's-ease—there's none in honeysuckle."

Frere's brow cleared as if by magic.

"My little darling," he said, fixing his deep-set eyes greedily on the girl's beautiful face. "Forgive me for being such a brute to you, Hetty. Here —give me the flowers."

"No, not until you pay for them. You don't deserve them for being so nasty and suspicious."

"Give me the flowers, Hetty; I promise never to doubt you again."

"Yes, you will; it is your nature to doubt."

"I have no words to say what I feel for you."

Frere's eyes emphasized this statement so emphatically, that the empty-headed girl by his side felt her heart touched for the moment.

"What do you want me to do, Mr. Horace?" she asked, lowering her eyes.

"To give me the flowers, and to be nice to me."

"Come down to the brook after supper, perhaps I'll give them to you then. There's aunt calling me—don't keep me, please." She rushed off.

"Hetty," said Mrs. Armitage, the innkeeper's wife, "did I hear you talking to Mr. Horace Frere in the porch?"

"Yes, Aunt Fanny, you did," replied Hetty.

"Well, look here, your uncle and I won't have it. Just because you're pretty——"

Hetty tossed back her wealth of black curls.

"It's all right," she said in a whisper, her eyes shining as she spoke. "He wants me to be his wife—he asked me this morning."

"He doesn't mean that, surely," said Mrs. Armitage, incredulous and pleased.

"Yes, he does; he'll speak to uncle to-morrow—that is, if I'll say 'Yes.' He says he has no one to consult—he'll make me a lady—he has plenty of money."

"Do you care for him, Hetty?"

"Oh, don't ask me whether I do or not, Aunt Fanny—I'm sure I can't tell you."

Hetty moved noisily about. She put plates and dishes on a tray preparatory to taking them into the parlor for the young men's supper.

"Look here," said her aunt, "I'll see after the parlor lodgers to-night." She lifted the tray as she spoke.

Hetty ran up to her bedroom. She took a little square of glass from its place on the wall and gazed earnestly at the reflection of her own charming face. Presently she put the glass down, locked her hands together, went over to the open window and looked out.

"Shall I marry him?" she thought. "He has plenty of money—he loves me right enough. If I were his wife, I'd be a lady—I needn't worry about household work any more. I hate household work—I hate drudgery. I want to have a fine time, with nothing to do but just to think of my dress and how I look. He has plenty of money, and he loves me—he says he'll make me his wife as soon as ever I say the word. Uncle and aunt would be pleased, too, and the people in the village would say I'd made a good match. Shall I marry him? I don't love him a bit, but what does that matter?"

She sighed—the color slightly faded on her blooming cheeks—she poked her head out of the little window.

"I don't love him," she said to herself. "When I see Mr. Awdrey my heart beats. Ever since I was a little child I have thought more of Mr. Awdrey than of any one else in all the world. I never told—no, I never told, but I'd rather slave for Mr. Robert Awdrey than be the wife of any one else on earth. What a fool I am! Mr. Awdrey thinks nothing of me, but he is never out of my head, nor out of my heart. My heart aches for him—I'm nearly mad sometimes about it all. Perhaps I'll see him to-night if I go down to the brook. He's sure to pass the brook on his way to the Court. Mr. Everett likes me too, I know, and he's a gentleman as well as Mr. Frere. Oh, dear, they both worry me more than please me. I'd give twenty men like them for one sight of the young Squire. Oh, what folly all this is!"

She went again and stood opposite to her little looking-glass.

"The young ladies up at the Court haven't got a face like mine," she murmured. "There isn't any one all over the place has a face like mine. I wonder if Mr. Awdrey really thinks it pretty? Why should I worry myself about Mr. Frere? I wonder if Mr. Awdrey would mind if I married him—would it make him jealous? If I thought that, I'd do it fast enough—yes, I declare I would. But of course he wouldn't mind—not one bit; he has scarcely ever said two words to me—not since we were little 'uns together, and pelted each other with apples in uncle's orchard. Oh, Mr. Awdrey, I'd give all the world for one smile from you, but you think nothing at all of poor Hetty. Dear, beautiful Mr. Awdrey—won't you love me even a little—even as you love your dog? Yes, I'll go and walk by the brook after supper. Mr. Frere will meet me there, of course, and perhaps Mr. Awdrey will go by—perhaps he'll be jealous. I'll take my poetry book and sit by the brook just where the forget-me-nots grow. Yes, yes—oh, I wonder if the Squire will go by."

These thoughts no sooner came into Hetty's

brain than she resolved to act upon them. She snatched up a volume of L. E. L.'s poems—their weak and lovelorn phrases exactly suited her style and order of mind—and ran quickly down to a dancing rivulet which ran its merry course about a hundred yards back of the Inn. She sat by the bank, pulled a great bunch of forget-me-nots, laid them on the open pages of her book, and looked musingly down at the flowers. Footsteps were heard crunching the underwood at the opposite side. A voice presently sounded in her ears. Hetty's heart beat loudly.

"How do you do?" said the voice.

"Good-evening, Mr. Robert," she replied.

Her tone was demure and extremely respectful. She started to her feet, letting her flowers drop as she did so. A blush suffused her lovely face, her dancing eyes were raised for a quick moment, then as suddenly lowered. She made a beautiful picture. The young man who stood a few feet away from her, with the running water dividing them, evidently thought so. He had a boyish figure—a handsome, manly face. His eyes were very dark, deeply set, and capable of much thought. He looked every inch the gentleman.

"Is Armitage in?" he asked after a pause.

"I don't know, Mr. Robert, I'll go and inquire if you like."

"No, it doesn't matter. The Squire asked me to call and beg of your uncle to come to the Court to-morrow morning. Will you give him the message?"

"Yes, Mr. Robert."

There was a perceptible pause. Hetty looked down at the water. Awdrey looked at her.

"Good-evening," he said then.

"Good-evening, sir," she replied.

He turned and walked slowly up the narrow path which led toward the Court.

"His eyes told me to-night that he thought me pretty," muttered Hetty to herself, "why doesn't he say it with his lips? I—I wish I could make him. Oh, is that you, Mr. Frere?"

"Yes, Hetty. I promised to come, and I am here. The evening is a perfect one, let us follow the stream a little way."

Hetty was about to say "No," when suddenly lifting her eyes, she observed that the young Squire had paused under the shade of a great elm-tree a little further up the bank. A quick idea darted into her vain little soul. She would walk past the Squire without pretending to see him, in Frere's company. Frere should make love to her in the Squire's presence. She gave her lover a coy and affectionate glance.

"Yes, come," she said: "it is pretty by the stream; perhaps I'll give you some forget-me-nots presently."

"I want the heart's-ease which you have already picked for me," said Frere.

"Oh, there's time enough."

Frere advanced a step, and laid his hand on the girl's arm.

"Listen," he said: "I was never more in earnest in my life. I love you with all my heart and soul. I love you madly. I want you for my wife. I mean to marry you, come what may. I have plenty of money and you are the wife of all others for me. You told me this morning that you loved me, Hetty. Tell me again; say that you love me better than any one else in the world."

Hetty paused, she raised her dark eyes; the Squire was almost within earshot.

"I suppose I love you—a little," she said, in a whisper.

"Then give me a kiss—just one."

She walked on. Frere followed.

"Give me a kiss—just one," he repeated.

"Not to-night," she replied, in a demure voice.

"Yes, you must—I insist."

"Don't, Mr. Frere," she called out sharply, uttering a cry as she spoke.

He didn't mind her. Overcome by his passion he caught her suddenly in his arms, and pressed his lips many times to hers.

"Hold, sir! What are you doing?" shouted Awdrey's voice from the opposite side of the bank.

"By heaven, what is that to you?" called Frere back.

He let Hetty go with some violence, and retreated one or two steps in his astonishment. His face was crimson up to the roots of his honest brow.

Awdrey leaped across the brook. "You will please understand that you take liberties with Miss

Armitage at your peril," he said. "What right have you to take such advantage of an undefended girl? Hetty, I will see you home."

Hetty's eyes danced with delight. For a moment Frere felt too stunned to speak.

"Come with me, Hetty," said Awdrey, putting a great restraint upon himself, but speaking with irritation. "Come—you should be at home at this hour."

"You shall answer to me for this, whoever you are," said Frere, whose face was white with passion.

"My name is Awdrey," said the Squire; "I will answer you in a way you don't like if you don't instantly leave this young girl alone."

"Confound your interference," said Frere. "I am not ashamed of my actions. I can justify them. I am going to marry Miss Armitage."

"Is that true, Hetty?" said Awdrey, looking at the girl in some astonishment.

"No, there isn't a word of it true," answered Hetty, stung by a look on the Squire's face. "I don't want to have anything to do with him—he shan't kiss me. I—I'll have nothing to do with him." She burst into tears.

"I'll see you home," said Awdrey.

CHAPTER II.

THE Awdreys of "The Court" could trace their descent back to the Norman Conquest. They were a proud family with all the special characteristics which mark races of long descent. Among the usual accompaniments of race, was given to them the curse of heredity. A strange and peculiar doom hung over the house. It had descended now from father to son during many generations. How it had first raised its gorgon head no one could tell. People said that it had been sent as a punishment for the greed of gold. An old ancestor, more than a hundred and fifty years ago, had married a West Indian heiress. She had colored blood in her veins, a purse of enormous magnitude, a deformed figure, and, what was more to the point, a particularly crooked and obtuse order of mind. She did her duty by her descendants, leaving to each of them a gift. To one, deformity of person—to another, a stammering tongue—to a third, a squint—to a fourth, imbecility. In each succeeding generation, at least one man and woman of the house of Awdrey had cause to regret the gold which had certainly brought a curse with it. But beyond and above all these

things, it was immediately after the West Indian's
entrance into the family that that strange doom began to assail the male members of the house which
was now more dreaded than madness.   The doom
was unique and curious. It consisted of one remarkable phase.   There came upon those on whom
it descended an extraordinary and complete lapse
of memory for the grave events of life, accompanied
by perfect retention of memory for all minor
matters.   This curious phase once developed, other
idiosyncrasies immediately followed.   The victim's
moral sense became weakened—all physical energy
departed—a curious lassitude of mind and body
became general. The victim did not in the least
know that there was anything special the matter
with him, but as a rule the doomed man either became idiotic, or died before the age of thirty.

All the great physicians of their time had been
consulted with regard to this curious family trait,
but in the first place no one could understand it,
in the second no possible cure could be suggested
as a remedy. The curse was supposed to be due
to a brain affection, but brain affections in the old
days were considered to be_ special visitations
from God, and men of science let them alone.

In their early life, the Awdreys were particularly
bright, clever sharp fellows, endowed with excellent animal spirits, and many amiable traits of
character. They were chivalrous to women, kind
to children, full of warm affections, and each and
all of them possessed much of the golden gift of

hope. As a rule the doom of the house came upon each victim with startling suddenness. One of the disappointments of life ensued—an unfortunate love affair—the death of some beloved member—a money loss. The victim lost all memory of the event. No words, no explanations could revive the dead memory—the thing was completely blotted out from the phonograph of the brain. Immediately afterward followed the mental and physical decay. The girls of the family quite escaped the curse. It was on the sons that it invariably descended.

Up to the present time, however, Robert Awdrey's father had lived to confute the West Indian's dire curse. His father had married a Scotch lassie, with no bluer blood in her veins than that which had been given to her by some rugged Scotch ancestors. Her health of mind and body had done her descendants much good. Even the word "nerves" had been unknown to this healthy-minded daughter of the North—her children had all up to the present escaped the family curse, and it was now firmly believed at the Court that the spell was broken, and that the West Indian's awful doom would leave the family. The matter was too solemn and painful to be alluded to except under the gravest conditions, and young Robert Awdrey, the heir to the old place and all its belongings, was certainly the last person to speak of it.

Robert's father was matter-of-fact to the back bone, but Robert himself was possessed of an essentially reflective temperament. Had he been less healthily brought up by his stout old grandmother. and by his mother, he might have given way to morbid musings. Circumstances, however, were all in his favor, and at the time when this strange story really opens, he was looking out at life with a heart full of hope and a mind filled with noble ambitions. Robert was the only son—he had two sisters, bright, good-natured, every-day sort of girls. As a matter of course his sisters adored him. They looked forward to his career with immense pride. He was to stand for Parliament at the next general election. His brains belonged to the highest order of intellect. He had taken a double first at the University—there was no position which he might not hope to assume.

Robert had all the chivalrous instincts of his race toward women. As he walked quickly home now with Hetty by his side, his blood boiled at the thought of the insult which had been offered to her. Poor, silly little Hetty was nothing whatever to him except a remarkably pretty village girl Her people, however, were his father's tenants; he felt it his duty to protect her. When he parted with her just outside the village inn, he said a few words.

"You ought not to allow those young men to take liberties with you, Hetty," he said. "Now, go home. Don't be out so late again in the future, and don't forget to give your uncle my father's message."

She bent her head, and left him without replying. She did not even thank him. He watched her until she disappeared into the house, then turned sharply and walked up the village street home with a vigorous step.

He had come to the spot where he had parted with Frere, and was just about to leap the brook, when that young man started suddenly from under a tree, and stood directly in his path.

"I must ask you to apologize to me," he said.

Awdrey flushed.

"What do you mean?" he replied.

"What I say. My intentions toward Miss Armitage are perfectly honest. She promised to marry me this morning. When you chose to interfere, I was kissing my future wife."

"If that is really the case, I beg your pardon," said Awdrey; "but then," he continued, looking full at Frere, "Hetty Armitage denies any thought of marrying you."

"She does, does she?" muttered Frere. His face turned white.

"One word before you go," said Awdrey. "Miss Armitage is a pretty girl——"

"What is that to you?" replied Frere, "I don't mean to discuss her with you."

"You may please yourself about that, but allow me to say one thing. Her uncle is one of my father's oldest and most respected tenants; Hetty is therefore under our protection, and I for one will see that she gets fair play. Any one who

takes liberties with her has got to answer to me.
That's all.   Good-evening."

Awdrey slightly raised his hat, leaped the brook,
and disappeared through the underwood in the
direction of the Court.

Horace Frere stood and watched him.

His rage was now almost at white heat. He
was madly in love, and was therefore not quite responsible for his own actions.   He was determined
at any cost to make Hetty his wife. The Squire's
interference awoke the demon of jealousy in his
heart. He had patiently borne Everett's marked
attentions to the girl of his choice—he wondered
now at the sudden passion which filled him. He
walked back to the inn feeling exactly as if the
devil were driving him.

"I'll have this thing out with Hetty before I am
an hour older," he cried aloud.   "She promised
to marry me this very morning. How dare that
jackanapes interfere! What do I care for his position in the place? If he's twenty times the Squire
it's nothing to me. Hetty had the cool cheek to
eat her own words to him in my presence. It's
plain to be seen what the thing means. She's a
heartless flirt—she's flying for higher game than
honest Horace Frere, but I'll put a spoke in her
wheel, and in his wheel too, curse him. He's in
love with the girl himself—that's why he interferes.
Well, she shall choose between him and me to-
night, and if she does choose him it will be all the
worse for him."

As he rushed home, Frere lashed himself into greater and greater fury. Everett was standing inside the porch when the other man passed him roughly by.

"I say, Frere, what's up?" called Everett, taking the pipe out of his mouth.

"Curse you, don't keep me, I want to speak to Miss Armitage."

Everett burst into a somewhat discordant laugh.

"Your manners are not quite to be desired at the present moment, old man," he said. "Miss Armitage seems to have a strangely disquieting effect upon her swains."

"I do not intend to discuss her with you, Everett. I must speak to her at once."

Everett laughed again.

"She seems to be a person of distinction," he said. "She has just been seen home with much ceremony by no less a person than Awdrey, of The Court."

"Curse Awdrey and all his belongings. Do you know where she is?"

A sweet, high-pitched voice within the house now made itself heard.

"I can see you in Aunt's parlor if you like, Mr. Horace."

"Yes."

Frere strode into the house—a moment later he was standing opposite to Hetty in the little hot gaslit parlor.

Hetty had evidently been crying. Her tears

had brought shadows under her eyes—they added pathos to her lovely face, giving it a look of depth which it usually lacked. Frere gave her one glance, then he felt his anger dropping from him like a mantle.

"For God's sake, Hetty, speak the truth, ' said the poor fellow.

"What do you want me to say, Mr. Horace?" she asked.

Her voice was tremulous, her tears nearly broke forth anew. Frere made a step forward. He would have clasped her to his breast, but she would not allow him.

"No," she said with a sob, "I can't have anything to do with you."

"Hetty, you don't know what you are saying. Hetty, remember this morning."

"I remember it, but I can't go on with it. Forget everything I said—go away—please go away."

"No, I won't go away. By heaven, you shall tell me the truth. Look here, Hetty, I won't be humbugged—you've got to choose at once."

"What do you mean, Mr. Horace?"

"You've got to choose between that fellow and me."

"Between you and the Squire!" exclaimed Hetty.

She laughed excitedly; the bare idea caused her heart to beat wildly. Her laughter nearly drove Frere mad. He strode up to her, took her hands with force, and looked into her frightened eyes.

"Do you love him? The truth, girl, I will have it."

"Let me go, Mr. Horace."

"I won't until you tell me the truth. It is either the Squire or me; I must hear the truth now or never—which is it, Squire Awdrey or me?"

"Oh, I can't help it," said Hetty, bursting into tears—"it's the Squire—oh, sir, let me go."

CHAPTER III.

FRERE stood perfectly still for a moment after Hetty had spoken, then without a word he turned and left her. Everett was still standing in the porch. Everett had owned to himself that he had a decided penchant for the little rustic beauty, but Frere's fierce passion cooled his. He did not feel particularly inclined, however, to sympathize with his friend.

"How rough you are, Frere!" he said angrily; "you've almost knocked the pipe out of my mouth a second time this evening."

Frere went out into the night without uttering a syllable.

"Where are you off to?" called Everett after him.

"What is that to you?" was shouted back.

Everett said something further. A strong and very emphatic oath left Frere's lips in reply. The innkeeper, Armitage, was passing the young man at the moment. He stared at him, wondering at the whiteness of his face, and the extraordinary energy of his language. Armitage went indoors to supper, and thought no more of the circumstance. He was destined, however, to remember it later. Everett continued to smoke his pipe with philosophical calm. He hoped against hope that pretty little Hetty might come and stand in the porch with him. Finding she did not appear, he resolved to go out and look for his friend. He was leaving the Inn when Armitage called after him:

"I beg your pardon, Mr. Everett, but will you be out late?"

"I can't say," replied Everett, stopping short; "why?"

"Because if so, sir, you had better take the latchkey. We're going to shut up the whole place early to-night; the wife is dead beat, and Hetty is not quite well."

"I'm sorry for that," said Everett, after a pause; "well, give me the key. I dare say I'll return quite soon; I am only going out to meet Mr. Frere."

Armitage gave the young man the key and returned to the house.

Meanwhile Frere had wandered some distance from the pretty little village and the charming rustic inn. His mind was out of tune with all harmony and beauty. He was in the sort of condition when men will do mad deeds not knowing in the least why they do them. Hetty's words had, as he himself expressed it, "awakened the very devil in him."

"She has owned it," he kept saying to himself. "Yes, I was right in my conjecture—he wants her himself. Much he regards honor and behaving straight to a woman. I'll show him a thing or two. Jove, if I meet him to-night, he'll rue it."

The great solemn plain of Salisbury lay not two
miles off. Frere made for its broad downs without knowing in the least that he was doing so. By
and by, he found himself on a vast open space,
spreading sheer away to the edge of the horizon.
The moon, which had been bright when he had
started on his walk, was now about to set—it was
casting long shadows on the ground; his own
shadow in gigantic dimensions walked by his side
as he neared the vicinity of the plain. He walked
on and on; the further he went the more fiercely
did his blood boil within him. All his life hitherto
he had been calm, collected, reasonable. He had
taken the events of life with a certain rude philoso-
phy. He had intended to do well for himself—to
carve out a prosperous career for himself, but although he had subdued his passions both at college
and at school, he had never blinded his eyes to the
fact that there lived within his breast, ready to be
awakened when the time came, a devil. Once, as
a child, he had given way to this mad fury. He
had flung a knife at his brother, wounding him in
the temple, and almost killing him. The sight of
the blood and the fainting form of his only brother
had awakened his better self. -He had lived
through agony while his brother's life hung in the
balance. The lad eventually recovered, to die in
a year or two of something else, but Frere never
forgot that time of mental torture. From that
hour until the present, he had kept his "devil,"
as he used to call it, well in check.

It was rampant to-night, however—he knew it, he took no pains to conceal the fact from his own heart—he rather gloried in the knowledge.

He walked on and on, across the plain.

Presently in the dim distance he heard Everett calling him.

"Frere, I say Frere, stop a moment, I'll come up to you."

A man who had been collecting underwood, and was returning home with a bagful, suddenly appeared in Frere's path. Hearing the voice of the man shouting behind he stopped.

"There be some-un calling yer," he said in his rude dialect.

Frere stared at the man blindly. He looked behind him, saw Everett's figure silhouetted against the sky, and then took wildly to his heels; he ran as if something evil were pursuing him.

At this moment the moon went completely down, and the whole of the vast plain lay in dim gray shadow. Frere had not the least idea where he was running. He and Everett had spent whole days on the plain revelling in the solitude and the splendid air, but they had neither of them ever visited it at night before. The whole place was strange, uncanny, unfamiliar. Frere soon lost his bearings. He tumbled into a hole, uttered an exclamation of pain, and raised himself with some difficulty.

"Hullo!" said a voice, "you might have broken your leg. What are you doing here?"

Frere stood upright; a man slighter and taller than himself faced him about three feet away. Frere could not recognize the face, but he knew the tone.

"What the devil have you come to meet me for?" he said. "You've come to meet a madman. Turn back and go home, or it will be the worse for you."

"I don't understand you," said Awdrey.

Frere put a tremendous restraint upon himself.

"Look here," he said, "I don't want to injure you, upon my soul I don't, but there's a devil in me to-night, and you had better go home without any more words."

"I shall certainly do nothing of the kind," answered Awdrey. "The plain is as open to me as to you. If you dislike me take your own path."

"My path is right across where you are standing," said Frere.

"Well, step aside and leave me alone!"

It was so dark the men only appeared as shadows one to the other. Their voices, each of them growing hot and passionate, seemed scarcely to belong to themselves. Frere came a step nearer to Awdrey.

"You shall have it," he cried. "By the heaven above, I don't want to spare you. Let me tell you what I think of you."

"Sir," said Awdrey, "I don't wish to have anything to do with you—leave me, go about your business."

"I will after I've told you a bit of my mind.

You're a confounded sneak—you're a liar—you're no gentleman. Shall I tell you why you interfered between me and my girl to-night—because you want her for yourself!"

This sudden accusation so astounded Awdrey that he did not even reply. He came to the conclusion that Frere was really mad.

"You forget yourself," he said, after a long pause. "I excuse you, of course, I don't even know what you are talking about!"

"Yes, you do, you black-hearted scoundrel. You interfered between Hetty Armitage and me because you want her yourself—she told me so much to-night!"

"She told you!—it's you who lie."

"She told me—so much for your pretended virtue. Get out of the way, or I'll strike you to the earth, you dog!"

Frere's wild passion prevented Awdrey's rising. The accusation made against him was so preposterous that it did not even rouse his anger.

"I'm sorry for you," he said after a pause, "you labor under a complete misapprehension. I wish to protect Hetty Armitage as I would any other honest girl. Keep out of my path now, sir, I wish to continue my walk."

"By Heaven, that you never shall."

Frere uttered a wild, maniacal scream. The next instant he had closed with Awdrey, and raising a heavy cane which he carried, aimed it full at the young Squire's head.

"I could kill you, you brute, you scoundrel, you low, base seducer," he shouted.

For a moment Awdrey was taken off his guard. But the next instant the fierce blood of his race awoke within him. Frere was no mean antagonist —he was a stouter, heavier, older man than Awdrey. He had also the strength which mad-ness confers. After a momentary struggle he flung Awdrey to the ground. The two young men rolled over together. Then with a quick and sudden movement Awdrey sprang to his feet. He had no weapon to defend himself with but a slight stick which he carried. Frere let him go for a moment to spring upon him again like a tiger. A sudden memory came to Awdrey's aid—a memory which was to be the undoing of his entire life. He had been told in his boyhood by an old prize-fighter who taught him boxing, that the most effective way to use a stick in defending himself from an enemy was to use it as a bayonet.

"Prod your foe in the mouth," old Jim had said —"be he dog or man, prod him in the mouth. Grasp your stick in both hands, and when he comes to you, prod him in the mouth or neck."

The words flashed distinctly now through Awdrey's brain. When Frere raised his heavy stick to strike him he grasped his own slender weapon and rushed forward. He aimed full at Frere's open mouth. The stick went a few inches higher and entered the unfortunate man's right eye. He fell with a sudden groan to the ground.

In a moment Awdrey's passion was over. He bent over the prostrate man and examined the wound which he had made. Frere lay perfectly quiet; there was an awful silence about him. The dark shadows of the night brooded heavily over the place. Awdrey did not for several moments realize that something very like a murder had been committed. He bent over the prostrate man—he took his limp hand in his, felt for a pulse—there was none. With trembling fingers he tore open the coat and pressed his hand to the heart—it was strangely still. He bent his ear to listen—there was no sound. Awdrey was scarcely frightened yet. He did not even now in the least realize what had happened. He felt in his pocket for a flask of brandy which he sometimes carried about with him. An oath escaped his lips when he found he had forgotten it. Then taking up his stick he felt softly across the point. The point of the stick was wet—wet with blood. He felt carefully along its edge. The blood extended up a couple of inches. He knew then what had happened. The stick had undoubtedly entered Frere's brain through the eye, causing instant death.

When ths knowledge came to Awdrey he laughed. His laugh sounded queer, but he did not notice its strangeness. He felt again in his pocket—discovered a box of matches which he pulled out eagerly. He struck a match, and by the weird, uncertain light which it cast looked for an instant at the dead face of the man whose life he had taken.

"I don't even know his name," thought Awdrey. "What in the world have I killed him for? Yes, undoubtedly I've killed him. He is dead, poor fellow, as a door-nail. What did I do it for?"

He struck another match, and looked at the end of his stick. The stick had a narrow steel ferrule at the point. Blood bespattered the end of the stick.

"I must bury this witness," said Awdrey to himself.

He blew out the match, and began to move gropingly across the plain. His step was uncertain. He stooped as he walked. Presently he came to a great copse of underwood. Into the very thick of the underwood he thrust his stick.

Having done this, he resolved to go home. Queer noises were ringing in his head. He felt as if devils were pursuing him. He was certain that if he raised his eyes and looked in front of him, he must see the ghost of the dead man. It was early in the night, not yet twelve o'clock. As he entered the grounds of the Court, the stable clock struck twelve.

"I suppose I shall get into a beastly mess about this," thought Awdrey. "I never meant to kill that poor fellow. I ran at him in self-defence. He'd have had my blood if I hadn't his. Shall I see my father about it now? My father is a magistrate; he'll know what's best to be done."

Awdrey walked up to the house. His gait was uncertain and shambling, so little characteristic of him that if any one had met him in the dark he would not have been recognized. He opened one of the side doors of the great mansion with a latch key. The Awdreys were early people—an orderly household who went to roost in good time—the lamps were out in the house—only here and there was a dim illumination suited to the hours of darkness. Awdrey did not meet a soul as he went up some stairs, and down one or two corridors to his own cheerful bedroom. He paused as he turned the handle of his door.

"My father is in bed. There's no use in troubling him about this horrid matter before the morning," he said to himself.

Then he opened the door of his room, and went in.

To his surprise he saw on the threshold, just inside the door, a little note. He picked it up and opened it.

It was from his sister Ann. It ran as follows:

"DEAREST BOB.—I have seen the Cuthberts, and they can join us on the plain to-morrow for a picnic. As you have gone early to bed, I thought I'd let you know in case you choose to get up at cockcrow, and perhaps leave us for the day. Don't forget that we start at two o'clock, and that Margaret will be there. Your loving sister, ANN."

Awdrey found himself reading the note with interest. The excited beating of his heart cooled down. He sank into a chair, took off his cap, and wiped the perspiration from his brow.

"I wouldn't miss Margaret for the world," he said to himself.

A look of pleasure filled his dark gray eyes. A moment or two later he was in bed, and sound asleep. He awoke at his usual hour in the morning. He rose and dressed calmly. He had forgotten all about the murder — the doom of his house had fallen upon him.

CHAPTER IV.

" I wish you would tell me about him, Mr. Awdrey," said Margaret Douglas.

She was a handsome girl, tall and slightly made —her eyes were black as night, her hair had a raven hue, her complexion was a pure olive. She was standing a little apart from a laughing, chattering group of boys and girls, young men and young ladies, with a respectable sprinkling of fathers and mothers, uncles and aunts. Awdrey stood a foot or two away from her—his face was pale, he looked subdued and gentle.

" What can I tell you?" he asked.

" You said you met him last night, poor fellow. The whole thing seems so horrible, and to think of it happening on this very plain, just where we are having our picnic. If I had known it, I would not have come."

" The murder took place several miles from here," said Awdrey. " Quite close to the Court, in fact. I've been over the ground this morning with my father and one of the keepers. The body was removed before we came."

" Didn't it shock you very much?"

"Yes; I am sorry for that unfortunate Everett."

"Who is he? I have not heard of him."

"He is the man whom they think must have done it. There is certainly very grave circumstantial evidence against him. He and Frere were heard quarrelling last night, and Armitage can prove that Everett did not return home until about two in the morning. When he went out he said he was going to follow Frere, who had gone away in a very excited state of mind."

"What about, I wonder?"

"The usual thing," said Awdrey, giving Margaret a quick look, under which she lowered her eyes and faintly blushed.

"Tell me," she said, almost in a whisper. "I am interested—it is such a tragedy."

"It is; it is awful. Sit down here, won't you, or shall we walk on a little way? We shall soon get into shelter if we go down this valley and get under those trees yonder."

"Come then," said Margaret.

She went first, her companion followed her. He looked at her many times as she walked on in front of him. Her figure was full of supple and easy grace, her young steps seemed to speak the very essence of youth and springtime. She appeared scarcely to touch the ground as she walked over it; once she turned, and the full light of her dark eyes made Awdrey's heart leap. Presently she reached the shadow caused by a copse of young trees, and stood still until the Squire came up to her.

"Here's a throne for you, Miss Douglas. Do you see where this tree extends two friendly arms? Do you observe a seat inlaid with moss? Take your throne."

She did so immediately and looked up at him with a smile.

"The throne suits you," he said.

She looked down—her lips faintly trembled—then she raised her eyes.

"Why are you so pale?" he asked anxiously.

"I can't quite tell you," she replied, "except that notwithstanding the beauty of the day, and the summer feeling which pervades the air, I can't get rid of a sort of fear. It may be superstitious of me, but I think it is unlucky to have a picnic on the very plain where a murder was committed."

"You forget over what a wide extent the plain extends," said Awdrey; "but if I had known"—he stopped and bit his lips.

"Never mind," she answered, endeavoring to smile and look cheerful, "any sort of tragedy always affects me to a remarkable degree. I can't help it—I'm afraid there is something in me akin to trouble, but of course it would be folly for us to stay indoors just because that poor young fellow came to a violent end some miles away."

"Yes, it is quite some miles from here—I am truly sorry for him."

"Sit down here, Mr. Awdrey, here at my feet if you like, and tell me about it."

"I will sit at your feet with all the pleasure in

the world, but why should we talk any more on this gruesome subject?"

"That's just it," said Margaret, "if I am to get rid of it, I must know all about it. You said you met him last night?"

"I did," said Awdrey, speaking with unwillingness.

"And you guess why he came by his end?"

"Partly, but not wholly."

"Well, do tell me."

"I will—I'll put it in as few words as possible. You know that little witch Hetty, the pretty niece of the innkeeper Armitage?"

"Hetty Armitage—of course I know her. I tried to get her into my Sunday class, but she wouldn't come."

"She's a silly little creature," said Awdrey.

"She is a very beautiful little creature," corrected Miss Douglas.

"Yes, I am afraid her beauty was too much for this unfortunate Frere's sanity. I came across him last night, or rather they passed me by in the underwood, enacting a love scene. The fact is, he was kissing her. I thought he was taking a liberty and interfered. He told me he intended to mary her—but Hetty denied it. I saw her back to the Inn—she was very silent and depressed. Another man, a handsome fellow, was standing in the porch. It just occurred to me at the time, that perhaps he also was a suitor for her hand, and might be the favored one. She went indoors. On my way home I met Frere again. He tried to pick a quarrel with me, which of course I nipped in the bud. He referred to his firm intention of marrying Hetty Armitage, and when I told him that she had denied the engagement, he said he would go back at once and speak to her. I then returned to the Court.

"The first thing I heard this morning was the news of the murder. My father as magistrate was of course made acquainted with the fact at a very early hour. Poor Everett has been arrested on suspicion, and there's to be a coroner's inquest to-morrow. That is the entire story as far as I know anything about it. Your face is whiter than ever, Miss Douglas. Now keep your word —forget it, since you have heard all the facts of the case."

She looked down again. Presently she raised her eyes, brimful of tears, to his face.

"I cannot forget it," she said. "That poor young fellow—such a fearfully sudden end, and that other poor fellow; surely if he did take away a life it must have been in a moment of terrible madness?"

"That is true," said Awdrey.

"They cannot possibly convict him of murder, can they?"

"My father thinks that the verdict will be manslaughter, or, at the worst, murder under strong provocation; but it is impossible to tell."

Awdrey looked again anxiously at his companion. Her pallor and distress aroused emotion in his breast which he found almost impossible to quiet.

"I'm sorry to my heart that you know about this," he said. "You are not fit to stand any of the roughness of life."

"What folly!" she answered, with passion. "What am I that I should accept the smooth and reject the rough? I tell you what I would like to do. I'd like to go this very moment to see that poor Mr. Everett, in order to tell him how deeply sorry I am for him. To ask him to tell me the story from first to last, from his point of view. To clear him from this awful stain. And I'd like to lay flowers over the breast of that dead boy. Oh, I can't bear it. Why is the world so full of trouble and pain?"

She burst into sudden tears.

"Don't, don't! Oh! Margaret, you're an angel. You're too good for this earth," said Awdrey.

"Nonsense," she answered; "let me have my cry out; I'll be all right in a minute."

Her brief tears were quickly over. She dashed them aside and rose to her feet.

"I hear the children shouting to me," she said. "I'm in no humor to meet them. Where shall we go?"

"This way," said Awdrey quickly; "no one knows the way through this copse but me."

He gave her his hand, pushed aside the trees, and they soon found themselves in a dim little world of soft green twilight. There was a narrow path on which they could not walk abreast. Awdrey now t ok the lead, Margaret following him. After walking for half a mile the wood grew thinner, and they found themselves far away from their compani ns, and on a part of the plain which was quite new ground to Margaret.

"How lovely and enchanting it is here," she said, giving a low laugh of pleasure.

"I am glad you like it," said Awdrey. "I discovered that path to these heights only a week ago. I never told a soul about it. For all you can tell your feet may now be treading on virgin ground."

As Awdrey spoke he panted slightly, and put his hand to his brow.

"Is anything the matter with you?" asked Margaret.

"Nothing; I was never better in my life."

"You don't look well; you're changed."

"Don't say that," he answered, a faint ring of anxiety in his voice.

She gazed at him earnestly.

"You are," she repeated. "I don't quite recognize the expression in your eyes."

"Oh, I'm all right," he replied, "only——"

"Only what? Do tell me."

"I don't want to revert to that terrible tragedy again," he said, after a pause. "There is something, however, in connection with it which surprises myself."

"What is that?"

"I don't seem to feel the horror of it. I feel everything else; your sorrow, for instance—the beauty of the day—the gladness and fulness of life, but I don't feel any special pang about that poor dead fellow. It's queer, is it not?"

"No," said Margaret tenderly. "I know—I quite understand your sensation. You don't feel it simply because you feel it too much—you are slightly stunned."

"Yes, you're right—we'll not talk about it any more. Let us stay here for a little while."

"Tell me over again the preparations for your coming of age."

Margaret seated herself on the grass as she spoke. Her white dress—her slim young figure—a sort of spiritual light in her dark eyes, gave her at that moment an unearthly radiance in the eyes of the man who loved her. All of a sudden, with an impulse he could not withstand, he resolved to put his fortunes to the test.

"Forgive me," he said, emotion trembling in his voice—"I can only speak of one thing at this moment."

He dropped lightly on one knee beside her. She did not ask him what it was. She looked down.

"You know perfectly well what I am going to say," he continued; "you know what I want most when I come of age—I want my wife—I want you. Margaret, you must have guessed my secret long ago?"

She did not answer him for nearly a minute—then she softly and timidly stretched out one of her hands—he grasped it in his.

"You have guessed—you do know—you're not astonished nor shocked at my words?"

"Your secret was mine, too," she answered in a whisper.

"You will marry me, Margaret—you'll make me the happiest of men?"

"I will be your wife if you wish it, Robert," she replied.

She stood up as she spoke. She was tall, but he was a little taller—he put his arms round her, drew her close to him, and kissed her passionately.

Half-an-hour afterward they left the woods side by side.

"Don't tell anybody to-day," said Margaret.

"Why not? I don't feel as if I could keep it to myself even for an hour longer."

"Still, humor me, Robert; remember I am superstitious."

"What about?"

"I am ashamed to confess it—I would rather that our engagement was not known until the day of the murder has gone by."

CHAPTER V.

MARGARET DOUGLAS lived with her cousins, the Cuthberts. Sir John Cuthbert was the Squire of a parish at a little distance from Grandcourt. He was a wealthy man and was much thought of in his neighborhood. Margaret was the daughter of a sister who had died many years ago—she was poor, but this fact did not prevent the county assigning her a long time ago to Robert Awdrey as his future wife. The attachment between the pair had been the growth of years. They had spent their holidays together, and had grown up to a great extent in each other's company—it had never entered into the thoughts of either to love any one else. Awdrey, true to his promise to Margaret, said nothing about his engagement, but the secret was after all an open one. When the young couple appeared again among the rest of Sir John Cuthbert's guests, they encountered more than one significant glance, and Lady Cuthbert even went to the length of kissing Margaret with much fervor in Awdrey's presence.

"You must come back with us to Cuthbertstown to supper," she said to the young Squire.

"Yes, come, Robert," said Margaret, with a smile.

He found it impossible to resist the invitation in her eyes. It was late, therefore, night, in fact, when he started to walk back to Grandcourt. He felt intensely happy as he walked. He had much reason for this happiness—had he not just won the greatest desire of his life? There was nothing to prevent the wedding taking place almost immediately. As he strode quickly over the beautiful summer landscape he was already planning the golden future which lay before him. He would live in London, he would cultivate the considerable abilities which he undoubtedly possessed. He would lead an active, energetic, and worthy life. Margaret already shared all his ambitions. She would encourage him to be a man in every sense of the word. How lucky he was—how kind fate was to him! Why were the things of life so unevenly divided? Why was one man lifted to a giddy pinnacle of joy and another hurled into an abyss of despair? How happy he was that evening— whereas Everett—he paused in his quick walk as the thought of Everett flashed before his mind's eye. He didn't know the unfortunate man who was now awaiting the coroner's inquest, charged with the terrible crime of murder, but he had seen him twenty-four hours ago. Everett had looked jolly and good-tempered, handsome and strong, as he stood in the porch of the pretty little inn, and smoked his pipe and looked at Hetty when Awdrey.

brought her home. Now a terrible and black doom was overshadowing him. Awdrey could not help feeling deeply interested in the unfortunate man. He was young like himself. Perhaps he, too, had dreamed dreams, and been full of ambition, and perhaps he loved a girl, and thought of making her his wife. Perhaps Hetty was the girl—if so—Awdrey stamped his foot with impatience.

"What mischief some women do," he muttered; "what a difference there is between one woman and another. Who would suppose that Margaret Douglas and Hetty Armitage belonged to the same race? Poor Frere, how madly in love he was with that handsome little creature! How little she cared for the passion which she had evoked. I hope she won't come in my path; I should like to give her a piece of my mind.

This thought had scarcely rushed through Awdrey's brain before he was attracted by a sound in the hedge close by, and Hetty herself stood before him.

"I thought you would come back this way, Mr. Robert," she said. "I've waited here by the hedge for a long time on purpose to see you."

The Squire choked down a sound of indignation —the hot color rushed to his cheeks—it was with difficulty he could keep back his angry words. One glance, however, at Hetty's face caused his anger to fade. The lovely little face was so completely changed that he found some difficulty in recognizing it. Hetty's pretty figure had always been the perfection of trim neatness. No London belle could wear her expensive dresses more neatly nor more becomingly. Her simple print frocks fitted her rounded figure like a glove. The roses on her cheeks spoke the perfection of perfect health; her clear dark eyes were wont to be as open and untroubled as a child's. Her wealth of coal-black hair was always neatly coiled round her shapely head. Now, all was changed, the pretty eyes were scarcely visible between their swollen lids—the face was ghastly pale in parts—blotched with ugly red marks in others; there were great black shadows under the eyes, the lips were parched and dry, they drooped wearily as if in utter despair. The hair was untidy, and one great coil had altogether escaped its bondage, and hung recklessly over the girl's neck and bosom. Her cotton dress was rumpled and stained, and the belt with which she had hastily fastened it together, was kept in its place by a large pin.

Being a man, Awdrey did not notice all these details, but the *tout ensemble*, the abject depression of intense grief, struck him with a sudden pang.

"After all, the little thing loved that poor fellow," he said to himself; "she was a little fool to trifle with him, but the fact that she loved him alters the complexion of affairs."

"What can I do for you?" he said, speaking in a gentle and compassionate voice.

"I have waited to tell you something for nearly two hours, Mr. Robert."

4

"Why did you do it? If you wanted to say anything to me, you could have come to the Court, or I'd have called at the Inn. What is it you want to say?"

"I could not come to the Court, sir, and I could not send you a message, because no one must know that we have met. I came out here unknown to any one; I saw you go home from Cuthbertstown with Miss Douglas." Here Hetty choked down a sob. "I waited by the hedge, for I knew you must pass back this way. I wished to say, Mr. Robert, to tell you, sir, that whatever happens, however matters turn out, I'll be true to you. No one shall get a word out of me. They say it's awful to be cross-examined, but I'll be true. I thought I'd let you know, Mr. Awdrey. To my dying day I'll never let out a word—you need have no fear."

"I need have no fear," said Awdrey, in absolute astonishment. "What in the world do you mean? What are you talking about?"

Hetty looked full up into the Squire's face. The unconscious and unembarrassed gaze with which he returned her look evidently took her breath away.

"I made a mistake," she said in a whisper. "I see that I made a mistake. I'd rather not say what I came to say."

"But you must say it, Hetty; you have something more to tell me, or you wouldn't have taken all this trouble to wait by the roadside on the chance of my passing. What is it? Out with it now, like a good girl."

"May I walk along a little bit with you, Mr. Robert?"

"You may as far as the next corner. There our roads part, and you must go home."

Hetty shivered. She gave the Squire another furtive and undecided glance.

"Shall I tell him?" she whispered to herself.

Awdrey glanced at her, and spoke impatiently.

"Come, Hetty; remember I'm waiting to hear your story. Out with it now, be quick about it."

"I was out last night, sir."

"You were out—when? Not after I saw you home?"

"Yes, sir." Hetty choked again. "It was after ten o'clock."

"You did very wrong. Were you out alone?"

"Yes, sir. I—I followed Mr. Frere on to the Plain."

"You did?" said Awdrey. "Is that fact known? Did you see anything?"

"Yes, sir."

"Then why in the name of Heaven didn't you come up to the Court this morning and tell my father. Your testimony may be most important. Think of the position of that poor unfortunate young Everett."

"No, sir, I don't think of it."

"What do you mean, girl?"

"Let me tell you my story, Mr. Awdrey. If it

is nothing to you—it is nothing. You will soon know if it is nothing or not. I had a quarrel with Mr. Frere last night. Nobody was by; Mr. Frere came into Aunt's parlor and he spoke to me very angrily, and I—I told him something which made him wild."

"What was that?"

Hetty gave a shy glance up at the young Squire; his face looked hard, his lips were firmly set. He and she were walking on the same road, but he kept as far from her side as possible.

"I will not tell him—at least I will not tell him yet," she said to herself.

"I think I won't say, sir," she replied. "What we talked about was Mr. Frere's business and mine. He asked me if I loved another man better than him, and I—I said that I did, sir."

"I thought as much," reflected Awdrey; "Everett is the favored one. If this fact is known it will go against the poor fellow."

"Well, Hetty," he interrupted, "it's my duty to tell you that you behaved very badly, and are in a great measure responsible for the awful tragedy that has occurred. There, poor child, don't cry. Heaven knows, I don't wish to add to your trouble; but see, we have reached the cross-roads where we are to part, and you have not yet told me what you saw when you went out."

"I crept out of my bedroom window," said Hetty. "Aunt and uncle had gone to bed. I can easily get out of the window, it opens right on the

cow-house, and from there I can swing myself into
the laburnum-tree, and so reach the ground. I
got out, and followed Mr. Frere. Presently I saw
that Mr. Everett was also out, and was following
him. I knew every yard of the Plain well, far better than Mr. Everett did. I went to it by a short
cut round by Sweetbriar Lane—you know the
part there—not far from the Court. I had no
sooner got on the Plain than I saw Mr. Frere—he
was running—I thought he was running to meet
me—he came forward by leaps and bounds very
fast—suddenly he stumbled and fell. I wanted to
call him, but my voice, sir, it wouldn't rise, it
seemed to catch in my throat. I couldn't manage
to say his name. All of a sudden the moon went
down, and the plain was all gray with black shadows. I felt frightened—awfully. I was determined to get to Mr. Frere. I stumbled on—presently I fell over the trunk of a tree. My fall
stunned me a bit—when I rose again there were
two men on the Plain. They were standing facing
each other. Oh, Mr. Awdrey, I don't think I'll
say any more."

"Not say any more? You certainly must, girl,"
cried Awdrey, his face blazing with excitement.
"You saw two men facing each other—Frere and
Everett, no doubt."

Hetty was silent. After a moment, during which
her heart beat loudly, she continued to speak in a
very low voice.

"It was so dark that the men looked like shadows. Presently I heard them talking—they were quarrelling. All of a sudden they sprang together like—like tigers, and they—fought. I heard the sound of blows—one of them fell, the taller one— he got on to his feet in a minute: they fought a second time, then one gave a cry, a very sharp, sudden cry, and there was the sound of a body falling with a thud on the ground—afterward, si- lence—not a sound. I crept behind the furze bush. I was quite stunned. After a long time—at least it seemed a long time to me—one of the men went away, and the other man lay on his back with his face turned up to the sky. The man who had killed him turned in the direction of——"

"In what direction?" asked Awdrey.

"In the direction of——" Hetty looked full up at the Squire; the Squire's eyes met hers. "The town, sir." •

"Oh, the town," said Awdrey, giving vent to a short laugh. "From the way you looked at me, I thought you were going to say The Court."

"Sir, Mr. Robert, do you think it was Mr. Everett?"

"Who else could it have been?" replied Awdrey.

"Very well, sir, I'll hold to that. Who else could it have been? I thought I'd tell you, Mr. Awdrey. I thought you'd like to know that I'd hold to that. When the steps of the murderer died away, I stole back to Mr. Frere, and I tried to bring him back to life, but he was as dead as a stone. I left him and I went home. I got back to

my room about four in the morning. Not a soul
knew I was out; no one knows it now but you, sir.
I thought I'd come and tell you, Mr. Robert, that
I'd hold to the story that it was Mr. Everett who
committed the murder. Good-night, sir."

"Good-night, Hetty. You'll have to tell my
father what you have told me, in the morning."

"Very well, sir, if you wish it."

Hetty turned and walked slowly back toward
the village, and Awdrey stood where the four roads
met and watched her. For a moment or two he
was lost in anxious thought—then he turned
quickly and walked home. He entered the house
by the same side entrance by which he had come
in on the previous night. He walked down a long
passage, crossed the wide front hall, and entered
the drawing-room where his sister Ann was seated.

"Is that you, Bob?" she said, jumping up when
she saw him. "I'm so glad to have you all to myself. Of course, you were too busy with Margaret
to take any notice of us all day, but I've been dying to hear your account of that awful tragedy.
Sit here like a dear old fellow and tell me the
story."

"Talk of women and their tender hearts," said
Awdrey, with irritation.

Then the memory of Margaret came over him
and his face softened. Margaret, whose heart was
quite the tenderest thing in all the world, had also
wished to hear of the tragedy.

"To tell the truth, Ann," he said, sinking into a

chair by his sister's side, "you can scarcely ask
me to discuss a more uncongenial theme. Of
course, the whole thing will be thoroughly inves-
tigated, and the local papers will be filled with
nothing else for weeks to come. Won't that content you? Must I, too, go into this painful subject?"

Ann was a very good-natured girl.

"Certainly not, dear Bob, if it worries you,"
she replied; "but just answer me one question.
Is it true that you met the unfortunate man last
night?"

"Quite true. I did. We had a sort of quarrel."

"Good gracious! Why, Robert, if you had
been out late last night they might have suspected
you of the murder."

Awdrey's face reddened.

"As it happens, I went to bed remarkably early,"
he said; "at least, such is my recollection." As
he spoke he looked at his sister with knitted
brows.

"Why, of course, don't you remember, you said
you were dead beat. Dorothy and I wanted you
to sing with us, but you declared you were as
hoarse as a raven, and went off to your bedroom
immediately after supper. For my part, I was so
afraid of disturbing you that I wouldn't even knock
when I pushed that little note about Margaret
under the door."

Ann gave her brother a roguish glance when she

mentioned Margaret's name. He did not notice it. He was thinking deeply.

"I am tired to-night, too," he said. "I have an extraordinary feeling in the back of my head, as if it were numbed. I believe I want more sleep. This horrid affair has upset me. Well, good-night, Ann, I'm off to bed at once."

"But supper is ready."

"I had something at Cuthbertstown; I don't want anything more. Good-night."

CHAPTER VI.

HETTY dragged herself wearily home—she had waited to see the young Squire in a state of intense and rapt excitement. He had received her news with marvellous indifference. The excitement he had shown was the ordinary excitement which an outsider might feel when he received startling and unlooked for tidings. There was not a scrap of personal emotion in his manner. Was it possible that he had forgotten all about the murder which he himself had committed? Hetty was not a native of Grandcourt without knowing something of the tragedy which hung over the Court. Was it possible that the doom of the house had really overtaken Robert Awdrey? Hetty with her own eyes had seen him kill Horace Frere. Her own eyes could surely not deceive her. She rubbed them now in her bewilderment. Yes, she had seen the murder committed. Without any doubt Awdrey was the man who had struggled with Frere. Frere had thrown him to the ground; he had risen quickly again. Once more the two men had rushed at each other like tigers eager for blood—there had been a scuffle—a fierce, awful wrestle. A wrestle which had been followed by a sudden leap forward on the part of the young Squire—he had used his

stick as men use bayonets in battle—there had
come a groan from Frere's lips—he had staggered
—his body had fallen to the ground with a heavy
thud—then had followed an awful silence. Yes,
Hetty had seen the whole thing. She had watched
the terrible transaction from beginning to end.
After he had thrown his man to the ground the
Squire had struck a match, and had looked hard
into the face of the dead. Hetty had seen the lu-
rid light flash up for an instant on the Squire's
face—it had looked haggard and gray—like the
face of an old man. She had watched him as he
examined the slender stick with which he had
killed his foe. She observed him then creep across
the Plain to a copse of young alders. She had
seen him push the stick out of sight into the middle of the alders—she had then watched him as he
went quickly home. Yes, Robert Awdrey was the
guilty man—Frank Everett was innocent, as innocent as a babe. All day long Hetty's head had
been in a mad whirl. She had kept her terrible
knowledge to herself. Knowing that a word from
her could save him, she had allowed Everett to be
arrested. She had watched him from behind her
window when the police came to the house for the
purpose, she had seen Everett go away in the company of two policemen. He was a square-built
young fellow with broad shoulders—he had held
himself sturdily as an Englishman should, when
he walked off, an innocent man, to meet an awful
doom. Hetty, as she watched, crushed down the.

cry in her heart—it had clamored to save this man.
There was a louder cry there—a fiercer instinct.
The Squire belonged to her own people—she was
like a subject, and he was her king—to the people
of Grandcourt the king could do nothing wrong.
They were old-fashioned in the little village, and
had somewhat the feeling of serfs to their feudal
lord. Hetty shared the tradition of her race. But
over and above these minor matters, the unhappy
girl loved Robert Awdrey with a fierce passion.
She would rather die herself than see him die.
When she saw Everett arrested, she watched the
whole proceeding in dull amazement. She wondered why the Squire had not acted a man's part.
Why did he not deliver himself up to the course of
justice? He had killed Frere in a moment of mad
passion. Hetty's heart throbbed. Could that
passion have been evoked on her account? Of
course, he would own to his sin. He had not done
so; on the contrary, he had gone to a picnic. He
had been seen walking about with the young lady
whom he loved. Did Robert Awdrey really love
Margaret Douglas?

"If that is the case, why should not I give him
up?" thought Hetty. "He cares nothing for me.
I am less than the thistle under his feet. Why
should I save him? Why should Mr. Everett die
because of him? The Squire cares nothing for me.
Why should I sin on his account?"

These thoughts, when they came to her, were
quickly hurled aside by others.

"I'd die twenty times over rather than he should suffer," thought the girl. "He shan't die, he's my king, and I'm his subject. It does not matter whether he loves me or not, he shan't die. Yes, he loves that beautiful Miss Douglas—she belongs to his set, and she'll be his wife. Perhaps she thinks that she loves him. Oh, oh!"

Hetty laughed wildly to herself.

"After all, she doesn't know what real love is. She little guesses what I feel; she little guesses that I hold his life in my hands. O God, keep me from going mad!"

It was dark when Hetty re-entered the Inn. The taproom was the scene of noisy excitement. It was crowded with eager and interested villagers. The murder was the one and only topic of conversation. Armitage was busy attending to his numerous guests, and Mrs. Armitage kept going backward and forward between the taproom and the little kitchen at the back.

When she saw Hetty she called out to her in a sharp tone.

"Where have you been, girl?" she cried. "Now just look here, your uncle won't have you stealing out in this fashion any more. You are to stay at home when it is dark. Why, it's all over the place, it's in every one's mouth, that you have been the cause of the murder. You encouraged that poor Mr. Frere with your idle, flighty, silly ways and looks, and then you played fast and loose with him. Don't you know that this is just the thing

that will ruin us? Yes, you'll be the ruin of us,
Hetty, and times so bad, too. When are we likely
to have parlor lodgers again?"

"Oh, Aunt, I wish you wouldn't scold me," answered Hetty. She sank down on the nearest
chair, pushed her hat from her brow, and pressed
her hand to it.

"Sakes, child!" exclaimed her aunt, "you do
look white and bad to be sure."

Mrs. Armitage stood in front of her niece, and
eyed her with a critical gaze.

"It's my belief, after all, that you really cared
for the poor young man," she said. "For all your
silly, flighty ways you gave him what little heart
you possess. If he meant honest by you, you
couldn't have done better—they say he had lots of
money, and not a soul to think of but himself. I
don't know how your uncle is to provide for you.
But there, you've learned your lesson, and I hope
you'll never forget it."

"Aunt Fanny, may I go up-stairs to my room?"

"Hoity toity! nothing of the kind. You've got
to work for your living like the rest of us. Put on
your apron and help me to wash up the dishes."

Hetty rose wearily from her chair. The body
of the murdered man lay out straight and still in
the little front parlor. Many people had been in
and out during the afternoon; many people had
gazed solemnly at the white face. The doctor had
examined the wound in the eye. The coroner had
come to view the dead. All was in readiness for

the inquest, which was to take place at an early
hour on the following day. No one as yet had
wept a single tear over the dead man. Mrs. Armitage came to Hetty now and asked her to go and
fetch something out of the parlor. A paper which
had been left on the mantelpiece was wanted by
Armitage in a hurry.

"Go, child, be quick!" said the aunt. "You'll
find the paper by that vase of flowers on the mantelpiece."

Hetty obeyed, never thinking of what she was to
see. There was no artificial light in the room.
On the centre-table, in a rude coffin which had
been hastily prepared, lay the body. It was covered by a white sheet. The moon poured in a
ghastly light through the window. The form of
the dead man was outlined distinctly under the
sheet. Hetty almost ran up against it when she
entered the room. Her nerves were overstrung;
she was not prepared for the sight which met her
startled eyes; uttering a piercing shriek, she
rushed from the room into her Aunt Fanny's arms.

"Now, whatever is the matter?" said the elder
woman.

"You shouldn't have sent me in there," panted
Hetty. "You should have told me that it was
there."

"Well, well, I thought you knew. What a silly
little good-for-nothing you are! Stay quiet and
I'll run and fetch the paper. Dear, dear, I'm glad
you are not my niece; it's Armitage you belong to."

Mrs. Armitage entered the parlor, fetched the required paper, and shut the door behind her. As she walked down the passage Hetty started quickly forward and caught her arm.

"If I don't tell somebody at once I'll go mad," she said. "Aunt Fanny, I must speak to you at once. "I can't keep it to myself another minute."

"Good gracious me! whatever is to be done, Hetty? How am I to find time to listen to your silly nonsense just now? There's your uncle nearly wild with all the work being left on his hands."

"It isn't silly nonsense, Aunt Fanny. I've got to say something. I know something. I must tell it to you. I must tell it to you at once."

"Why, girl," said Mrs. Armitage, staring hard at her niece, "you are not making a fool of me, are you?"

"No. I'll go up to my room. Come to me as soon as ever you can. Tell Uncle that you are tired and must go to bed at once. Tell any lie, make any excuse, only come to me quickly. I'm in such a state that if you don't come I'll have to go right into the taproom and tell every one what I know. Oh, Aunt Fanny! have mercy on me and come quickly."

"You do seem in a way, Hetty," replied the aunt. "For goodness sake do keep yourself calm. There, run up-stairs and I'll be with you in a minute or two."

Mrs. Armitage went into the taproom to her husband.

"Look here, John," she sad, "I've got a split-ting headache, and Hetty is fairly knocked up. Can't you manage to do without us for the rest of the evening?"

"Of course, wife, if you're really bad," replied Armitage. "There's work here for three pairs of hands," he added, "but that can't be helped, if you are really bad."

"Yes, I am, and as to that child, she is fairly done."

"I'm not surprised. I wonder she's alive when she knows the whole thing is owing to her. Little hussy, I'd like to box her ears, that I would."

"So would I for that matter," replied the wife, "but she's in an awful state, poor child, and if I don't get her to bed, she'll be ill, and there will be more money out of pocket."

"Don't waste your strength sitting up with her, wife, she ain't worth it," Armitage called out, as his wife left the room.

A moment later, Mrs. Armitage crept softly up-stairs. She entered Hetty's little chamber, which was also flooded with moonlight. It was a tiny room, with a sloping roof. Its little lattice window was wide open. Hetty was kneeling by the window looking out into the night. The moment she saw her aunt she rose to her feet, and ran to meet her.

"Lock the door, Aunt Fanny," she said, in a hoarse whisper.

"Oh, child, whatever has come to you?"

"Lock the door, Aunt Fanny, or let me do it."

"There, I'll humor you. Here's the key. I'll put it into my pocket. Why don't you have a light, Hetty?"

"I don't want it—the moon makes light enough for me. I have something to say to you. If I don't tell it, I shall go mad. You must share it with me, Aunt Fanny. You and I must both know it, and we must keep it to ourselves forever and ever and ever."

"Lor, child! what are you talking about?"

"I'll soon tell you. Let me kneel close to you. Hold my hand. I never felt so frightened in all my life before."

"Out with it, Hetty, whatever it is."

"Aunt, before I say a word, you've got to make me a promise."

"What's that?"

"You won't tell a soul what I am going to say to you."

"I hate making promises of that sort, Hetty."

"Never mind whether you hate it or not. Promise or I shall go mad."

"Oh, dear me!" exclaimed Mrs. Armitage, "why should a poor woman be bothered in this way, and you neither kith nor kin to me. Don't you forget that it's Armitage you belong to. You've no blood of mine, thank goodness, in your veins."

"What does that matter. You're a woman, and I'm another. I'm just in the most awful position a girl could be in. But whatever happens, I'll be true to him. Yes, Aunt Fanny, I'll be true to him. I'm nothing to him, no more than if I were a weed, but I love him madly, deeply, desperately. He is all the world to me. He is my master, and I am his slave. Of course I'm nothing to him, but he's everything to me, and he shan't die. Aunt Fanny, you and I have got to be true to him. We must share the thing together, for I can't keep the secret by myself. You must share it with me, Aunt Fanny."

Up to this point, Mrs. Armitage had regarded Hetty's words as merely those of a hysterical and overwrought girl. Now, however, she began to perceive method in her madness.

"Look here, child," she said, "if you've got anything to say, say it, and have done with it. I'm not blessed with over much patience, and I can't stand beating round the bush. If you have a secret, out with it, you silly thing. Oh, yes, of course I won't betray you. I expect it's just this, you've gone and done something you oughtn't to. Oh, what have I done to be blessed with a niece-in-law like you?

"It's nothing of that sort, Aunt Fanny. It is this—I don't mind telling you now, now that you have promised not to betray me. Aunt Fanny, I was out last night—I saw the murder committed."

Mrs. Armitage suppressed a sharp scream.

"Heaven preserve us!" she said, in a choking voice. "Were you not in bed, you wicked girl?"

"No, I was out. I had quarrelled with Mr.

Frere in the parlor, and I thought I'd follow him
and make it up. I went straight on to the Plain—
I saw him running. I hid behind a furze bush
and I saw the quarrel, and I heard the words—I
saw the awful struggle, and I heard the blows. I
heard the fall, too—and I saw the man who had
killed Mr. Frere run away."

"I wonder you never told all this to-day, Hetty
Armitage. Well, I'm sorry for that poor Mr.
Everett. Oh, dear, what will not our passions lead
us to; to think that two young gentlemen should
come to this respectable house, and that it should
be the case of Cain and Abel over again—one rising up and slaying the other."

Hetty, who had been kneeling all this time, now
rose. Her face was ghastly—her words came out
in strange pauses.

"It wasn't Mr. Everett," she said.

"Good Heavens! Hetty," exclaimed her aunt,
springng also to her feet, and catching the girl's
two hands within her own—"It wasn't Mr. Everett!
—what in the world do you mean?"

"What I say, Aunt Fanny—the man who killed
Mr. Frere was Mr. Awdrey. Our Mr. Awdrey,
Aunt Fanny, and I could die for him—and no one
must ever know—and I saw him this evening, and
—and he has forgotten all about it. He doesn't
know a bit about it—not a bit. Oh, Aunt Fanny,
I shall go quite mad, if you don't promise to help
me to keep my secret."

CHAPTER VII

"Sit down, Hetty, and keep yourself quiet," said Mrs. Armitage.

Her manner had completely changed. A stealthy, fearful look crept into her face. She went on tiptoe to the door to assure herself over again that it was locked. She then approached the window, shut it, fastened it, and drew a heavy moreen curtain across it.

"When one has secrets," she said, "it is best to be certain there are no eavesdroppers anywhere."

She then lit a candle and placed it on the centre of the little table.

Having done this, she seated herself—she didn't care to look at Hetty. She felt as if in a sort of way she had committed the murder herself. The knowledge of the truth impressed her so deeply that she did not care to encounter any eyes for a few minuttes.

"Aunt Fanny, why don't you speak to me?" asked the girl at last.

"You are quite sure, child, that you have told me the truth?" said Mrs. Armitage then.

"Yes—it is the truth—is it likely that I could invent anything so fearful?"

"No, it ain't likely," replied the elder woman, "but I don't intend to trust just to the mere word

of a slip of a giddy girl like you. You must swear
it—is there a Bible in the room?"

"Oh, don't, Aunt, I wish you wouldn't."

"Stop that silly whining of yours, Hetty; what
do your wishes matter one way or the other? If
you've told me the truth an awful thing has happened, but I won't stir in the matter until I know
it's gospel truth. Yes, there's your Testament—
the Testament will do. Now, Hetty Armitage,
hold this book in your hand, and say before God
in heaven that you saw Mr. Robert Awdrey kill Mr.
Horace Frere. Kiss the book, and tell the truth
if you don't want to lose your soul."

Hetty trembled from head to foot. Her nature
was impressionable—the hour—the terrible excitement she had just lived through—the solemn,
frightened expression of her aunt's face, irritated
her nerves to the last extent. She had the utmost
difficulty in keeping herself from screaming aloud.

"What do you want me to do?" she said, holding the Testament between her limp fingers.

"Say these words: 'I, Hetty Armitage, saw Mr.
Robert Awdrey kill Mr. Horace Frere on Salisbury Plain last night. This is the truth, so help
me God.'"

"I, Hetty Armitage, saw Mr. Robert Awdrey
kill Mr. Horace Frere on Salisbury Plain last
night. This is the truth, so help me God," repeated Hetty, in a mechanical voice.

"Kiss the Book now, child," said the aunt.

Hetty raised it to her lips.

"Give me the Testament."

Mrs. Armitage took it in her hands.

"Aunt Fanny, what in the world do you mean to do now?" said the girl.

"You are witness, Hetty; you are witness to what I mean to do. It is all for the sake of the Family. What are poor folks like us and our consciences, and our secrets, compared to the Family? This book has not done its work yet. Now I am going to take an oath on the Testament. I, Frances Armitage, swear by the God above, and the Bible He has given us, that I will never tell to mortal man the truth about this murder."

Mrs. Armitage finished her words by pressing the Testament to her lips.

"Now you swear," she said, giving the book back again to her niece.

Hetty did so. Her voice came out in broken sobs. Mrs. Armitage replaced the Testament on the top shelf of Hetty's little bookcase.

"There," she said, wiping her brow, "that's done. You saw the murder committed; you and I have sworn that we'll never tell what we know. We needn't talk of it any more. Another man will swing for it. Let him swing. He is a nice fellow, too. He showed me the photograph of his mother one day. She had white hair and eyes like his; she looked like a lady every inch of her. Mr. Everett said, 'I am her only child, Mrs. Armitage; I'm all she has got.' He had a pleas-ant smile—wonderful, and a good face. Poor lad, if it wasn't the Family I had to be true to I wouldn't let him swing. They say down-stairs that the circumstantial evidence is black against him."

"Perhaps, after all, they cannot convict him, Aunt."

"What do you know about it? I say they can and will, but don't let us talk of it any more. The one thing you and I have to do is to be true to the Family. There's not a second thought to be given to the matter. Sit down, Hetty; don't keep hovering about like that. I think I had better send you away from home; only I forgot, you are sure to be called upon as a witness. You must see that your face doesn't betray you when you're cross-examined."

"No, it won't," said the girl. "I've got you to help me now. I can talk about it sometimes, and it won't lie so heavily on my heart. Aunt Fanny, do you really think Mr. Awdrey forgets?"

"Do I think it? I know it. I don't trouble to think about what I know. It's in their blood, I tell you. The things they ought to remember are wiped out of their brains as clean as if you washed a slate after using it. My mother was cook in the Family, and her mother and her mother before her again. We are Perrys, and the Perrys had always a turn for cooking. We've cooked the dinner up at the Court for close on a hundred years. Don't you suppose I know their ways by this time? Oh, I could tell you of fearful things. There have been dark deeds done before now, and the men who did them had no more memory of their own sin than if they were babies of a month old. There was a Squire—two generations back he was—my grandmother knew him—and he had a son. The mother was—! but there! where's the use of going into that. The mother died raving mad, and the Squire knew no more what he had done than the babe unborn. Folks call it the curse of God. It's an awful doom, and it always comes on just as it has fallen on the young Squire. There comes a fit of passion—a desperate deed is done or a desperate sorrow is met, and all is blank. They wither up afterward just as if the drought was in them. He'll die young, the young Squire will, just like his forefathers. What's the good of crying, Hetty? Crying won't save him—he'll die young. Blood for blood. God will require that young man's blood at his hands. He can't escape—it's in his race; but at least he shan't hang for it—if you and I can keep him from the gallows. Hetty, put your hand in mine and tell me all over again what you saw."

"I can't bear to go over it again, Aunt Fanny—it seems burnt into me like fire. I can think of nothing else—I can think of no face but Mr. Awdrey's—I can only remember the look on his face when he bent over the man he had killed. I saw his face just for a minute by the light of the match, and I never could have believed that human face could have looked like that before. It was old—like the face of an old man. But I met him this

evening, Aunt Fanny, and he had forgotten all
about it, and he was jolly and happy, and they
say he was seen with Miss Douglas to-day.   The
family had a picnic on the Plain, and Miss Douglas was there, with her uncle, Sir John Cuthbert,
and there were a lot of other young ladies.   Mr.
Awdrey went back to Cuthbertstown with Miss
Douglas.   It was when he was returning to the
Court I met him.   All the world knows he worships the ground she walks on.   I suppose he'll
marry her by and by, Aunt—he seemed so happy
and contented to-night."

"I suppose he will marry her, child—that is the
best thing that could happen to him, and she's a
nice young lady and his equal in other ways.   He
happy, did you say?   Maybe he is for a bit, but
he's a gone man for all that—nothing, nor no one
can keep the doom of his house from him.   What
are you squeezing my hand for, Hetty?"

"I can't bear to think of the Squire marrying
Miss Douglas."

"Stuff and nonsense!   What is the Squire to
you, except as one of the Family.   You'd better
mind your station, Hetty, and leave your betters
to themselves.   If you don't you'll get into awful
trouble some day.   But now the night is going on,
and we've got something to do.   Tell me again
how that murder was done."

"The Squire ran at Mr. Frere, and the point of
his stick ran into Mr. Frere's eye."

"What did he do with the stick?"

"He went to a copse of young alders and thrust it into the middle. Oh, it's safe enough."

"Nothing of the kind—it isn't safe at all. How do you know they won't cut those alders down and find the stick? Mr. Robert's walking-stick is well known—it has a silver plate upon it with his name. Years hence people may come across that stick, and all the county will know at once who it belonged to. Come along, Hetty—you and I have our work to do."

"What is that, Aunt Fanny?"

"Before the morning dawns we must bury that stick where no one will find it."

"Oh, Aunt, don't ask me—I can't go back to the Plain again."

"You can and must—I wouldn't ask you, but I couldn't find the exact spot myself. I'll go down first and have a word with Armitage, and then return to you."

Mrs. Armitage softly unlocked the door of her niece's room, and going first to her own bedroom, washed her ashen face with cold water; she then rubbed it hard with a rough towel to take some of the tell-tale expression out of it. Afterward she stole softly down-stairs. Her husband was busy in the taproom. She opened the door, and called his name.

"Armitage, I want you a minute."

"Mercy on us, I thought you were in bed an hour ago, wife," he said. "Why, you do look bad, what's the matter?"

"It isn't me, it's the child—she's hysterical. I've been having no end of a time with her; I came down to say that I'd sleep with Hetty to-night. Good-night, Armitage."

"Good-night," said the man. "I say, wife, though," he called after her, "see that you are up in good time to-morrow."

"Never fear," exclaimed Mrs. Armitage, as she ascended the creaking stairs, "I'll be down and about at six."

She re-entered her niece's bedroom and locked the door.

"How did you get out last night?" she asked.

"Through the window."

"Well, you're a nice one. This is not the time to scold you, however, and you and I have got to go out the same way now. They'll think we are in our bed—let them think it. Come, be quick—show me the way out. It's a goodish step from here to the Plain; we've not a minute to lose, and not a soul must see us going or returning."

Mrs. Armitage was nearly as slender and active as her niece. She accomplished the descent from the window without the least difficulty, and soon she and Hetty were walking quickly in the direction of the Plain—they kept well in the shadow of the road and did not meet a soul the entire way. During that walk neither woman spoke a word to the other. Presently they reached the Plain. Hetty trembled as she stood by the alder copse.

"Keep your courage up," whispered Mrs. Armitage, "we must bury that stick where no one can find it."

"Don't bury it, Aunt Fanny," whispered Hetty. "I have thought of something—there's the pond half a mile away. Let us weight the stick with stones and throw it into the pond."

"That's a good thought, child, we'll do it."

CHAPTER VIII.

THE village never forgot the week when the young Squire came of age. During that week many important things happened. The usual festivities were arranged to take place on Monday, for on that day the Squire completed his twenty-first year. On the following Thursday Robert Awdrey was to marry Margaret Douglas, and between these two days, namely, on Tuesday and Wednesday, Frank Everett was to be tried for the murder of Horace Frere at Salisbury. It will be easily believed, therefore, that the excitement of the good folks all over the country reached high-water mark. Quite apart from his position, the young Squire was much loved for himself. His was an interesting personality. Even if this had not been so, the fact of his coming of age, and the almost more interesting fact of his marriage, would fill all who knew him with a lively sense of pleasure. The public gaze would be naturally turned full upon this young man. But great as was the interest which all who knew him took in Awdrey, it was nothing to that which was felt with regard to a man who was a stranger in the county, but whose awful fate now filled all hearts and minds. The strongest circumstantial evidence was against

Frank Everett, but beyond circumstantial evidence there was nothing but good to be known of this young man. He had lived in the past, as far as all could tell, an immaculate life. He was the only son of a widowed mother. Mrs. Everett had taken lodgings in Salisbury, and was awaiting the issue of the trial with feelings which none could fathom.

As the week of her wedding approached, Margaret Douglas showed none of the happy expectancy of a bride. Her face began to assume a worn and anxious expression. She could hardly think of anything except the coming trial. A few days before the wedding she earnestly begged her lover to postpone the ceremony for a short time.

"I cannot account for my sensations, Robert," she said. "The shadow of this awful tragedy seems to shut away the sunshine from me. You cannot, of course, help coming of age on Monday, but surely there is nothing unreasonable in my asking to have the wedding postponed for a week. I will own that I am superstitious—I come of a superstitious race—my grandmother had the gift of second sight—perhaps I inherit it also, I cannot say. Do yield to me in the matter, Robert. Do postpone the wedding."

Awdrey stood close to Margaret. She looked anxiously into his eyes; they met hers with a curious expression of irritation in them. The young squire was pale; there were fretful lines round his mouth.

"I told you before," he said, "that I am affected

with a strange and unaccountable apathy with regard to this terrible murder. I try with all my
might to get up sympathy for that poor unfortunate Everett. Try as I may, however, I utterly
fail to feel even pity for him. Margaret, I would
confess this to no one in the world but yourself.
Everett is nothing to me—you are everything.
Why should I postpone my happiness on Everett's
account?"

"You are not well, dearest," said Margaret, looking at him anxiously.

"Yes, I am, Maggie," he replied. "You must
not make me fanciful. I never felt better in my
life, except——" Here he pressed his hand to his
brow.

"Except?" she repeated.

"Nothing really—I have a curious sensation of
numbness in the back of my head. I should think
nothing at all about it but for the fact——"

Here he paused, and looked ahead of him steadily.

"But for what fact, Robert?"

"You must have heard—it must have been whispered to you—every one all over the county knows
that sometimes—sometimes, Maggie, queer things
happen to men of our house."

"Of course, I have heard of what you allude to,"
she answered brightly. "Do you think I mind?
Do you think I believe in the thing? Not I. I am
not superstitious in that way. So you, dear old
fellow, are imagining that you are to be one of the

victims of that dreadful old curse. Rest assured
that you will be nothing of the kind. I have a
cousin—he is in the medical profession—you shall
know him when we go to London. I spoke to Dr.
Rumsey once about this curious phase in your
family history. He said it was caused by an extraordinary state of nerves, and that the resolute
power of will was needed to overcome it. Dr.
Rumsey is a very interesting man, Robert. He
believed in heredity; who does not? but he also
firmly believes that the power of will, rightly
exercised, can be more powerful than heredity.
Now, I don't mean you to be a victim to that old
family failing, so please banish the thought from
your mind once and for ever."

Awdrey smiled at her.

"You cheer me," he said. "I am a lucky man
to have found such a woman as you to be my wife.
You will help to bring forward all that is best in
me. Margaret, I feel that through you I shall
conquer the curse which lies in my blood."

"There is no curse, Robert. When your grandfather married a strong-minded Scotch wife the
curse was completely arrested — the spell removed."

"Yes," said Awdrey, "of course you are perfectly right. My father has never suffered from a
trace of the family malady, and as for me, I didn't
know what nervousness meant until within the last
month. I certainly have suffered from a stupid
lapse of memory during the last month."

6

"We all forget things at times," said Margaret. "What is it that worries you?"

"Something so trifling that you will laugh when I tell you. You know my favorite stick?"

"Of course. By the way, you have not used it lately."

"I have not. It is lost. I have looked for it high and low, and racked my memory in vain to know where I could have put it. When last I remember using it, I was talking to that unfortunate young Frere in the underwood. I wish I could find it—not for the sake of the stick, but because, under my circumstances, I don't want to forget things."

"Well, every one forgets things at times—you will remember where you have put the stick when you are not thinking of it."

"Quite true; I wish it didn't worry me, however. You know that poor Frere met his death in the most extraordinary manner. The man who killed him ran his walking-stick into his eye. The doctors say that the ferrule of the stick entered the brain, causing instantaneous death. Everett carried a stick, but the ferrule was a little large for the size of the wound made. Now my stick——"

"Really, Robert, I won't listen to you for another moment," exclaimed Margaret. "The next thing you will do is to assure me that your stick was the weapon which caused the murder."

"No," he replied, with a spasm of queer pain. "Of course, Maggie, there is nothing wrong, only with our peculiar idiosyncrasies, small lapses of memory make one anxious. I should be happy if I could find the stick, and happier still if this numbness would leave the back of my head. But your sweet society will soon put me right."

"I mean it to," she replied, in her firm way.

"You will marry me, dearest, on the twenty-fourth?"

"Yes," she answered, "you are first, first of all. I will put aside my superstition—the wedding shall not be postponed."

"Thank you a thousand times—how happy you make me!"

Awdrey went home in the highest spirits.

The auspicious week dawned. The young Squire's coming of age went off without a flaw. The day was a perfect one in August. All the tenants assembled at the Court to welcome Awdrey to his majority. His modest and graceful speech was applauded on all sides. He never looked better than when he stood on a raised platform and addressed the tenants who had known him from his babyhood. Some day he was to be their landlord. In Wiltshire the tie between landlord and tenant is very strong. The spirit of the feudal times still in a measure pervades this part of the country. The cheers which followed Awdrey's speech rose high on the evening air. Immediately afterward there was supper on the lawn, followed by a dance. Among those assembled, however, might have been seen two anxious faces—one of them belonged

to Mrs. Armitage.   She had been a young-looking
woman for her years, until after the night of the
murder—now she looked old, her hair was sprin-
kled with gray, her face had deep lines in it, there
was a touch of irritation also in her manner.   She
and Hetty kept close together.   Sometimes her
hand clutched hold of the hand of her niece and
gave it a hard pressure.   Hetty's little hand trembled, and her whole frame quivered with almost un-
controllable agony when Mrs. Armitage did this.
All the gay scene was ghastly mockery to poor
Hetty.   Her distress, her wasted appearance,
could not but draw general attention to her.   The
little girl, however, had never looked more beautiful nor lovely.   She was observed by many people;
strangers pointed her out to one another.

"Do you see that little girl with the beautiful
face?" they said.   "It was on her account that the
tragedy took place."

Presently the young Squire came down and
asked Mrs. Armitage to open the ball with him.

"You do me great honor, sir," she said.   She
hesitated, then placed her hand on his arm.

As he led her away, his eyes met those of
Hetty.

"I'll give you a dance later on," he said, nod-
ding carelessly to the young girl.

She blushed and pressed her hand to her heart.

There wasn't a village lad in the entire assembly
who would not have given a year of his life to
dance even once with beautiful little Hetty, but she

declined all the village boys' attentions that evening.

"She wasn't in the humor to dance," she said. "Oh, yes, of course, she would dance with the Squire if he asked her, but she would not bestow her favors upon any one else." She sat down presently in a secluded corner. Her eyes followed Awdrey wherever he went. By and by Margaret Douglas noticed her. There was something about the childish sad face which drew out the compassion of Margaret's large heart. She went quickly across the lawn to speak to her.

"Good-evening, Hetty," she said, "I hope you are well?"

Hetty stood up; she began to tremble.

"Yes, Miss Douglas, I am quite well," she answered.

"You don't look well," said Margaret. "Why are you not dancing?"

"I haven't the heart to dance," said Hetty, turning suddenly away. Her eyes brimmed with sudden tears.

"Poor little girl! how could I be so thoughtless as to suppose she would care to dance," thought Margaret. "All her thoughts must be occupied with this terrible trial—Robert told me that she would be the principal witness. Poor little thing."

Margaret stretched out her hand impulsively and grasped Hetty's.

I feel for you—I quite understand you," she said. Her voice trembled with deep and full sympathy. "I see that you are suffering a great deal, but you will be better afterward—you ought to go away afterward—you will want change."

"I would rather stay at home, please, Miss Douglas."

"Well, I won't worry you. Here is Mr. Awdrey. You have not danced once, Hetty. Would you not like to have a dance with the Squire, just for luck? Yes, I see you would. Robert, come here."

"What is it?" asked Awdrey. "Oh, is that you, Hetty? I have not forgotten our dance."

"Dance with her now, Robert," said Margaret. "There is a waltz just striking up—I will meet you presently on the terrace."

Margaret crossed the lawn, and Awdrey gave his arm to Hetty. She turned her large gaze upon him for a moment, her lips trembled, she placed her hand on his arm. "Yes, I will dance with him once," she said to herself. "It will please me—I am doing a great deal for him, and it will strengthen me—to have this pleasure. Oh, I hope, I do hope I'll be brave and silent, and not let the awful pain at my heart get the better of me. Please, God, help me to be true to Mr. Robert."

"Come, Hetty, why won't you talk?" said the Squire; he gave her a kindly yet careless glance.

They began to waltz, but Hetty had soon to pause for want of breath.

"You are not well," said Awdrey; "let me lead you out of the crowd. Here, let us sit the dance out under this tree; now you are better, are you not?"

"Yes, sir; oh, yes, Mr. Robert, I am much better now." She panted as she spoke.

"How pale you are," said Awdrey "and you used to be such a blooming, rosy little thing. Well, never mind," he added hastily, "I ought not to forget that you have a good deal to worry you just now. You must try to keep up your courage. All you have to do to-morrow when you go into court is to tell the entire and exact truth."

"You don't mean me to do that, you can't," said Hetty. She opened her eyes and gave a wild startled glance. The next moment her whole face was covered with confusion. "Oh, what have I said?" she cried, in consternation. "Of course, I will tell the exact and perfect truth."

"Of course," said Awdrey, surprised at her manner. "You will be under oath, remember." He stood up as he spoke. "Now let me take you to your aunt."

"One moment first, Mr. Robert; I'd like to ask you a question."

"Well, Hetty, what is it?" said the young man, kindly.

Hetty raised her eyes for a moment, then she lowered them.

"It's a very awful thing, the kind of thing that God doesn't forgive," she said in a whisper, "for —for a girl to tell a lie when she's under oath?"

"It is perjury," said Awdrey, in a sharp, short

voice. "Why should you worry your head about
such a matter?"

"Of course not, sir, only I'd like to know. I
hope you'll be very happy with your good lady,
Mr. Awdrey, when you're married. I think I'll
go home now, sir. I'm not quite well, and it
makes me giddy to dance. I wish you a happy
life, sir, and—and Miss Douglas the same. If you
see Aunt Fanny, Mr. Robert, will you tell her that
I've gone home?"

"Yes, to be sure I will. Good-by, Hetty.
Here, shake hands, won't you? God bless you,
little girl. I hope you will soon be all right."

Hetty crept slowly away; she looked like a little
gray shadow as she returned to the village, passing
silently through the lovely gardens and all the
sweet summer world. Beautiful as she was, she
was out of keeping with the summer and the time
of gayety.

Against Awdrey's wish Margaret insisted on being present during the first day of the trial. Everett's trial would in all probability occupy the
whole of two days. Awdrey was to appear in
court as witness. His evidence and that of Hetty
Armitage and the laborer who had seen Frere running across the plain would probably sum up the
case against the prisoner. Hetty's evidence, however, was the most important of all. Some of the
neighbors said that Hetty would never have strength
to go through the trial. But when the little creature stepped into the witness-box, there was no

perceptible want of energy about her—her cheeks
were pink with the color of excitement, her lovely
eyes shone brightly. She gave her testimony in a
clear, penetrating, slightly defiant voice. That
voice of hers never once faltered. Her eyes full of
desperate courage were fixed firmly on the face of
the solicitor who examined her. Even the terrible
ordeal of cross-examination was borne without
flinching; nor did Hetty once commit herself, or
contradict her own evidence. At the end of the
cross-examination, however, she fainted off. It
was noticed afterward by eye-witnesses that Hetty's
whole evidence had been given with her face
slightly turned away from that of the accused man.
It was after she had inadvertently met his eyes
that she turned white to the very lips, and fell
down fainting in the witness-box. She was carried
away immediately, and murmurs of sympathy followed her as she was taken out of the court.
Hetty was undoubtedly the heroine of the occasion.
Her remarkable beauty, her modesty, the ring of
truth which seemed to pervade all her unwilling
words, told fatally against poor Everett.

She was obliged to return to court on the second
day, but Margaret did not go to Salisbury on that
occasion. After the first day of the trial Margaret
spent a sleepless night. She was on the eve of her
own wedding, but she could think of nothing but
Everett and Everett's mother. Mrs. Everett was
present at the trial. She wore a widow's dress and
her veil was down, but once or twice she raised it

and looked at her son; the son also glanced at his mother. Margaret had seen these glances, and they wrung her heart to its depths. She felt that she could not be in court when the verdict was given. She was so excited with regard to the issue of the trial that she gave no attention to those minor matters which usually occupy the minds of young brides.

"It doesn't matter," she said to her maid; "pack anything you fancy into my travelling trunk. Oh, yes, that dress will do; any dress will do. What hats did you say? Any hats, I don't care. I'm going to Grandcourt now, there may be news from Salisbury."

"They say, Miss Douglas, that the Court won't rise until late to-night. The jury are sure to take a long time to consider the case."

"Well, I'm going to Grandcourt now. Mr. Awdrey may have returned. I shall hear the latest news."

Margaret arrived at the Court just before dinner. Her future sisters-in-law, Anne and Dorothy, ran out on the lawn to meet her.

"Oh, how white and tired you look!"

"I am not a bit tired; you know I am always pale. Dorothy, has any news come yet from Salisbury?"

"Nothing special," replied Dorothy. "The groom has come back to tell us that we are not to wait dinner for either father or Robert. You will come into the house now, won't you, Margaret?"

"No, I'd rather stay out here. I don't want any dinner."

"Nor do I. I will stay with you," said Dorothy. "Isn't there a lovely view from here? I love this part of the grounds better than any other spot. You can just get a peep of the Cathedral to the right and the Plain to the left."

"I hate the Plain," said Margaret, with a shiver. "I wish Grandcourt didn't lie so near it."

Dorothy Awdrey raised her delicate brows in surprise.

"Why, the Plain is the charm of Grandcourt," she exclaimed. "Surely, Margaret, you are not going to get nervous and fanciful, just because a murder was committed on the Plain."

"Oh, no!" Margaret started to her feet. "Excuse me, Dorothy, I see Robert coming up the avenue."

"So he is. Stay where you are, and I'll run and get the news."

"No, please let me go."

"Margaret, you are ill."

"I am all right," replied Margaret.

She ran swiftly down the avenue.

Awdrey saw her, and stopped until she came up to him.

"Well?" she asked breathlessly.

He put both his hands on her shoulders, and looked steadily into her eyes.

"The verdict," she said. "Quick, the verdict."

"Guilty, Maggie; but they have strongly recom-

mended him to mercy. Maggie, Maggie, my darling, what is it?"

She flung her arms round his neck, and hid her
trembling face against his breast.

"I can't help it," she said. "It is the eve of our
wedding-day. Oh, I feel sick with terror—sick
with sorrow."

CHAPTER IX.

ARTHUR RUMSEY, M.D., F.R.C.S., was one of the most remarkable men of his time. He was unmarried, and lived in a large house in Harley Street, where he saw many patients daily. He was on the staff of more than one of the big London hospitals, and one or two mornings in each week had to be devoted to this public service, which occupies so much of the life of a busy and popular doctor. Rumsey was not only a clever, all-round man, but he was also a specialist. The word nerve—that queer complex word, with its many hidden meanings, its daily and hourly fresh renderings—that word, which belongs especially to the end of our century, he seized with a grip of psychological intensity, and made it his principal study. By slow degrees and years of patient toil he began to understand the nerve power in man. From the study of the nerves to the study of the source of all nerves, aches and pains, joys and delights, the human brain, was an easy step. Rumsey was a brain specialist. It began to be reported of him, not only in the profession, but among that class of patients who must flock to such a man, when he had performed wonderful and extraordinary cures, that to him was given insight almost superhuman. It was said of

Rumsey that he could read motives and could also unravel the most complex problems of the psychological world.

Five years had passed since Margaret Douglas found herself the bride of Robert Awdrey. These five years had been mostly spent by the pair in London. Being well off, Awdrey had taken a good house in a fashionable quarter. He and Margaret began to entertain, and were popular from the very first, in their own somewhat large circle. They were now the parents of one beautiful child, a boy, and the outside world invariably spoke of them as a prosperous and a very happy couple.

Everett did not expiate his supposed crime by death. The plea of the jury for mercy resulted in fourteen years' penal servitude. Such a sentence meant, of course, a living death; he had quite sunk out of ken — almost out of memory. Except in the heart of his mother and in the tender heart of Margaret Awdrey, this young man, whose career had promised to be so bright, so satisfactory, such a blessing to all who knew him, was completely forgotten.

In his mother's heart, of course, he was safely enshrined, and Margaret also, although she had never spoken to him, and never saw his face until the day of the trial, still vividly remembered him.

When her honeymoon was over and she found herself settled in London, one of her first acts was to seek out Mrs. Everett, and to make a special friend of the forlorn and unhappy widow.

Both Margaret and Mrs. Everett soon found that they had a strong bond of sympathy between them. They both absolutely believed in Frank Everett's innocence. The subject, however, was too painful to the elder woman to be often alluded to, but knowing what was in Margaret's heart she took a great fancy to her, always spoke to her with affection, took a real interest in her concerns, and was often a visitor at her home.

Four years after the wedding the elder Squire died. He was found one morning dead in his bed, having passed peacefully and painlessly away. Awdrey was now the owner of Grandcourt, but for some reason which he could not explain, even to himself, he did not care to spend much time at the old place—Margaret was often there for months at a time, but Awdrey preferred London to the Court, and a week at a time was the longest period he would ever spend under the old roof. Both his sisters were now married and had homes of their own—the place in consequence began to grow a little into disuse, although Margaret did what she could for the tenantry, and whenever she was at the Court was extremely popular with her neighbors. But she did not think it right to leave her husband long alone—he clung to her a good deal, seeking her opinion more and more as the months and years went by, and leaning upon her to an extraordinary extent for a young and clever man.

Awdrey had grown exceptionally old for his age in the five years since his marriage. He was only

twenty-six, but some white streaks were already to
be found in his thick hair, and several wrinkles
were perceptible round his dark gray eyes. He
had not gone into Parliament—he had not distin-
guished himself by any literary work. His own
ambitious dreams and his wife's longings for him
faded one by one out of sight. He was a gentle,
kindly mannered man—generous with his money,
sympathetic up to a certain point over every tale of
woe, but there was a curious want of energy about
him, and as the days and months flew by, Margaret's sense of trouble, which always lay near her
heart, unaccountably deepened.

The great specialist, Arthur Rumsey, was about
to give a dinner. It was his custom to give one
once a fortnight during the London season. To
these dinners he not only invited his own friends
and the more favored among his patients, but many
celebrated men of science and literature; a few also
of the better sort of the smart people of society
were to be met on these occasions. Although there
was no hostess, Rumsey's dinners were popular,
his invitations were always eagerly accepted, and
the people who met each other at his house often
spoke afterward of these occasions as specially de-
lightful.

In short, the dinners partook of that intellectual
quality which makes, to quote an old-world phrase,
"the feast of reason and the flow of soul." On
Rumsey's evenings, the forgotten art of conversation
seemed once again to struggle to re-assert itself,

Robert Awdrey and his wife were often among the favored guests, and were to be present at this special dinner. Margaret was a distant cousin of the great physician, and shortly after her arrival in London had consulted him about her husband. She had told him all about the family history, and the curious hereditary taint which had shown itself from generation to generation in certain members of the men of the house. He had listened gravely, and with much interest, saying very little at the time, and endeavoring by every means in his power to soothe the anxieties of the young wife.

"The doom you dread may never fall upon your husband," he said finally. "The slight inertia of mind which he complains of is probably more due to nervous fear than to anything else. It is a pity he is so well off. If he had to work for his living, he would soon use his brain to good and healthy purpose. That fiat which fell upon Adam is in reality a blessing in disguise. There is no surer cure for most of the fads and fancies of the present day than the command which ordains to man that 'In the sweat of thy brow shalt thou eat bread.'"

Margaret's anxious eyes were fixed upon the great doctor while he was speaking.

"Your husband must make the best of his circumstances," he continued, in a cheerful tone. "Crowd occupation upon him; get him to take up any good intellectual work with strength and vigor. If you see he is really tired out, do not over-worry him. Get him to travel with you; get him to read

books with real stuff in them; occupy his mind at
any risk. When he begins to forget serious matters it will be time enough to come to the conclusion that the hereditary curse has descended upon
him. Up to the present he has never forgotten
anything of consequence, has he?"

"Nothing that I know of," answered Margaret.
Then she added, with a half-smile, "The small
lapse of memory which I am about to mention, you
will probably consider beneath your notice, nevertheless it has irritated my husband to a strange
degree. You have doubtless heard of the tragic
murder of Horace Frere, which took place on
Salisbury Plain a few weeks before our wedding?"

Rumsey nodded.

"On the night of the murder my husband lost
his favorite walking-stick. He has worried cease-
lessly over that small fact, referring to it constantly
and always complaining of a certain numbness in
the back of his head when he does so. The fact is
he met the unfortunate man who was murdered
early in the afternoon. At that time he had his
stick with him. He can never recall anything
about it from that moment, nor has he seen it from
then to now."

The doctor laughed good-humoredly.

"There is little doubt," he said, "that the fear
that the doom of his house may fasten upon him
has affected your husband's nerves. The lapse of
memory to which you refer means nothing at all.

Keep him occupied, Mrs. Awdrey, keep him occupied. That is my best advice to you."

Margaret went away feeling reassured and almost happy, but since the date of that conversation Rumsey never forgot Awdrey's queer case. He possessed that extraordinary and perfect memory himself, which does not allow the smallest detail, however apparently unimportant, to escape observation, and often as he talked to his guest across his dinner table, he observed him with a keenness of interest which he could himself scarcely account for.

On this particular evening more guests than usual were assembled at the doctor's house. Sixteen people had sat down to dinner and several fresh arrivals were expected in the evening. Among the dining guests was Mrs. Everett. She was a tall, handsome woman of about forty-five years of age. Her hair was snow-white and was piled high up over her head—her face was of a pale olive hue, with regular features, and very large, piercing, dark eyes. The eyebrows were well arched and somewhat thickly marked—they were still raven black, and afforded a striking contrast to the lovely thick hair which shone like a mass of silver above her brow.

Everett's mother always wore black, but, curious to relate, she had discarded widow's weeds soon after her son's incarceration. Before that date she had been in character, and had also lived the life of an ordinary, affectionate, and thoroughly amiable woman. Keen as her sorrow in parting with the husband of her youth was, she contrived to weave a happy nest in which her heart could take shelter, in the passionate love which she gave to her only son. But from the date of his trial and verdict, the woman's whole character, the very expression on her face, had altered. Her eyes had now a watchful and intent look. She seemed like some one who had set a mission before herself. She had the look of one who lived for a hidden purpose. She no longer eschewed society, but went into it even more frequently than her somewhat slender means afforded. She made many new acquaintances and was always eager to win the confidence of those who cared to confide in her. Her own story she never touched upon, but she gave a curious kind of watchful sympathy to others which was not without its charm.

On this particular night, the widow's eyes were brighter and more restless than usual. Dr. Rumsey knew all about her story, and had often counselled her with regard to her present attitude toward society at large.

"My boy is innocent," she had said many times to the doctor. "The object of my life is to prove this. I will quietly wait, I will do nothing rash, but it is my firm conviction that I shall yet be permitted to find and expose the man who killed Horace Frere."

Rumsey had warned her as to the peril which she ran in fostering too keenly a fixed idea—he had taken pains to give her psychological reasons for the danger which she incurred—but nothing he could say or do could alter the bias of her mind. Her fixed and unwavering assurance that her boy was absolutely innocent could not be imperilled by any words which man could speak.

"If I had even seen my boy do the murder I should still believe it to be a vision of my own brain," she had said once, and after that Rumsey had ceased to try to guide her thoughts into a healthier channel.

On this particular night when the doctor came up-stairs after wine, accompanied by the rest of the men of the party, Mrs. Everett seemed to draw him to her side by her watchful and excited glances.

There was something about the man which could never withstand an appeal of human need—he went straight now to the widow's side as a needle is attracted to a magnet.

"Well," he said, drawing a chair forward, and seating himself so as almost to face her.

"You guessed that I wanted to see you?" she said eagerly.

"I looked at you and that was sufficient," he said.

"When can you give me an interview?" she replied.

"Do you want to visit me as a patient?"

"I do not—that is, not in the ordinary sense. I want to tell you something. I have a story to relate, and when it is told I should like to get

your verdict on a certain peculiar case—in short, I
believe I have got a clue, if only a slight one, to
the unravelling of the mystery of my life—you
quite understand?"

"Yes, I understand," replied Dr. Rumsey in a
gentle voice, "but, my dear lady, I am not a detective."

"Not in the ordinary sense, but surely as far as
the complex heart is concerned."

Dr. Rumsey held up his hand.

"We need not go into that," he said.

"No, we will not. May I see you to-morrow
for a few minutes?"

The doctor consulted his note-book.

"I cannot see you as a patient," he said, "but
as a friend it is possible. Can you be here at
eight o'clock to-morrow morning? I breakfast at
eight—my breakfast generally occupies ten minutes—that time is at your disposal."

"I will be with you. Thank you a thousand
times," she replied.

Her eyes grew bright with exultation. The
doctor favored her with a keen glance and moved
aside. A few minutes later he found himself in
Margaret Awdrey's vicinity. Margaret was now a
very beautiful woman. As a girl she had been
lovely, but her early matronhood had developed
her charms, had added to her stateliness, and had
brought out many new and fresh expressions in
her mobile and lovely face.

As Rumsey approached her side, she was in the

act of taking leave of an old friend of her husband's, who was going away early. The Doctor was therefore able to watch her for a minute without her observing him—then she turned slightly, saw him, flushed vividly, and went eagerly and swiftly to his side.

"Dr. Rumsey," said Margaret, "I know this is not the place to make appointments, but I am anxious to see you on the subject of my husband's health. How soon can you manage——"

"I can make an appointment for to-morrow," he interrupted. "Be with me at half-past one. I can give you half an hour quite undisturbed then."

She did not smile, but her eyes were raised fully to his face. Those dark, deep eyes so full of the noblest emotions which can stir the human soul, looked at him now with a pathos that touched his heart. He moved away to talk to other friends, but the thought of Margaret Awdrey returned to him many times during the ensuing night.

CHAPTER X.

AT the appointed hour on the following morning Mrs. Everett was shown into Dr. Rumsey's presence. She found him in his cosy breakfast-room, in the act of helping himself to coffee.

"Ah!" he said, as he placed a chair for her, "what an excellent thing this punctuality is in a woman. Sit down, pray. You shall have your full ten minutes—the clock is only on the stroke of eight."

Mrs. Everett looked too disturbed and anxious even to smile. She untied her bonnet-strings, threw back her mantle, and stared straight at Dr. Rumsey.

"No coffee, thank you," she said. "I breakfasted long ago. Dr. Rumsey, I am nearly wild with excitement and anxiety. I told you long ago, did I not, that a day would come when I should get a clue which might lead to establishing my boy's"—she wet her lips—"my only boy's innocence? Nothing that can happen now will ever, of course, repair what he has lost—his lost youth, his lost healthy outlook on life—but to set him free, even now! To give him his liberty once again! To feel the clasp of his hand on mine! Ah, I nearly go mad at times with longing, but thank God, thank the Providence which is above us all, I do believe I have found a clue at last."

"Tell me what it is," said the doctor, in a kind voice. "I know," he added, "you will make your story as brief as possible."

"I will, my good friend," she replied. She stood up now, her somewhat long arms hung at her sides, she turned her face in all its intense purpose full upon the doctor.

"You know my restless nature," she continued. "I can seldom or never sit still—even my sleep is broken by terrible dreams. All the energy which I possess is fixed upon one thought, and one only —I want to find the real murderer of Horace Frere."

"Yes," said Dr. Rumsey.

"A fortnight ago I made up my mind to do a queer thing. I determined to visit Grandcourt— I mean the village of that name."

The doctor started.

"You are surprised?" said Mrs. Everett; "nevertheless I can account for my longings."

"You need not explain. I quite understand."

"I believe you do. I felt drawn to the place— to the Inn where my son stayed, to the neighborhood. I travelled down to Grandcourt without announcing my intention to any one, and arrived at the Inn just as the dusk was setting in. The landlord, Armitage by name, came out to interview me. I told him who I was. He looked much disturbed, and by no means pleased. I asked him if he

would take me in. He went away to consult his
wife. She followed him after a moment into the
porch with a scared face.

"'I wonder, ma'am, that you like to come here,'
she said.

"'I come for one purpose,' I replied. 'I want
to see the spot where Horace Frere met his death.
I am drawn to this place by the greatest agony
which has ever torn a mother's heart. Will you
take me in, and will you give me the room in which
my son slept?'

"The landlady looked at me in anything but a
friendly manner. Her husband whispered something to her—after a time her brow cleared—she
nodded to him, and the next moment I was given
to understand that my son's old room would be at
my disposal. I took possession of it that evening,
and my meals were served to me in the little parlor where my boy and the unfortunate Horace
Frere had lived together.

"The next day I went out alone at an early hour
to visit the Plain. I had never ventured on Salisbury Plain before. The day was a gloomy and
stormy one. There were constant showers of rain,
and I was almost wet through by the time I
reached my destination. I had just got upon the
borders of the Plain when I saw a young woman
walking a little ahead of me. There was something in the gait which I seemed to recognize, although at first I had only a dim idea that I had
ever seen her before. Hurrying my footsteps I

came up to her, passed her, and as I did so looked her full in the face. I started then and stopped short. She was the girl who had seen the murder committed, and who had given evidence of the most damnatory kind against my son on the day of the trial. In that one swift glance I saw that she was much altered._ She had been a remarkably pretty girl. She had now nearly lost all her comeliness of appearance. Her face was thin, her dress negligent and untidy, on her brow there was a sullen frown. When she saw me she also stood still, her eyes dilated with a curious expression of fear.

" ' Who are you?' she said, with a pant.

" ' I am Mrs. Everett,' I replied, slowly. ' I am the mother of the man who once lodged in your uncle's house, and who is now expiating the crime of another at Portland prison.'

" She had turned red at first, now she became white.

" ' And your name,' I continued, ' is Hetty Armitage.'

" ' Why do you say that your son is expatiating the crime of another?' she asked.

" ' Because I am his mother. I have looked into his heart, and there is no murder there. But tell me, is not your name Hetty Armitage?'

" ' It is not Armitage now,' she answered. ' I am married. I live about three miles from Grandcourt, over in that direction. I am going home now. My husband's name is Vincent. He is a farmer.'

"'You don't look too well off,' I said, for I noticed her shabby dress and run-to-seed appearance.

"'These are hard times for farmers,' she answered.

"'Have you children?' I asked.

"'No,' she replied fiercely, 'I am glad to say I have not.'

"'Why are you glad?' I asked. 'Surely a child is the crown of a married woman's bliss.'

"'It would not be to me,' she cried. 'My heart is full to the brim. I have no room for a child in it.'

"'A full heart generally means happiness,' I said. 'Are you happy?'

"She gave me a queer glance.

"'No, ma'am,' she answered, 'my heart is full of bitterness, of sorrow.' Her eyes looked quite wild. She pressed one of her hands to her forehead,—then stepping out, she half turned round to me.

"'I wish you good-morning, Mrs. Everett,' she said. 'My way lies across here.'

"'Stay a moment before you leave me,' I said. 'I am coming to this plain on a mission which you perhaps can guess. If you are poor you will not despise half a sovereign. I'll give you half a sovereign if you'll show me the exact spot where the murder was committed.'

"She turned from white to red, and from red to white again.

"'I don't like that spot,' she said. 'That night was a terrible night to me; my nerves ain't what they were—I sleep bad, and sometimes I dream. Many and many a time I've seen that murder committed over again. I have seen the look on the face of the murdered man, and the look on the face of the man who did it—Oh, my God, I have seen——'

She pressed her two hands hard against her eyes.

"I waited quietly until she had recovered her emotion; then I held out the little gold coin.

"'You will take me to the spot?' I asked.

"She clutched the coin suddenly in her hand.

"'This will buy what I live for,' she cried, with passion. 'I can drown thought with this. Come along, ma'am, we are not very far from the place here. I'll take you, and then go on home.'

"She started off, walking in front of me, and keeping well ahead. She went quickly, and yet with a sort of tremulous movement, as though she were not quite certain of herself. We crossed the Plain not far from the Court. I saw the house in the distance, and the curling smoke which rose up out of the trees.

"'Don't walk so fast,' I said. 'I am an old woman, and you take my breath away.' She slackened her steps, but very unwillingly.

"'The family are not often at the Court?' I queried.

"'No,' she answered with a start—'since the old Squire died the place has been most shut up.'

"'I happen to know the present Squire and his wife,' I said.

"She flushed when I said this, gave me a furtive glance, and then pressing one hand to her left side, said abruptly:

"'If you know you can tell me summ'at—he is well, is he?'

"'They are both well,' I answered, surprised at the tone of her voice. 'I should judge them to be a happy couple.'

"'I thank the good God that Mr. Robert is happy,' she said, in a hoarse whisper.

"Once again she hurried her footsteps; at last she stood still on a rising knoll of ground.

"'Do you see this clump of alders?' she said. 'It was here I stood, just on this spot—I was sheltered by the alders, and even if the night had not been so dark they would never have noticed me. Over there to your right it was done. You don't want me to stay any longer now, ma'am, do you?'

"'You can go when I have asked you one or two questions. You stood here, you say—just here?'

"'Just here, ma'am,' she answered.

"'And the murder was committed there?'

"'Yes, where the grass seems to grow a bit greener—you notice it, don't you, just there, to your right.'

"'I see,' I replied with a shudder, which I could not repress. 'Do you mind telling me how it was that you happened to be out of your bed at such a late hour at night?'

"She looked very sullen, and set her lips tightly. I gazed full at her, waiting for her to speak.

"'The man whose blood was shed was my lover—we had just had a quarrel,' she said, at last.

"'What about?'

"'That's my secret,' she replied.

"'How is it you did not mention the fact of the quarrel at the trial?' I asked.

"She looked full up at me.

"'I was not asked,' she answered; 'that's my secret, and I don't tell it to anybody. It was here I stood, just where your feet are planted, and I saw it done—the moon came out for a minute, and I saw everything—even to the look on the dead man's face and the look on the face of the man who took his life. I saw it all. I ain't been the same woman since.'

"'I am not surprised,' I replied. 'You may leave me when I have said one thing.'

"'What is that, ma'am?'

"She raised her dark eyes. I saw fear in their depths.

"'You saw two men that night, Hetty Vincent,' I said—'one, the man who was murdered, was Horace Frere, but the other man, as there is a God above, was not Frank Everett. I am speaking the truth—you can go now.'

"My words seemed forced from me, Dr. Rumsey, but the effect was terrifying. The wretched creature fell on her knees—she clung to my dress, covering her face with a portion of the mantle which I was wearing.

"'Good God, why do you say that?' she gasped. 'How do you know? Who has told you? Why do you say awful words of that sort?'

"Her excitement made me calm. I stood perfectly silent, but with my heart beating with the queerest sense of exultation and victory.

"'Get up,' I said. She rose trembling to her feet. I laid my hand on her shoulder.

"'You have something to confess,' I said.

"She looked at me again and burst out laughing.

"'What a fool I made of myself just now!' she said. 'I have nothing to confess; what could I have? You spoke so solemn and the place is queer—it always upsets me. I'll go now.' She backed a few steps away.

"'I saw two men on the Plain,' she said then, raising her voice, 'one was Horace Frere—the other was your son, Frank Everett.' Before I could add another word she took to her heels and was quickly out of sight.

"I returned to the Inn and questioned Armitage and his wife. I did not dare to tell them what Hetty had said in her excitement, but I asked for her address and drove out early the following morning to Vincent's farm to visit her. I was told on my arrival that she had left home that morning; that she often did so to visit a relation at a distance. I asked for the address, which was

given me somewhat unwillingly. That night I
went there, but Hetty had not arrived and nothing
was known about her. Since then I have tried in
vain to get any clue to her present whereabouts.
That is my story, Dr. Rumsey. What do you
think of it? Are the wild stories of an excited and
over-wrought woman worthy of careful consideration? Is her sudden flight suspicious, or the reverse? I anxiously await your verdict."

Dr. Rumsey remained silent for a moment.

"I am inclined to believe," he said, then very
slowly, "that the words uttered by this young
woman were merely the result of overstrung nerves;
remember, she was in all probability in love with
the man who met his death in so tragic a manner.
From the remarkable change which you speak of
in her appearance, I should say that her nerves
had been considerably shattered by the sight she
witnessed, and also by the prominent place she was
obliged to take in the trial. She has probably
dreamt of this thing, and dwelt upon it year in
and year out, since it happened. Then, remember,
you spoke in a very startling manner and practically accused her of having committed perjury at
the time of the trial. Under such circumstances
and in the surroundings she was in at the time,
she would be very likely to lose her head. As to
her sudden disappearance, I confess I cannot quite
understand it, unless her nervous system is even
more shattered than you incline me to believe; but,
stay,—from words she inadvertently let drop, she

8

has evidently become addicted to drink, to opium eating, or some such form of self-indulgence. If that is the case she would be scarcely responsible for her actions. I do not think, Mrs. Everett, unless you can obtain further evidence, that there is anything to go upon in this."

"That is your carefully considered opinion?"

"It is—I am sorry if it disappoints you."

"It does not do that, for I cannot agree with you."

Mrs. Everett rose as she spoke, fastened her cloak, and tied her bonnet-strings.

"Your opinion is the cool one of an acute reasoner, but also of a person who is outside the circumstances," she continued.

Rumsey smiled.

"Surely in such a case mine ought to be the one to be relied upon?" he queried.

"No, for there is such a thing as mother's instinct. I will not detain you longer, Dr. Rumsey. You have said what I expected you would say."

CHAPTER XI.

RUMSEY began the severe routine of his daily work. He was particularly busy that day, and had many anxious cases to consider; it was also one of his hospital mornings, and his hospital cases were, he considered, some of the most important in his practice. Nevertheless Mrs. Everett's face and her words of excitement kept flashing again and again before his memory.

"There is a possibility of that woman losing her senses if her mind is not diverted into another channel, and soon too," he thought to himself. "If she allows her thoughts to dwell much longer on this fixed idea, she will see her son's murderer in the face of each man and woman with whom she comes in contact. Still there is something queer in her story—the young woman whom she addressed on Salisbury Plain was evidently the victim of nervous terror to a remarkable extent—can it be possible that she is concealing something?"

Rumsey thought for a moment over his last idea. Then he dismissed it from his mind.

"No," he said to himself, "a village girl could not stand cross-examination without betraying herself. I shall get as fanciful as Mrs. Everett if I dwell any longer upon this problem. After all there is no problem to consider. Why not accept the obvious fact? Poor Everett killed his friend in a moment of strong irritation—it was a very plain case of manslaughter."

At the appointed hour Margaret Awdrey appeared on the scene. She was immediately admitted into Dr. Rumsey's presence. He asked her to seat herself, and took a chair facing her. It was Margaret's way to be always very direct. She was direct now, knowing that her auditor's time was of extreme value.

"I have not troubled you about my husband for some years," she began.

"You have not," he replied.

"Do you remember what I last told you about him?"

"Perfectly. But excuse me one moment; to satisfy you I will look up his case in my case-book. Do you remember the year when you last spoke to me about him?"

Margaret instantly named the date, not only of year, but of month. Dr. Rumsey quickly looked up the case. He laid his finger on the open page in which he had entered all particulars, ran his eyes rapidly over the notes he had made at the time, and then turned to Mrs. Awdrey.

"I find, as I expected, that I have forgotten nothing," he said. "I was right in my conjectures, was I not? Your husband's symptoms were due to nervous distress?"

"I wish I could say so," replied Margaret.

Dr. Rumsey slightly raised his brows.

"Are there fresh symptoms?" he asked.

"He is not well. I must tell you exactly how he is affected."

The doctor bent forward to listen. Margaret began her story.

"Since the date of our marriage there has been a very gradual, but also a marked deterioration in my husband's character," she said. "But until lately he has been in possession of excellent physical health, his appetite has been good, he has been inclined for exercise, and has slept well. In short, his bodily health has been without a flaw. Accompanying this state of physical well-being there has been a very remarkable mental torpor."

"Are you not fanciful on that point?" asked Dr. Rumsey.

"I am not. Please remember that I have known him since he was a boy. As a boy he was particularly ambitious, full of all sorts of schemes for the future—many of these schemes were really daring and original. He did well at school, and better than well at Balliol. When we became engaged his strong sense of ambition was quite one of the most remarkable traits of his character. He always spoke of doing much with his life. The idea was that as soon as possible he was to enter the House, and he earnestly hoped that when that happy event took place he would make his mark there. One by one all these thoughts, all these hopes and aims, have dropped away from his mind; each

year has robbed him of something, until at last he
has come to that pass when even books fail to
arouse any interest in him. He sits for many
hours absolutely doing nothing, not even sleeping,
but gazing straight before him into vacancy. Our
little son is almost the only person who has any
power to rouse him. He is devoted to the child,
but his love even for little Arthur is tempered by
that remarkable torpor—he never plays with the
boy, who is a particularly strong-willed, spirited
child, but likes to sit with him on his knee, the
child's arms clasped round his neck. He has
trained the little fellow to sit perfectly still. The
child is devoted to his father, and would do anything for him. As the years have gone on, my
husband has become more and more a man of few
words—I now believe him to be a man of few
thoughts—of late he has been subject to moods of
deep depression, and although he is my husband,
I often feel, truly as I love him, that he is more
like a log than a man."

Tears dimmed Margaret's eyes; she hastily
wiped them away.

"I would not trouble you about all this," she
continued, "but for a change which has taken place
within the last few months. That change directly
affects my husband's physical health, and as such
is the case I feel it right to consult you about it."

"Yes, speak—take your own time—I am much
interested," said the doctor.

"The change in my husband's health of body

has also begun gradually," continued Mrs. Awdrey. "You know, of course, that he is now the owner of Grandcourt. He has taken a great dislike to the place—in my opinion, an unaccountable dislike. He absolutely refuses to live there. Now I am fond of Grandcourt, and our little boy always seems in better health and spirits there than anywhere else. I take my child down to the old family place whenever I can spare a week from my husband. Last autumn I persuaded Mr. Awdrey with great difficulty to accompany me to Grandcourt for a week. I have never ceased to regret that visit."

"Indeed, what occurred?" asked the doctor.

"Apparently nothing, and yet evidently a great deal. When we got into the country Robert's apathy seemed to change; he roused himself and became talkative and even excitable. He took long walks, and was particularly fond of visiting Salisbury Plain, that part which lies to the left of the Court. He invariably took these rambles alone, and often went out quite late in the evening, not returning until midnight.

"On the last of these occasions I asked him why he was so fond of walking by himself. He said with a forced laugh, and a very queer look in his eyes, that he was engaged trying to find a favorite walking-stick which he had lost years ago. He laid such stress upon what appeared such a trivial subject that I could scarcely refrain from smiling. When I did so he swore a terrific oath, and said, with blazing eyes, that life or death depended upon the matter which I thought so trivial. Immediately after his brief blaze of passion he became moody, dull, and more inert than ever. The next day we left the Court. It was immediately after that visit that his physical health began to give way. He lost his appetite, and for the last few months he has been the victim of a very peculiar form of sleeplessness."

"Ah, insomnia would be bad in a case like his." said Dr. Rumsey.

"It has had a very irritating effect upon him. His sleeplessness, like all other symptoms, came on gradually. At the same time he became intensely sensitive to the slightest noise. Against my will he tried taking small doses of chloral, but they had the reverse of a beneficial effect upon him. During the last month he has, toward morning, dropped off into uneasy slumber, from which he awakens bathed in perspiration and in a most curious state of terror. Night after night the same sort of thing occurs. He seizes my hand and asks me in a voice choking with emotion if I see anything in the room. 'Nothing,' I answer.

"'Am I awake or asleep?' he asks next.

"'Wide awake,' I say to him.

"'Then it is as I fear,' he replies. 'I see it, I see it distinctly. Can't you? Look, you must see it too. It is just over there, in the direction of the window. Don't you see that sphere of perfect light? Don't you see the picture in the middle?' He shivers; the drops of perspiration fall from his forehead.

"'Margaret,' he says, 'for God's sake look. Tell me that you see it too.'

"'I see nothing,' I answer him.

"'Then the vision is for me alone. It haunts me. What have I done to deserve it? Margaret, there is a circle of light over there—in the centre a picture—it is the picture of a murder. Two men are in it—yes, I know now—I am looking at the Plain near the Court—the moon is hidden behind the clouds—there are two men—they fight. God in heaven, one man falls—the other bends over him. I see the face of the fallen man, but I cannot see the face of the other. I should rest content if I could only see his face. Who is he, Margaret, who is he?'

"He falls back on his pillow half-fainting.

"This sort of thing goes on night after night, Dr. Rumsey. Toward morning the vision which tortures my unhappy husband begins to fade, he sinks into heavy slumber, and awakens late in the morning with no memory whatever of the horrible thing which has haunted him during the hours of darkness.

"The days which follow are more full than ever of that terrible inertia, and now he begins to look what he really is, a man stricken with an awful doom.

"The symptoms you speak of are certainly alarming," said Dr. Rumsey, after a pause. "They point to a highly unsatisfactory state of the nerve centres. These symptoms, joined to

what you have already told me of the peculiar
malady which Awdrey inherits, make his case a
grave one. Of course, I by no means give up
hope, but the recurrence of this vision nightly is a
singular symptom. Does Awdrey invariably speak
of not being able to see the face of the man who
committed the murder?"

"Yes, he always makes a remark to that effect.
He seems every night to see the murdered man
lying on the ground with his face upward, but the
man who commits the murder has his back to
him. Last night he shrieked out in absolute terror
on the subject:

"'Who is the man? That man on the ground is
Horace Frere—he has been hewn down in the first
strength of his youth—he is a dead man. There
stands the murderer, with his back to me, but who
is he? Oh, my God!' he cried out with great
passion, 'who is the one who has done this deed?
Who has murdered Horace Frere? I would give
all I possess, all that this wide world contains,
only to catch one glimpse of his face.'

"He sprang out of bed as he spoke, and went a
step or two in the direction where he saw the
peculiar vision, clasping his hands, and staring
straight before him like a person distraught, and
almost out of his mind. I followed him and tried
to take his hand.

"'Robert!' I said, 'you know, don't you, quite
well, who murdered Horace Frere? Poor fellow,
it was not murder in the ordinary sense. Frank

Everett is the name of the man whose face you cannot see. But it is an old story now, and you have nothing to do with it, nothing whatever— don't let it dwell any longer on your mind.'

"'Ha, but he carries my stick,' he shrieked out, and then he fell back in a state of unconsciousness against the bed."

"And do you mean to tell me that he remembered nothing of this agony in the morning?" queried Dr. Rumsey.

"Nothing whatever. At breakfast he complained of a slight headache and was particularly dull and moody. When I came off to you he had just started for a walk in the Park with our little boy."

"I should like to see your husband, and to talk to him," said Dr. Rumsey, rising abruptly. "Can you manage to bring him here?"

"I fear I cannot, for he does not consider himself ill."

"Shall you be at home this evening?"

"Yes, we are not going out to-night."

"Then I'll drop in between eight and nine on a friendly visit. You must not be alarmed if I try to lead up to the subject of these nightly visions, for I would infinitely rather your husband remembered them than that they should quite slip from his memory."

"Thank you," answered Margaret. "I will leave you alone with him when you call to-night."

"It may be best for me to see him without any-one else being present."

Margaret Awdrey soon afterward took her leave.

That night, true to his appointment, Dr. Rumsey made his appearance at the Awdreys' house in Seymour Street. He was shown at once into the drawing-room, where Awdrey was lying back in a deep chair on one side of the hearth, and Margaret was softly playing a sonata of Beethoven's in the distance. She played with great feeling and power, and did not use any notes. The part of the room where she sat was almost in shadow, but the part round the fire where Awdrey had placed himself was full of bright light.

Margaret's dark eyes looked full of painful thought when the great doctor was ushered into the room. She did not see him at first, then she noticed him and faltered in her playing. She took her fingers from the piano, and rose to meet him.

"Pray go on, Margaret. What are you stopping for?" cried her husband. "Nothing soothes me like your music. Go on, go on. I see the moonlight on the trees, I feel the infinite peace, the waves are beating on the shore, there is rest." He broke off abruptly, starting to his feet. "I beg your pardon, Dr. Rumsey, I assure you I did not see you until this moment."

"I happened to have half-an-hour at my disposal, and thought I would drop in for a chat," said Dr. Rumsey in his pleasant voice.

Awdrey's somewhat fretful brow relaxed.

"You are heartily welcome," he said. "Have you dined? Will you take anything?"

"I have dined, and I only want one thing," said Dr. Rumsey.

"Pray name it; I'll ring for it immediately."

"You need not do that, for the person to give it to me is already in the room."

The doctor bowed to Margaret as he spoke.

"I love the 'Moonlight Sonata' beyond all other music," he said. "Will you continue playing it, Mrs. Awdrey? Will you rest a tired physician as well as your husband with your music?"

"With all the pleasure in the world," she replied. She returned at once to her shady corner, and the soothing effects of the sonata once more filled the room. For a short time Awdrey sat upright, forced into attention of others by the fact of Dr. Rumsey's presence, but he soon relaxed the slight effort after self-control, and lay back in his chair once again with his eyes half shut.

Rumsey listened to the music and watched his strange patient at the same time.

Margaret suddenly stopped, almost as abruptly as if she had had a signal. She walked up the room, and stood in the bright circle of light. She looked very lovely, and almost spiritual—her face was pale—her eyes luminous as if lit from within —her pathetic and perfect lips were slightly apart. Rumsey thought her something like an angel who was about to utter a benediction.

"I am going up now to see little Arthur," she said. She glanced at her husband, and left the room.

Rumsey had not failed to observe that Awdrey did not even glance at his wife when she stood on the hearth. There was a full moment's pause after she left the room. Awdrey's eyes were half closed, they were turned in the direction of the bright blaze. Rumsey looked full at him.

"Strange case, strange man," he muttered under his breath. "There is something for me to un-ravel here. The man who is insensate enough not to see the beauty in that woman's face, not to revel in the love she bestows on him—he is a log, not a man—and yet——"

"Are you well?" cried the doctor abruptly. He spoke on purpose with great distinctness, and his words had something the effect of a pistol-shot.

Awdrey sat bolt upright and stared full at him.

"Why do you ask me that question?" he replied, irritation in his tone.

"Because I wish to question you with regard to your health," said Dr. Rumsey. "Whether you feel it or not, you are by no means well."

"Indeed! What do I look like?"

"Like a man who sees more than he ought," re-plied the doctor with deliberation. "But before we come to that may I ask you a question?"

Awdrey looked disturbed—he got up and stood with his back to the fire.

"Ask what you please," he said, rubbing up his hair as he spoke. "As there is a heaven above, Dr. Rumsey, you see a wretched man before you to-night."

"My dear fellow, what strong words! Surely, you of all people——"

Awdrey interrupted with a hollow laugh.

"Ah," he said, "it looks like it, does it not? In any circle, among any concourse of people, I should be pointed out as the fortunate man. I have money—I have a very good and beautiful wife —I am the father of as fine a boy as the heart of man could desire. I belong to one of the old and established families of our country, and I also, I suppose, may claim the inestimable privilege to youth, for I am only twenty-six years of age— nevertheless——" He shuddered, looked down the long room, and then closed his eyes.

"I am glad I came here," said Dr. Rumsey. "Believe me, my dear sir, the symptoms you have just described are by no means uncommon in the cases of singularly fortunate individuals like yourself. The fact is, you have got too much. You want to empty yourself of some of your abundance in order that contentment and health of mind may flow in."

Awdrey stared at the doctor with lack-lustre eyes. Then he shook his head.

"I am past all that," he said. "I might at the first have managed to make a superhuman effort; but now I have no energy for anything. I have not even energy sufficient to take away my own life, which is the only thing on all God's earth that I crave to do."

"Come, come, Awdrey, you must not allow

yourself to speak like that. Now sit down. Tell me, if you possibly can, exactly what you feel."

"Why should I tell you? I am not your patient."

"But I want you to be."

"Is that why you came here this evening?"

Dr. Rumsey paused before he replied; he had not expected this question.

"I will answer you frankly," he said, with a pause. "Your wife came to see me about you. She did not wish me to mention the fact of her visit, but I believe I am wise in keeping nothing back from you. You love your wife, don't you?"

"I suppose I do; that is, if I love anybody."

"Of course, you love her. Don't sentimentalize over a fact. She came to see me because her love for you is over-abundant. It makes her anxious; you have given her, Awdrey, a great deal of anxiety lately.

"I cannot imagine how. I have done nothing."

"That is just it. You have done too little. She is naturally terribly anxious. She told me one or two things about your state which I do not consider quite satisfactory. I said it would be necessary for me to have an interview with you, and asked her to beg of you to call at my house. She said you did not consider yourself ill, and might not be willing to come to me. I then resolved to come to you, and here I am."

"It is good of you, Rumsey, but you can do nothing; I am not really ill. It is simply that something—I have not the faintest idea what—has killed my soul. I believe, before heaven, that I have stated the case in a nutshell. You may be, and doubtless are, a great doctor, but you have not come across living men with dead souls before."

"I have not Awdrey; nor is your soul dead. You state an impossibility."

Awdrey started excitedly. His face, which had been deadly pale, now blazed with animation and color.

"Learned as you are," he cried, "you will gain some fresh and valuable experience from me to-night. I am the strangest patient you ever attempted to cure. You have roused me, and it is good to be roused. Perhaps my soul is not dead after all—perhaps it is struggling with a demon which crushes it down."

9

CHAPTER XII.

DR. RUMSEY did not reply to this for a moment, then he spoke quietly.

"Tell me everything," he said. "Nothing you can say will startle me, but if there is any possibility of my helping you I must know the case as far as you can give it me."

"I have but little to say," replied Awdrey. "I am paralyzed day after day simply by want of reeling. Even a sense of pain, of irritation, is a relief—the deadness of my life is so overpowering. Do you know the history of my house?"

"Your wife has told me. It is a queer story."

"It is a damnable story," said Awdrey. "With such a fate hanging over me, why was I born? Why did my father marry? Why did my mother bring a man-child into the world? Men with dooms like mine ought never to have descendants. I curse the thought that I have a child myself. It is all cruel, monstrous."

"But the thing you fear has not fallen upon you," said Dr. Rumsey.

"Has it not? I believe it has."

"How can you possibly imagine what is not the case?"

"Dr. Rumsey," said Awdrey, advancing a step

or two to meet him, "I don't imagine what I know. Look at me. I am six-and-twenty. Do I look that age?"

"I must confess that you look older than your years."

"Aye, I should think so. See my hair already mingled with gray. Feel this nerveless hand. Is this the hand of the English youth of six-and-twenty? Look at my eyes—how dull they are; are they the eyes of a man in his prime? No, no, I am going down to the grave as the other men of my house have gone, simply because I cannot help it. Like those who have gone before me I slip, and slip, and slip, and cannot get a grip of life anywhere, and so I go out, or go over the precipice into God knows what—anyhow I go."

"Poor fellow, he is far worse than I had any idea of," thought the doctor. He took his patient's hand, and led him to a seat.

"You are quite ill enough to see a doctor," he said, "and ought to have had advice long ago. I mean to take you up, Awdrey. From this moment you must consider yourself my patient."

"If you can do anything for me I shall be glad—that is, no, I shall not be glad, for I am incapable of the sensation, but I am aware it is the right thing to put myself into your hands. What do you advise?"

"I cannot tell you until I know more. My present impression is that you are simply the victim of nerve terrors. You have dwelt upon the doom of your house for so long a time that you are now fully convinced that you are one of the victims. But you must please remember that the special feature of the tragedy, for tragedy it is, has not occurred in your case, for you have never forgotten anything of consequence."

"Only one thing—it sounds stupid even to speak of it, but it worries me inconceivably. There was a murder committed on Salisbury Plain the night before I got engaged to Margaret. On that night I lost a walking-stick which I was particularly fond of."

"Your wife mentioned to me that you were troubled on that point," broke in Dr. Rumsey. "Pray dismiss it at once and forever from your mind. The fact of your having forgotten such a trifle is not of the slightest consequence."

"Do you think so? The fret about it has fastened itself very deeply into my mind."

"Well, don't think of it again—the next time it occurs to torment you, just remember that I, who have made brain troubles like yours my special study, think nothing at all about it."

"Thank you, I'll try to remember."

"Do so. Now, I wish to talk to you about another matter. You sleep badly."

"Do I?" Awdrey raised his brows. "I cannot recall that fact."

"Nevertheless you do. Your wife speaks of it. Now in your state of health it is most essential that you should have good nights."

"I always feel an added sense of depression when I am going to bed," said Awdrey, "but I am unconscious that I have bad nights—what can Margaret mean?"

"I trust that your wife's natural nervousness with regard to you makes her inclined to exaggerate your symptoms, but I may as well say frankly that some of the things she has mentioned, as occurring night after night, have given me uneasiness. Now I should like to be with you during one of your bad nights."

"What do you mean?"

"Come home with me to-night, my good fellow," said the doctor, laying his hand on Awdrey's shoulder—"we will pass this night together. What do you say?"

"Your request surprises me very much, but it would be a relief—I will go," said Awdrey.

He turned and rang the bell as he spoke—a servant appeared, who was sent with a message to Mrs. Awdrey. She came to the drawing-room in a few minutes. Her face of animation, wakefulness of soul and feeling, made a strong contrast to Awdrey's haggard, lifeless expression.

He went up to his wife and put his hand on her shoulder.

"You have been telling tales of me, Maggie," he said. "You complain of something I know nothing about—my bad nights."

"They are very bad, Robert, very terrible," she replied.

"I cannot recall a single thing about them."

"I wish you could remember," she said.

"I have made a suggestion to your husband," interrupted Dr. Rumsey, "which I am happy to say he approves of. He returns with me to my house to-night. I will promise to look after him. If he does happen to have a bad night I shall be witness to it. Now pray go to bed yourself and enjoy the rest you sorely need."

Margaret tried to smile in reply, but her eyes filled with tears. Rumsey saw them, but Awdrey took no notice—he was staring straight into vacancy, after his habitual fashion.

A moment later he and Rumsey left the house together. Ten minutes afterward Rumsey opened his own door with a latch-key.

"It is late," he said to his guest. He glanced at the clock as he spoke. "At this hour I always indulge in supper—it is waiting for me now. Will you come and have a glass of port with me?"

Awdrey murmured something in reply—the two men went into the dining-room, where Rumsey, without apparently making any fuss, saw that his guest ate and drank heartily. During the meal the doctor talked, and Awdrey replied in monosyllables—sometimes, indeed, not replying at all. Dr. Rumsey took no notice of this. When the meal, which really only took a few minutes, was over, he rose.

"I am going to take you to your bedroom now," he said.

"Thanks," answered Awdrey. "The whole thing seems extraordinary," he added. "I cannot make out why I am to sleep in your house."

"You sleep here as my patient. I am going to sit up with you."

"You! I cannot allow it, doctor!"

"Not a word, my dear sir. Pray don't overwhelm me with thanks. Your case is one of great interest to me. I shall certainly not regret the few hours I steal from sleep to watch it."

Awdrey made a dull reply. The two men went up-stairs. Rumsey had already given orders, and a bedroom had been prepared. A bright fire burned in the grate, and electric light made the room cheerful as day. The bed was placed in an alcove by itself. In front of the fire was drawn up a deep, easy chair, a small table, a reading-lamp ready to be lighted, and several books.

"For me?" said Awdrey, glancing at these. "Excuse me, Dr. Rumsey, but I do not appreciate books. Of late months I have had a difficulty in centring my thoughts on what I read. Even the most exciting story fails to arouse my attention."

"These books are for me," said the doctor. "You are to go straight to bed. You will find everything you require for the night in that part of the room. Pray undress as quickly as possible —I shall return at the end of a quarter of an hour."

"Will you give me a sleeping draught? I generally take chloral."

"My dear sir, I will give you nothing. It is my

impression you will have a good night without
having recourse to sedatives. Get into bed now—
you look sleepy already."

The doctor left the room. When he came back
at the end of the allotted time, Awdrey was in bed
—he was lying on his back, with his eyes already
closed. His face looked very cadaverous and
ghastly pale; but for the gentle breathing which
came from his partly opened lips he might almost
have been a dead man.

"Six-and-twenty," muttered the doctor, as he
glanced at him, "six-and-forty, six-and-fifty,
rather. This is a very queer case. There is
something at the root of it. I can no longer make
light of Mrs. Awdrey's fears—something is killing
that man inch by inch. He has described his own
condition very accurately. He is slipping out of
life because he has not got grip enough to hold it.
Nevertheless, at the present moment, no child
could sleep more tranquilly."

The doctor turned off the electric light, and returned to his own bright part of the room. The
bed in which Awdrey lay was now in complete
shadow. Dr. Rumsey opened a medical treatise,
but he did not read. On the contrary, the book
lay unnoticed on his knee, while he himself stared
into the blaze of the fire—his brows were contracted
in anxious thought. He was thinking of the sleeper
and his story—of the tragedy which all this meant
to Margaret. Then, by a queer chain of connection, his memory reverted to Mrs. Everett—her

passionate life quest—her determination to consider her son innocent. The queer scene she had described as taking place between Hetty and herself returned vividly once more to the doctor's retentive memory.

"Is it possible that Awdrey can in any way be connected with that tragedy?" he thought. "It looks almost like it. According to his own showing, and according to his wife's showing, the strange symptoms which have brought him to his present pass began about the date of that somewhat mysterious murder. I have thought it best to make light of that lapse of memory which worries the poor fellow so much in connection with his walking-stick, but is there not something in it after all? Can he possibly have witnessed the murder? Would it be possible for him to throw any light upon it and save Everett? If I really thought so? But no, the hypothesis is too wild."

Dr. Rumsey turned again to his book. He was preparing a lecture of some importance. As he read he made many notes. The sleeper in the distant part of the room slept on calmly—the night gradually wore itself away—the fire smouldered in the grate.

"If this night passes without any peculiar manifestation on Awdrey's part, I shall begin to feel assured that the wife has overstated the case," thought the doctor. He bent forward as this thought came to him to replenish the fire. In the act of doing so he made a slight noise. Whether

this noise disturbed the sleeper or not no one can
say—Awdrey abruptly turned in bed, opened his
eyes, uttered a heavy groan, and then sat up.

"There it is again," he cried.   "Margaret, are
you there?—Margaret, come here."

Dr. Rumsey immediately approached the bed.

"Your wife is not in the room, Awdrey," he
said—"you remember, don't you, that you are
passing the night with me."

Awdrey rubbed his eyes—he took no notice of
Dr. Rumsey's words.   He stared straight before
him in the direction of one of the windows.

"There it is," he said, "the usual thing—the
globe of light and the picture in the middle.   There
lies the murdered man on his back.   Yes, that is
the bit of the Plain that I know so well—the moon
drifts behind the clouds—now it shines out, and I
see the face of the murdered man—but the murderer, who is he?   Why will he keep his back to
me?!   Good God! why can't I see his face?   Look,
can't you see for yourself?   Margaret, can't you
see?—do you notice the stick in his hand?—it is
my   stick—and—the   scoundrel,   he   wears   my
clothes.   Yes, those clothes are mine.   My God,
what does this mean?"

CHAPTER XIII.

"Come, Awdrey, wake up, you don't know what you are talking about," said the doctor. He grasped his patient firmly by one arm, and shook him slightly. The dazed and stricken man gazed at the doctor in astonishment.

"Where am I, and what is the matter?" he asked.

"You are spending the night in my house, and have just had a bad dream," said Dr. Rumsey. "Don't go back to bed just yet. Come and sit by the fire for a few minutes."

As the doctor spoke, he put a warm padded dressing-gown of his own over his shivering and cowed-looking patient.

Awdrey wrapped himself in it, and approached the fire. Dr. Rumsey drew a chair forward. He noticed the shaking hands, thin almost to emaciation, the sunken cheeks, the glazed expression of the eyes, the look of age and mental irritation which characterized the face.

"Poor fellow? no wonder that he should be simply slipping out of life if this kind of thing continues night after night," thought the doctor. "What is to be done with him? His is one of the cases which baffle Science. Well, at least, he wants heaps of nourishment to enable him to bear up. I'll go downstairs and prepare a meal for him."

He spoke aloud.

"You shiver, Awdrey, are you cold?"

"Not very," replied Awdrey, trying to smile, although his lips chattered. He looked into the fire, and held out one hand to the grateful blaze.

"You'll feel much better after you have taken a prescription which I mean to make up for you. I'll go and prepare it now. Do you mind being left alone?"

"Certainly not. Why should I?"

"He has already forgotten his terrors," thought Dr. Rumsey. "Queer case, incomprehensible. I never met one like it before. In these days, it is true, one comes across all forms of psychological distress. Nothing now ought to be new or startling to medical science, but this certainly is marvellous."

The doctor speedily returned with a plate of cold meat, some bread and butter, and a bottle of champagne.

"As we are both spending the night other than it should be spent," he said, "we must have nourishment. I am going to eat, will you join me?"

"I feel hungry," answered Awdrey. "I should be glad of something."

The doctor fed him as though he were an infant. He drank off two glasses of champagne, and then the color returned to his cheeks, and some animation to his sunken eyes.

"You look better," said the doctor. "Now, you will get back to bed, won't you? After that champagne a good sleep will put some mettle into you. It is not yet four o'clock. You have several hours to devote to slumber."

The moment Rumsey began to speak, Awdrey's eyes dilated.

"I remember something," he said.

"I dare say you do—many things—what are you specially alluding to?"

"I saw something a short time ago in this room. The memory of it comes dimly back to me. I struggle to grasp it fully. Is your house said to be haunted, Dr. Rumsey?"

Dr. Rumsey laughed.

"Not that I am aware of," he replied.

"Well, haunted or not, I saw something." Awdrey rose slowly as he spoke—he pointed in the direction of the farthest window.

"I was sleeping soundly but suddenly found myself broad awake," he began—"I saw over there" —he pointed with his hand to the farthest window, "what looked like a perfect sphere or globe of light —in the centre of this light was a picture. I see the whole thing now in imagination, but the picture is dim—it worries me, I want to see it better. No, I will not get back to bed."

"You had a bad dream and are beginning to remember it," said Rumsey.

"It was not a dream at all. I was wide awake. Stay—don't question me—my memory becomes more vivid instant by instant. I was wide awake as I said—I got up—I approached the thing. It never swerved from the one position—it was there by the window—a sphere of light and the picture in the middle. There were two men in the picture."

"A nightmare, a nightmare," said the doctor. "What did you eat for dinner last night?"

"It was not an ordinary nightmare—my memory is now quite vivid. I recall the whole vision. I saw a picture of something that happened. Years ago, Dr. Rumsey—over five years ago now—there was a murder committed on the Plain near my place. Two men, undergraduates of Oxford, were staying at our village inn—they fought about a girl with whom they were both in love. One man killed the other. The murder was committed in a moment of strong provocation and the murderer only got penal servitude. He is serving his time now. It seems strange, does it not, that I should have seen a complete picture of the murder! The whole thing was very vivid and distinct—it has, in short, burnt itself into my brain."

Awdrey raised his hand as he spoke and pressed it to his forehead. "My pulse is bounding just here," he said—he touched his temple. "I have only to shut my eyes to see in imagination what I saw in reality half an hour ago. Why should I be worried with a picture of a murder committed five years ago?"

"It probably made a deep impression on you at the time," said Dr. Rumsey. "You are now weak and your nerves much out of order—your brain has simply reverted back to it. If I were you I would only think of it as an ordinary nightmare. Pray let me persuade you to go back to bed."

"I could not—I am stricken by the most indescribable terror."

"Nonsense! You a man!"

"You may heap what opprobrium you like on me, but I cannot deny the fact. I am full of cowardly terror. I cannot account for my sensations. The essence of my torture lies in the fact that I am unable to see the face of the man who committed the murder."

"Oh, come, why should you see his face—you know who he was?"

"That's just it, doctor. I wish to God I did know." Awdrey approached close to Dr. Rumsey, and stared into his eyes. His own eyes were queer and glittering. He seemed instinctively to feel that he had said too much, for he drew back a step, putting his hand again to his forehead and staring fixedly out into vacancy.

"You believe that I am talking nonsense," he said, after a pause.

"I believe that you are a sad victim to your own nervous fears. You need not go to bed unless you like. Dress yourself and sit here by the fire. You will very likely fall asleep in this arm-chair. I shall remain close to you."

"You are really good to me, and I would thank you if I were capable of gratitude. Yes, I'll get into my clothes."

Rumsey turned on the electric light, and Awdrey with trembling fingers dressed himself. When he came back to his easy-chair by the warm fire he said suddenly:

"Give me a sheet of paper and a pencil, will you?"

The doctor handed him a blank sheet from his own note-paper, and furnished him with a pencil.

"Now I will sketch what I saw for you," he said.

He drew with bold touches a broad sphere of light. In the centre was a picture, minute but faithful.

At one time Awdrey had been fond of dabbling in art. He sketched a night scene now, with broad effects—a single bar of moonlight lit up everything with vivid distinctness. A man lay on the ground stretched out flat and motionless—another man bent over him in a queer attitude—he held a stick in his hand—he was tall and slender—there was a certain look about his figure! Awdrey dropped his pencil and stared furtively with eyes dilated with horror at his own production. Then he put his sketch face downward on the table, and turned a white and indescribably perplexed countenance to Dr. Rumsey.

"What I have drawn is not worth looking at," he said, simulating a yawn as he spoke. "After all I cannot quite reproduce what I saw. I believe I shall doze off in this chair."

"Do so," said the doctor.

A few minutes later, when the patient was sound asleep, Dr. Rumsey lifted the paper on which Awdrey had made his sketch. He looked fixedly at the vividly worked-up picture.

"The man whose back is alone visible has an unmistakable likeness to Awdrey," he muttered. "Poor fellow, what does this mean!—diseased nerves of course. The next thing he will say is that he committed the murder himself. He certainly needs immediate treatment. But what to do is the puzzle."

CHAPTER XIV

WHEN he awoke Awdrey felt much better. He expressed surprise at finding himself sitting up instead of in bed, and Rumsey saw that he had once more completely forgotten the occurrence of the night. The doctor resolved that he should not see the sketch he had made—he put it carefully away therefore in one of his own private drawers, for he knew that it might possibly be useful later on. At the present moment the patient was better without it.

The two men breakfasted together, and then Rumsey spoke.

"Now," he said, "I won't conceal the truth from you. I watched you last night with great anxiety— I am glad I sat up with you, for I am now able to make a fairly correct diagnosis of your case. You are certainly very far from well—you are in a sort of condition when a very little more might overbalance your mind. I tell you this because I think it best for you to know the exact truth—at the same time pray do not be seriously alarmed, there is nothing as yet in your case to prevent you from completely recovering your mental equilibrium, but, in my opinion, to do so you must

have complete change of air and absolutely fresh
surroundings.   I recommend therefore that you
go away from home immediately.   Do not take
your child nor yet your wife with you.   If you
commission me to do so, I can get you a companion in the shape of a clever young doctor who
will never intrude his medical knowledge on you,
but yet will be at hand to advise you in case the
state of your nerves requires such interference.   I
shall put him in possession of one or two facts with
regard to your nervous condition, but will not tell
him too much.   Make up your mind to go away at
once, Awdrey, within the week if possible.   Start
with a sea voyage—I should recommend to the
Cape.   The soothing influence of the sea on nerves
like yours could not but be highly beneficial.
Take a sea voyage—to the Cape by preference, but
anywhere.   It does not greatly matter where you
go.   The winter is on us, don't spend it in England.   Keep moving about from one place to another.   Don't over-fatigue yourself in any way, but
at the same time allow heaps of fresh impressions
to filter slowly through your brain.   They will have
a healthy and salutary effect.   It is my opinion
that by slow but sure degrees, if you fully take my
advice in this matter, you will forget what now as-
sumes the aspect of monomania.   In short, you
will forget yourself, and other lives and other interests mingling with yours will give you the
necessary health and cure.   I must ask you to leave
me now, for it is the hour when my patients arrive

for consultation, but I will call round at your house late this evening.   Do you consent to my scheme?

"I must take a day to think it over—this kind of thing cannot be planned in a hurry."

"In your case it can and ought to be.   You have heaps of money, which is, as a rule, the main difficulty.   Go home to your wife, tell her at once what I recommend.   This is Wednesday, you ought to be out of London on Saturday.   Well, my dear fellow, if you have not sufficient energy to carry out what I consider essential to your recovery, some one else must have energy in your behalf and simply take you away.   Good-by—good-by."

Awdrey shook hands with the doctor and slowly left the house.   When he had gone a dozen yards down the street he had almost forgotten the prescription which had been given to him.   He had a dull sort of wish, which scarcely amounted to a wish in his mind, to reach home in time to take little Arthur for his morning walk.   Beyond that faint desire he had no longing of any sort.

He had nearly reached his own house when he was conscious of footsteps hurrying after him. Presently they reached his side, and he heard the hurried panting of quickened breath.   He turned round with a vague sort of wonder to see who had dared to come up and accost him in this way.   To his surprise he saw that the intruder was a woman. She was dressed in the plain ungarnished style of the country.   She wore an old-fashioned and somewhat seedy jacket which reached down to her knees, her dress below was of a faded summer tint, and thin in quality. Her hat was trimmed with rusty velvet, she wore a veil which only reached half way down her face. Her whole appearance was odd, and out of keeping with her surroundings.

"Mr. Awdrey, you don't know me?" she cried, in a panting voice.

"Yes, I do," said Awdrey. He stopped in his walk and stared at her.

"Is it possible," he continued, "that you are little Hetty Armitage?"

"I was, sir, I ain't now; I'm Hetty Vincent now. I ventured up to town unbeknown to any one to see you, Mr. Awdrey. It is of the greatest importance that I should have a word with you, sir. Can you give me a few minutes all alone?"

"Certainly I can, Hetty," replied Awdrey, in a kind voice. A good deal of his old gentleness and graciousness of manner returned at sight of Hetty. He overlooked her ugly attire—in short, he did not see it. She recalled old times to him—gay old times before he had known sorrow or trouble. She belonged to his own village, to his own people. He was conscious of a grateful sense of refreshment at meeting her again.

"You shall come home with me," he said. "My wife will be glad to welcome you. How are all the old folks at Grandcourt?"

"I believe they are well, sir, but I have not been to Grandcourt lately. My husband's farm is three

miles from the village. Mr. Robert," dropping
her voice, "I cannot go home with you. It would
be dangerous if I were to be seen at your
house."

"Dangerous!" said Awdrey in surprise. "What
do you mean?"

"What I say, sir; I must not be seen talking
to you. On no account must we two be seen together. I have come up to London unbeknown
to anybody, because it is necessary for me to tell
you something, and to ask you—to ask you—Oh,
my God!" continued Hetty, raising her eyes sky-
ward as she spoke, "how am I to tell him?"

She turned white to her lips now; she trembled
from head to foot.

"Sir," she continued, "there's some one who
suspects."

"Suspects?" said Awdrey, knitting his brows,
"Suspects what? What have suspicious people to
do with me? You puzzle me very much by this
extraordinary talk. Are you quite well yourself?
I recall now that you always were a mysterious
little thing; but you are greatly changed, Hetty."
He turned and gave her a long look.

"I know I am, sir, but that don't matter now. I
did not run this risk to talk about myself. Mr.
Robert, there's one living who suspects."

"Come home with me and tell me there," said
Awdrey—he was conscious of a feeling of irritation, otherwise Hetty's queer words aroused no
emotion of any sort within him.

·I cannot go home with you, sir—I came up to London at risk to myself in order to warn you."

"Of what—of whom?"

"Of Mrs. Everett, sir." .

"Mrs. Everett! my wife's friend!—you must have taken leave of your sense. See, we are close to the Green Park; if you won't come to my house, let us go there. Then you can tell me quickly what you want to say."

Awdrey motioned to Hetty to follow him. They crossed the road near Hyde Park Corner, and soon afterward were in the shelter of the Green Park.

"Now, speak out," said the Squire. "I cannot stay long with you, as I want to take my little son for his customary walk. What extraordinary thing have you to tell me about Mrs. Everett?"

"Mr. Robert, you may choose to make light of, but in your heart . . . there, I'll tell you every- thing. Mrs. Everett was down at Grandcourt lately —she was stopping at uncle's inn in the village. She walked out one day to the Plain—by ill-luck she met me on her road. She got me to show her the place where the murder was committed. I stood just by the clump of elders where—but of course you have forgotten, sir. Mrs. Everett stood with me, and I showed her the very spot. I de- scribed the scene to her, and showed her just where the two men fought together."

The memory of his dream came back to Awdrey. He was very quiet now—his brain was quite alert.

"Go on, Hetty," he said. "Do you know this

interests me vastly. I have been troubled lately
with visions of that queer murder. Only last night
I had one. Now why should such visions come to
one who knows nothing whatever about it?"

"Well, sir, they do say——"

"What?"

"It is the old proverb," muttered Hetty.
"'Murder will out.'"

"I know the proverb, but I don't understand
your application," replied Awdrey, but he looked
thoughtful. "If you were troubled, with these bad
visions or dreams I should not be surprised," he
continued, "for you really witnessed the thing.
By the way, as you are here, perhaps you can help
me. I lost my stick at the time of the murder, and
never found it since. I would give a good deal to
find it. What is that you say?"

"You'll never find it, sir. Thank the good God
above, you'll never find it."

"I am glad that you recognize the loss not to be
a trifle. Most people laugh when I speak of anything so trivial as a stick. You say I shall never
find it again—perhaps so. The forgetting it so
completely troubles me, however. Hetty, I had a
bad dream last night—no, it was not really a
dream, it was a vision. I saw that murder—I witnessed the whole thing. I saw the dead man, and
I saw the back of the man who committed the
murder. I tried hard, but I could not get a glimpse
of his face. I wanted to see his face badly. What
is the matter, girl? How white you look."

"Don't say another word, sir. I have borne much for you and for your people, but there are limits, and if you say another word, I shall lose my self-control."

"I am sorry my talk has such an effect upon you, Hetty. You don't look too happy, my little girl. Your face is old—I hope your husband is good to you."

"He is as good as I deserve, Mr. Awdrey. I never had any love to give him—he knew that from the first. He married me five years ago because I was pretty, and Aunt Fanny thought I'd best be married—she thought it would make things safer—but it is a mistake to marry when your heart is given to another."

"Ah yes, poor Frere—you were in love with him, were you not?"

"No, sir, that I was not."

"I forgot—it was with Everett—poor girl, no wonder you look old."

Awdrey gave Hetty a weary glance—his attention was already beginning to flag.

"It was not with Mr. Everett," whispered Hetty in a low tone which thrilled with passion.

Awdrey took no notice. His apathy calmed her, and saved her from making a terrible avowal.

"I'll just tell you what I came to say and then leave you, sir," she said in a broken voice. "It is all about Mrs. Everett. She stood with me close to the alders, and I described the scene of the murder and how it took place, and all of a sudden she looked me in the eyes and said something. She said that Mr. Horace Frere was the man who was murdered—but the man who committed the murder was not her son, Mr. Everett. She spoke in an awful sort of voice, and said she knew the truth—she knew that her son was innocent. Oh, sir, I got so awfully frightened—I nearly let the truth out."

"You nearly let the truth out—the truth? What do you mean?"

"Mr. Robert, is it possible that you do not know?"

"I only know what all the rest of the world knows—that Everett is guilty."

"I see, sir, that you still hold to that, and I am glad of it, but Mrs. Everett is the sort of woman to frighten a body. Her eyes seem to pierce right down to your very heart—they seem to read your secret. Mr. Awdrey, will you do what I ask you? Will you leave England for a bit? It would be dreadful for me to have done all that I have done and to find it useless in the end."

Whatever reply Awdrey might have made to this appeal was never uttered. His attention was at this moment effectually turned into another channel. He saw Mrs. Everett, his wife, and boy coming to meet him. The boy, a splendid little fellow with rosy cheeks and vigorous limbs, ran down the path with a glad cry to fling himself into his father's arms. He was a princely looking boy, a worthy scion of the old race. Awdrey, absorbed with his son, took no notice of Hetty. Unperceived by him she slipped down a side path and was lost to view.

"Dad," cried the child, in a voice of rapture.

Margaret and Mrs. Everett came up to the pair.

"I hope you are better, Robert," said his wife.

"I suppose I am," he answered. "I had a fairly good night. How well Arthur looks this morning."

"Poor little boy, he was fretting to come to meet you," said Mrs. Awdrey.

Awdrey turned to speak to Mrs. Everett. There was a good deal of color in her cheeks, and her dark eyes looked brighter and more piercing than ever.

"Forgive me," she said, "for interrupting this conversation. I want to ask you a question. Mr. Awdrey, I saw you walking just now with a woman. Who was she?"

Awdrey laughed.

"Why, she has gone," he said, glancing round. "Who do you think my companion was?" he continued, glancing at Margaret. "None other than an old acquaintance—pretty little Hetty Armitage. She has some other name now, but I forget what it is. She said she came up to town on purpose to see me, but I could not induce her to come to the house. What is the matter, Mrs. Everett?"

"I should like to see Hetty Armitage. Did she give you her address?"

"No, I did not ask her. I wonder why she

hurried off so quickly; but she seemed in a queer, excitable state. I don't believe she is well."

"I want to see her again," continued Mrs. Everett. "I may as well say frankly that I am fully convinced there is something queer about that woman—a very little more and I should put a detective on her track. I suspect her. If ever a woman carried a guilty secret she does."

"Oh, come," said Margaret, "you must not allow your prejudices to run away with you. Please remember that Hetty grew up at Grandcourt. My husband and I have known her almost from her birth."

"A giddy little thing, but wonderfully pretty," said Awdrey.

"Well, never mind about her now," interrupted Margaret, a slight touch of impatience in her manner. "Please, Robert, tell me exactly what Dr. Rumsey ordered for you."

"Nothing very alarming," he replied; "the doctor thinks my nerves want tone. No doubt they do, although I feel wonderfully better this morning. He said something about my leaving England for a time and taking a sea voyage. I believe he intends to call round this evening to talk over the scheme. Now, little man, are you ready for your walk?"

"Yes," said the child. He stamped his sturdy feet with impatience. Awdrey took his hand and the two went off in the direction of the Serpentine. Mrs. Everett and Margaret followed slowly in the background.

Awdrey remained out for some time with the boy. The day, which had begun by being mild and spring-like, suddenly changed its character. The wind blew strongly from the north—soon it rose to a gale. Piles of black clouds came up over the horizon and covered the sky, then heavy sleet showers poured down with biting intensity. Awdrey and the child were quite in the open when they were caught by one of these, and before they could reach any shelter they were wet through. They hurried into the first hansom they met, but not before the mischief was done. Awdrey took a chill, and before the evening was over he was shivering violently, huddled up close to the fire. The boy, whose lungs were his weak point, seemed, however, to have escaped without any serious result —he went to bed in his usual high spirits, but his mother thought his pretty baby voice sounded a little hoarse. Early the next morning the nurse called her up; the child had been disturbed in the night by the hoarseness and a croupy sensation in his throat; his eyes were now very bright and he was feverish. The nurse said she did not like the look of the little fellow; he seemed to find it difficult to breathe, and he was altogether very unlike himself.

"I'll send a messenger immediately for Dr. Rumsey," said Margaret.

She returned to her bedroom and awoke her husband, who was in a heavy sleep. At Margaret's first words he started up keen and interested.

"What are you saying, Maggie? The boy—little Arthur—ill?"

"Yes, he seems very ill; I do not like his look at all," she replied. "It is I know, very early, but I think I'll send a messenger round at once to ask Dr. Rumsey to call."

"We ought not to lose a minute," said Awdrey. "I'll go for him myself."

"You!" she exclaimed in surprise. "But do you feel well enough?"

"Of course I do, there's nothing the matter with me."

He sprang out of bed, and rushed off to his dressing-room, hastily put on his clothes, and then went out. As he ran quickly downstairs Margaret detected an almost forgotten quality in his steps.

"Why, he is awake again," she cried. "How strange that this trouble about the child should have power to give him back his old vigorous health!"

Rumsey quickly obeyed Awdrey's summons, and before eight o'clock that morning he was bending over the sick child's cot.

It needed but a keen glance and an application of the stethoscope to tell the doctor that there was grave mischief at work.

"It is a pity I was not sent for last night," he said. Then he moved away from the cot, where the bright eyes of the sick baby were fixing him with a too penetrating stare.

He walked across the large nursery. Awdrey followed him.

"The child is very ill," said the doctor.

"What do you mean?" replied Awdrey. "Very ill—do you infer that the child is in danger?"

"Yes, Awdrey, he is undoubtedly in danger. Double pneumonia has set in. Such a complaint at his tender age cannot but mean very grave danger. I only hope we may pull him through."

"We must pull him through, doctor. Margaret," continued her husband, his face was white as death, "Dr. Rumsey says that the child is in danger."

"Yes," answered Margaret. She was as quiet in her manner as he was excited and troubled. She laid her hand now with great tenderness on his arm. The touch was meant to soothe him, and to assure him of her sypmathy. Then she turned her eyes to fix them on the doctor.

"I know you will do what you can," she said. There was suppressed passion in her words.

"Rest assured I will," he answered.

"Of course," cried Awdrey. "Listen to me, Dr. Rumsey, not a stone must be left unturned to pull the child through. You know what his life means to us—to his mother and me. We cannot possibly spare him—he must be saved. Had we not better get other advice immediately?"

"It is not necessary, but you must please yourselves," answered Rumsey. "I am not a specialist as regards lung affections, although this case is perfectly straightforward. If you wish to have a specialist I shall be very glad to consult with Edward Cowley."

"What is his address? I'll go for him at once," said Awdrey.

Dr. Rumsey sat down, wrote a short note and gave it to Awdrey, who hurried off with it.

Dr. Rumsey looked at Mrs. Awdrey after her husband had left the room.

"It is marvellous," he said, "what a change for the better this illness has made in your husband's condition."

Her eyes filled slowly with tears.

"Is his health to be won back at such a price?" she asked—she turned once again to the sick child's bed.

"God grant not," said the doctor—"rest satisfied that what man can do to save him I will do."

"I know that," she replied.

In an hour's time the specialist arrived and the two doctors had their consultation. Certain remedies were prescribed, and Dr. Rumsey hurried away promising to send in two trained nurses immediately. He came back again himself at noon to find the boy, as he expected, much worse. The child was now delirious. All during that long dreadful day the fever rose and rose. The whole aspect of the house in Seymour Street was altered. There were hushed steps, anxious faces, whispered consultations. As the hours flew by the prognostications of the medical men became graver and graver. Margaret gave up hope as the evening approached. She knew that the little life could not long stand the strain of that all-consuming fever. Awdrey alone was full of bustle, excitement, and confidence.

"The child will and must recover," he said to his wife several times. When the night began Dr. Rumsey resolved not to leave the child.

"A man like Rumsey must save him," cried the father. He forgot all about his own nervous symptoms—he refused even to listen to his wife's words of anxiety.

"Pooh!" he said, "when children are ill they are always very bad. I was at death's door once or twice myself as a child. Children are bad one moment and almost themselves the next. Is not that so, doctor?"

"In some cases," replied the doctor.

"Well, in this case? You think the boy will be all right in the morning—come now, your honest opinion."

"My honest opinion is a grave one, Mr. Awdrey."

Awdrey laughed. There was a wild note in his merriment.

"You and Cowley can't be up to much if between you you can't manage to keep the life in a little mite like that," he said.

"The issues of life and death belong to higher than us," answered the doctor slowly.

Awdrey looked at him again, gave an incredulous smile, and went into the sick-room.

During the entire night the father sat up with the boy. The sick child did not know either parent. His voice grew weaker and weaker—the struggle to breathe became greater. When he had strength to speak, he babbled continually of his playthings, of his walk by the Serpentine the previous day, and the little ships as they sailed on the water. Presently he took a fancy into his head that he was in one of the tiny ships, and that he was sailing away from shore. He laughed with feeble pleasure, and tried to clap his burning hands. Toward morning his baby notes were scarcely distinguishable. He dozed off for a little, then woke again, and began to talk—he talked now all the time of his father.

"'Ittle boy 'ove dad," he said. "'Ittle Arthur 'oves dad best of anybody—best of all."

Awdrey managed to retain one of the small hands in his. The child quieted down then, gave him a look of long, unutterable love, and about six in the morning, twenty-four hours after the seizure had declared itself, the little spirit passed away. Awdrey, who was kneeling by the child's cot, still holding his hand, did not know when this happened. There was a sudden bustle round the bed, he raised his head with a start, and looked around him.

"What is the matter? Is he better?" he asked. He looked anxiously at the sunken face of the dead child. He noticed that the hurried breathing had ceased.

"Come away with me, Robert," said his wife.

"Why so?" he asked. "Do you think I will leave the child?"

"Darling, the child is dead."

Awdrey tottered to his feet.

"Dead!" he cried. You don't mean it—impossible." He bent over the little body, pulled down the bedclothes, and put his hand to the heart, then bending low he listened intently for any breath to come from the parted lips.

"Dead—no, no," he said again.

"My poor fellow, it is too true," said Dr. Rumsey.

"Then before God," began Awdrey—he stepped back, the words were arrested on his lips, and he fell fainting to the floor.

Dr. Rumsey had him removed to his own room, and with some difficulty the unhappy man was brought back to consciousness. He was now lying on his bed.

"Where am I?" he asked.

"In your room, on your bed. You are better now, dearest," said Margaret. She bent over him, trying valiantly to conceal her own anguish in order to comfort him.

"But what has happened?" he asked. He suddenly sat up. "Why are you here, Rumsey? Margaret, why are your eyes so red?"

Margaret Awdrey tried to speak, but the words would not come to her lips.

Rumsey bent forward and took Awdrey's hand.

"It has pleased Providence to afflict you very sorely, my poor fellow," he said, "but I know for your wife's sake you will be man enough to endure this fearful blow with fortitude."

"What blow, doctor?"

"Your child," began the doctor.

"My child?" said Awdrey. He put his feet on the floor, and stood up. There was a strange note of query in his tone.

"My child?" he repeated. "What child?"

"Your child is dead, Awdrey. We did what we could to save him."

Awdrey uttered a wild laugh.

"Come, this is too much," he exclaimed. "You talk of a child of mine—I, who never had a child. What are you dreaming about?"

CHAPTER XV.

On the evening of that same day Awdrey entered the room where his wife was silently giving way to her bitter anguish. She was quite overcome by her grief—her eyelids were swollen by much weeping, her dress was disarranged, the traces of a sleepless night, and the fearful anguish through which she was passing, were visible on her beautiful face. Awdrey, who had come into the room almost cheerfully, started and stepped back a pace or two when he saw her—he then knit his brows with marked irritation.

"What can be the matter with you, Margaret?" he cried. "I cannot imagine why you are crying in that silly way."

"I'll try not to cry any more, Robert," she answered.

"Yes, but you look in such dreadful distress; I assure you, it affects me most disagreeably, and in my state of nerves!—you know, don't you, that nothing ever annoys me more than weak, womanish tears."

"It is impossible for me to be cheerful to-night," said the wife. "The pain is too great. He was our only child, and such—such a darling."

Awdrey laughed.

"Forgive me, my dear," he said, "I really would not hurt your feelings for the world, but you must know, if you allow your common sense to speak, that we never had a child. It has surely been one of our great trials that no child has been given to us to carry on the old line. My poor Maggie," he went up to her quite tenderly, put his arm round her neck, and kissed her, "you must be very unwell to imagine these sort of things."

She suddenly took the hand which lay on her shoulder between both her own.

"Come with me, Robert," she said, an expression of the most intense despair on all her features, "come, I cannot believe that this blight which has passed over you can be final. I'll take you to the room where the little body of our beautiful child is lying. When you see that sweet face, surely you will remember."

He frowned when she began to speak; now he disengaged his hand from her clasp.

"It would not be right for me to humor you," he said. "You ought to see a doctor, Maggie, for you are really suffering from a strong delusion. If you encourage it it may become fixed, and even assume the proportions of a sort of insanity. Now, my dear wife, try and restrain yourself and listen to me."

She gazed at him with wide-open eyes. As he spoke she had difficulty in believing her own ears. A case like his was indeed new to her. She had

never really believed in the tragedy of his house—
but now at last the suspected and dreaded blow had
truly fallen. Awdrey, like his ancestors before
him, was forgetting the grave events of life. Was
it possible that he could forget the child, whose
life had been the joy of his existence, whose last
looks of love had been directed to him, whose last
faltering words had breathed his name? Yes, he
absolutely forgot all about the child. The stern
fact stared her in the face, she could not shut her
eyes to it.

"You look at me strangely, Margaret," said
Awdrey. "I cannot account for your looks, nor
indeed for your actions during the whole of to-day.
Now I wish to tell you that I have resolved to carry
out Rumsey's advice—he wants me to leave home
at once. I spent a night with him—was it last
night? I really forget—but anyhow, during that
time he had an opportunity of watching my symptoms. You know, don't you, how nervous I am,
how full of myself? You know how this inertia
steals over me, and envelops me in a sort of cloud.
The state of the case is something like this, Maggie; I feel as if a dead hand were pressed against
my heart; sometimes I have even a difficulty in
breathing, at least in taking a deep breath. It
seems to me as if the stupor of death were creeping up my body, gradually day by day, enfeebling
all my powers more and more. Rumsey, who
quite understands these symptoms, says that they
are grave, but not incurable. He suggests that I

should leave London and at once. I propose to take the eight o'clock Continental train. Will you come with me?"

"I?" she cried. "I cannot; our child's little body lies upstairs."

"Why will you annoy me by referring to that delusion of yours? You must know how painful it is to listen to you. Will you come, Maggie?"

"I cannot. Under any other circumstances I would gladly, but to-night, no, it is impossible."

"Very well then, I'll go alone. I have just been up in my room packing some things. I cannot possibly say how long I shall be absent—perhaps a few weeks, perhaps a day or two—I must be guided in this matter by my sensations."

"If you come back in a day or two, Robert, I'll try and go abroad with you, if you really think it would do you good," said Margaret.

"I'll see about that," he replied. "I cannot quite tell you what my plans are to-night. Meanwhile I find I shall want more money than I have in the house. Have you any by you?"

"I have twenty-five pounds."

"Give it to me; it will be quite sufficient. I have about fifteen pounds here." He touched his breast-pocket. "If I don't return soon I'll write to you. Now good-by, Maggie. Try and conquer that queer delusion, my dear wife. Remember, the more you think of it, the more it will feed upon itself, until you will find it too strong for you. Good-by, darling."

She threw her arms round his neck.

"I cannot describe what my feelings are at this awful moment," she said. "Is it right for me to let you go alone?"

"Perfectly right, dearest. What possible harm can come to me?" he said with tenderness. He pushed back the rich black hair from her brow as he spoke.

"You love me, Robert?" she cried suddenly— "at least your love for me remains?"

He knit his brows.

"If there is any one I love, it is you," he said, "but I do not know that I love any one—it is this inertia, dearest"—he touched his breast—"it buries love beneath it, it buries all emotion. You are not to blame. If I could conquer it my love for you would be as full, as fresh, and strong as ever. Good-by now. Take care of yourself. If those strange symptoms continue pray consult Dr. Rumsey."

He went out of the room.

Margaret was too stricken and stunned to follow him.

A few days later a child's funeral left the house in Seymour Street. Margaret followed her child to the grave. She then returned home, wondering if she could possibly endure the load which had fallen upon her. The house seemed empty—she did not think anything could ever fill it again. Her own heart was truly empty—she felt as if there were a gap within it which could never by

any possibility be closed up again.   Since the night
after her child's death she had heard nothing from
her husband—sometimes she wondered if he were
still alive.

Dr. Rumsey tried to reassure her on this point—
he did not consider Awdrey the sort of man to
commit suicide.

Mrs. Everett came to see Margaret every day
during this time of terrible grief, but her excited
face, her watchful attitude, proved the reverse
of soothing.   She was sorry for Margaret, but
even in the midst of Margaret's darkest grief
she never forgot the mission she had set before
herself.

On the morning of the funeral she followed the
procession at a little distance.   She stood behind
the more immediate group of mourners as the body
of the beautiful child was laid in his long home.
Had his father been like other men, Margaret
would never have consented to the child's being
buried anywhere except at Grandcourt.   Under ex-
isting circumstances, however, she had no energy
to arrange this.

About an hour after Mrs. Awdrey's return, Mrs.
Everett was admitted into her presence.

Margaret was seated listlessly by one of the tables
in the drawing-room.   A pile of black-edged paper
was lying near her—a letter was begun.   Heaps of
letters of condolence which had poured in lay near.
She was endeavoring to answer one, but found the
task beyond her strength.

"My poor dear!" said Mrs. Everett. She walked up the long room, and stooping down by Margaret, kissed her.

Margaret mechanically returned her embrace. Mrs. Everett untied her bonnet-strings and sat by her side.

"Don't try to answer those letters yet," she said. "You are really not fit for it. Why don't you have a composing draught and go to bed?"

"I would rather not; the awakening would be too terrible," said Margaret.

"You will knock yourself up and get really ill if you go on like this."

"It does not matter, Mrs. Everett, whether I am ill or well. Nothing matters," said Margaret, in a voice of despair.

"Oh, my poor love, I understand you," said the widow. "I do not know in what words to approach your terribly grieved heart—there is only one thing which I feel impelled to say, and which may possibly at some time comfort you. Your beautiful boy's fate is less tragical than the fate which has fallen upon my only son. When Frank was a little child, Margaret, he had a dreadful illness—I thought he would die. I was frantic, for his father had died not long before. I prayed earnestly to God. I vowed a vow to train the boy in the paths of righteousness, as never boy had been trained before. I vowed to do for Frank what no other mother had ever done, if only God would leave him to me. My prayer was answered, and my child was saved. Think of him now, Margaret. Margaret, think of him now."

"I do," answered Margaret. "I have always felt for you—my heart has always been bitter with grief for you—don't you know it?"

"I do, I do—you have been the soul of all that could be sweet and dear to me. Except Frank himself, I love no one as I love you. Ah!"—Mrs. Everett suddenly started to her feet—the room door had been slowly opened and Awdrey walked in. His face was very pale and more emaciated looking than ever—his eyes were bright, and had sunk into his head.

"Well," he said, with a sort of queer assumption of cheerfulness, "here I am. I came back sooner than I expected. How are you Maggie?" He went up to his wife and kissed her. "How do you do, Mrs. Everett?"

"I am well," said Mrs. Everett. "How are you, are you better?"

"Yes, I am much better—in fact, there is little or nothing the matter with me."

He sat down on a sofa as he spoke and stared at his wife with a puzzled expression between his brows.

"What in the world are you in that heavy black for?" he said suddenly.

"I must wear it," she said. "You cannot ask me to take it off."

"Why should I ask you?" he replied. "Do not excite yourself in that way, Maggie. If you like to look hideous, do so. Black, heavy black, of that sort, does not suit you—and you are absolutely in crêpe—what does all this mean? It irritates me immensely."

"People wear crêpe when those they love die," said Margaret.

"Have you lost a relation?—Who?"

She did not answer. A moment later she left the room.

When she did so Awdrey got up restlessly, walked to the fire and poked it, then he approached the window and looked out. After a time he returned to his seat. Mrs. Everett sat facing him. It was her wont to sit very still—often nothing seemed to move about her except her watchful eyes. To-day she had more than ever the expression of a person who is quietly watching and waiting. Awdrey, inert as he doubtlessly was, seemed to feel her gaze—he looked at her.

"Where have you been, Mr. Awdrey?" she asked gently. "Did you visit the Continent?"

He favored her with a keen, half-suspicious glance.

"No," he said. "I changed my mind about that. I did not wish the water to divide me from my quest. I have been engaged on a most important search."

"And what was that?" she asked gently.

"I have been looking for a stick which I missed some years ago."

"I have heard you mention that before," said

Mrs. Everett—the color flushed hotly into her face. "You seem to attribute a great deal of importance to that trifle."

"To me it is no trifle," he replied. "I regard it as a link," he continued slowly, "between me and a past which I have forgotten. When I find that stick I shall remember the past."

As he spoke he rose again and going to the hearth-rug stood with his back to the fire.

At that moment Margaret re-entered the room in white—she was in a soft, flowing, white robe, which covered her from top to toe—it swept about her in graceful folds, and exposed some of the lovely contour of her arms. Her face was nearly as colorless as her dress; only the wealth of thick dark hair, only the sombre eyes, relieved the monotony of her appearance. Awdrey gave her a smile and a look of approval.

"Come here," he said: "now you are good—how sweet you look. Your appearance makes me recall, recall——" He pressed his hand to his forehead. "I remember now," he said; "I recall the day we were engaged—don't you remember it?—the picnic on Salisbury Plain; you were all in white then, too, and you wore somewhat the same intense expression in your eyes. Margaret, you are a beautiful woman."

She stood close to him—he did not offer to kiss her, but he laid one emaciated hand on her shoulder and looked earnestly into her face.

"You are very beautiful," he said; "I wonder I

do not love you." He sighed heavily, and removed his gaze to look intently into the fire.

Mrs. Everett rose.

"I'll come again soon," she said to Margaret. Margaret took no notice of her, nor did Awdrey see when she left the room.

After a moment Margaret went up to her husband and touched him.

"You must have something to eat," she said. "It is probably a long time since you had a proper meal."

"I don't remember," he replied, "but I am not hungry. By the way, Maggie, I recall now what I came back for." His eyes, which seemed to be lit from within, became suddenly full of excitement.

"Yes," she said as gently as she could.

"I came back because I wanted you."

Her eyes brightened.

"I wanted you to come with me. I do not care to be alone, and I am anxious to leave London again to-night."

Before Margaret could reply the butler threw open the door and announced Dr. Rumsey. The doctor came quickly forward.

"I am glad you have returned, Awdrey," he said, holding out his hand as he spoke. "I called to inquire for your wife, and the man told me you were upstairs."

"Yes, and I am better," said Awdrey. "I came back because I thought perhaps Margaret—but by the way, why should I speak so much about my-

self? My wife was not well when I left her. I
hope, doctor, that she consulted you, and that she
is now much better."

"Considering all things, Mrs. Awdrey is fairly
well," said Rumsey.

"And she has quite got over that delusion?"

"Quite." The doctor's voice was full of decision.
Margaret shuddered and turned away.

Rumsey seated himself at a little distance from
the fire, but Awdrey remained standing. He stood
in such a position that the doctor could get a perfect view of him. Rumsey did not fail to avail
himself of so excellent a moment for studying this
queer case. He observed the wasted face of his
patient; the unnaturally large and bright eyes; the
lips which used to be firm as a line, and which gave
considerable character to the face, but which had
now become loose and had a habit of drooping
slightly open; the brows, too, worked at times
spasmodically, and the really noble forehead, which
in old times betokened intelligence to a marked degree, was now furrowed with many lines. While
Rumsey watched he also made up his mind.

"I must tear the veil from that man's eyes at any
cost," he said to himself. He gave Margaret a
glance and she left the room. The moment she did
so the doctor stood up.

"I am glad you have returned," he said.

"How strange of you to say that," answered
Awdrey. "Do you not remember you were the
man who ordered me away?"

"I do remember that fact perfectly, but since I gave you that prescription a very marked change has taken place in your condition."

"Do you think me worse?"

"In one sense you are."

Awdrey laughed.

"How queer that you should say that," he said, "for to tell you the truth, I really feel better; I am not quite so troubled by inertia."

"I must be frank with you, Awdrey. I consider you very ill."

Awdrey started when Rumsey said this.

"Pray speak out, doctor, I dislike riddles," he replied.

"I mean to speak out very plainly. Awdrey, my poor fellow, I am obliged to remind you of the strange history of your house."

"What do you mean?" said Awdrey—"the history of my house?" he continued; "there is a psychological history, which I dislike to think of; is it to that you refer?"

"Yes, I refer to the queer condition of brain which men of your house have inherited for several generations. It is a queer doom; I am forced to say it is an awful doom. Robert Awdrey, it has fallen upon you."

"I thought as much," said Awdrey, "but you never would believe it before."

"I had not cause to believe it before. Now I fully believe it. That lapse of memory, which is one of its remarkable symptoms, has taken place in

your case. You have forgotten a very important
fact in your life."

"Ah, you are wrong there," said Awdrey.   "I
certainly have forgotten my walking-stick.   I know
well that I am a queer fellow.   I know too that at
times my condition is the reverse of satisfactory,
but with this one exception I have never forgotten
anything of the least consequence.   Don't you remember telling me that the lapse of memory was
not of any moment?"

"It was not, but you have forgotten something
else, Awdrey, and it is my duty now to remind you
of it."

"I have forgotten?" began Awdrey.   "Well,
speak."

"You had a child—a beautiful child."

Awdrey interrupted with a laugh.

"I do declare you have got that delusion, too,"
he said.   "I tell you, Dr. Rumsey, I never had a
child."

"Your child is no longer with you, but you had
a child.   He lived for four years but is now dead.
This very afternoon he was laid in his grave.   He
was a beautiful child—more lovely than most.   He
died after twenty-four hours' illness.   His mother
is broken-hearted over his loss, but you, his father,
have forgotten all about it.   Here is the picture of
your child—come to the light and look at it."

Rumsey strode up to a table as he spoke, lifted
a large photograph from a stand, and held it before
Awdrey's eyes.

Awdrey favoured it with a careless glance.

"I do not know that face," he said. "How did the photograph get here?" Is Margaret's delusion really so bad? Does she imagine for a moment that the little boy represented in that picture has ever had anything to do with us?"

"The photograph is a photograph of your son," repeated Rumsey, in a slow, emphatic voice. As he spoke he laid the picture back again on its ebony stand. "Awdrey," he continued. "I cannot expect impossibilities—I cannot expect you to remember what you have absolutely forgotten, but it is my duty to tell you frankly that this condition of things, if not immediately arrested, will lead to complete atrophy of your mental system, and you, in short, will not long survive it. You told me once very graphically that you were a man who carried about with you a dead soul. I did not believe you then. Now I believe that nothing in your own description of your case has been exaggerated. In some way, Awdrey, you must get back your memory."

"How?" asked Awdrey. He was impressed in spite of himself.

"Whether you remember or not, you must act as though you remembered. You now think that you never had a child. It is your duty to act as if you had one."

Awdrey shrugged his shoulders.

"That is impossible," he said.

"It is not. Weak as your will now is, it is not

yet so inert that you cannot bring it to bear upon the matter. I observe that Mrs. Awdrey has taken off her mourning. She must put it on again. It would be the height of all that is heartless for her to go about now without showing proper respect to your beautiful child. You also, Awdrey, must wear mourning. You must allow your wife to speak of the child. In short, even though you have no belief, you must allow those who are in a healthy mental condition to act for you in this matter. By doing so you may possibly arrest the malady."

"I see what you mean," said Awdrey, "but I do not know how it is possible for me to act on your suggestions."

"For your wife's sake you must try, and also because it is necessary that you should show respect to the dead heir of your house."

"Then I am to put a band on my hat and all that sort of thing?"

"Yes."

"It is a trifle, doctor. If you and Margaret wish it, I cannot reasonably refuse. To come back to myself, however, you consider that I am quite doomed?"

"Not quite yet, although your case is a bad one. I believe you can be saved if only you will exert yourself."

"Do wishes go for anything in a case like mine?"

"Assuredly. To hear you express a wish is a capital sign. What do you want to do?"

"I have a strange wish to go down to the Court. I feel as if something or some one, whether angel or demon I do not know, were drawing me there. I have wished to be at the Court for some days. I thought at first of taking Margaret with me."

"Do so. She would be glad to accompany you. She is a wife in a thousand."

"But on second thoughts," continued Awdrey, "if I am obliged to listen to her bitter distress over the death of a child who never, as far as I can re-call, existed, I should prefer not having her."

"Very well then, go alone."

"I cannot go alone. In the condition which I am now in, a complete vacuum in all my thoughts may occur, and long before I reach the Court I may forget where I am going."

"That is possible."

"Then, Rumsey, will you come with me?"

The doctor thought a moment. "I'll go with you this evening," he said, "but I must return to town early to-morrow."

"Thanks," said Awdrey. "I'll ring the bell. We shall be in time, if we start at once, to catch the five o'clock train."

"Remember, Awdrey, that I shall treat you as the child's father. You will find all your tenantry in a state of poignant grief. That dear little fellow was much loved."

Awdrey pursed up his lips as if he would whistle. A smile dawned in his eyes and vanished.

CHAPTER XVI.

AT a late hour that evening Rumsey and his patient arrived at Grandcourt. A telegram had been sent to announce their visit, and all was in readiness for their reception. The old butler, Hawkins, who had lived in the family for nearly fifty years, came slowly down the steps to greet his master. Hawkins' face was pale, and his eyes dim, as if he had been indulging in silent tears. He was very much attached to little Arthur. Awdrey gave him a careless nod.

"I hope all is in readiness, Hawkins," he said, "I have brought my friend, Dr. Rumsey, with me; we should like supper—has it been prepared?"

"Yes, Mr. Robert—I beg your pardon, Squire—all is in readiness in the library."

"We'll go there after we have washed our hands," said Awdrey. "What room have you got ready for Dr. Rumsey?"

"The yellow room, Squire, in the west wing."

"That will do nicely. Rumsey, you and I will inhabit the same wing to-night. I suppose I am to sleep in the room I always occupy, eh, Hawkins?"

"Yes, sir; Mrs. Burnett, the housekeeper, thought you would wish that."

"It does not matter in the least where I sleep;

now order up supper, we shall be down directly. Follow me, doctor, will you?"

Dr. Rumsey followed Awdrey to the west wing. A few moments later the two men were seated before a cheerful meal in the library—a large fire burned in the huge grate, logs had been piled on, and the friendly blaze and the fragrance of the wood filled the room. The supper table was drawn into the neighborhood of the fire, and Awdrey lifted the cover from the dish which was placed before him with a look of appetite on his face.

"I am really hungry," he said—"we will have some champagne—Hawkins, take some from"—he named a certain bin. The man retired, coming back presently with some dusty-looking bottles. The cork was quickly removed from one, and the butler began to fill the glasses.

Supper came to an end. Hawkins brought in pipes and tobacco, and the two men sat before the fire. Awdrey, who had taken from two to three glasses of champagne, was beginning to feel a little drowsy, but Rumsey talked in his usual pleasant fashion. Awdrey replied by fits and starts; once he nodded and half fell asleep in his chair.

"You are sleepy," said Rumsey suddenly; "if you go to bed now you may have a really good night, which will do wonders for you—what do you say?"

"That I am quite agreeable," said Awdrey, rising as he spoke—"but is it not too early for you, doctor?"

"Not at all—an undisturbed night will be a treat to me."

"Well, then, I'll take you to your room."

They went upstairs together, and a moment later Rumsey found himself in the palatial chamber which had been prepared for him. He was not really sleepy and decided to sit up for a little. A fire burned in the grate, some books lay about—he drew his easy-chair forward and taking up a volume of light literature prepared to dip into it—he found that it was Stevenson's "Treasure Island," a book which he had not yet happened to read; the story interested him, and he read on for some time. Presently he closed the book, and laying his head against the cushion of the chair dropped fast asleep.

The events of the day made him dream; all his dreams were about his queer patient. He thought that he had followed Awdrey on to the Plain—that Awdrey's excitement grew worse and worse, until the last lingering doubt was solved, and the man was in very truth absolutely insane.

In the midst of his dream the doctor was awakened by a hand being laid on his shoulder—he started up suddenly—Awdrey, half-dressed and looking ghastly pale, stood before him.

"What is it?" said Rumsey. "Do you want anything?"

"I want you," said Awdrey. "Will you come with me?"

"Certainly—where am I to go? Why are you not in bed?"

Awdrey uttered a hollow laugh. There was a ring of horror in it.

"You could not sleep if you were me," he said. "Will you come with me now, at once?"

"In a moment or two when you are better—sit down, won't you—here, take my chair—where do you want me to go?"

"Out with me, doctor—out of doors. I want you to accompany me on to the Plain."

"All right, my dear fellow—but just allow me to get on my boots."

The doctor retired to a back part of the room to change his house shoes. While he was doing so, Awdrey sank down on a chair and laid his hands on his knees, took no notice of Rumsey, but stared straight before him into the centre of the room.

"I wish you'd be quick, doctor," he said at last. "I don't want to go alone, but I must follow it."

"Follow what?" said Rumsey.

"It—the queer vision—I have told you of it before."

"Oh, yes, that bad dream you are subject to. Well, I am at your service now."

Awdrey rose slowly. He pointed with one of his hands.

"Do you see that?" he said suddenly.

Rumsey following the direction of his eyes perceived that he was staring into the part of the room which was in deepest shadow.

"I see nothing, Awdrey," he replied in a kind and soothing voice, "but I perceive by your manner that you do.   What is it?"

"I wonder you cannot see it," replied Awdrey; "it is plain, too plain—it seems to fill all that part of the room."

"The old thing?" asked the doctor.

"Yes, the old thing but with a certain difference. There is the immense globe of light and the picture in the middle."

"The old picture, Awdrey?"

"Yes, yes, but with a difference.   The two men are fighting.   As a rule they stand motionless in the picture, but to-night they seem to have come alive—they struggle, they struggle hard; one stands with his back to me.   The face of the other I can recognize distinctly.   It is the face of that young fellow who stayed a few years ago at the inn in our village.   Ah! yes, of course, I know his name, Frere—Horace Frere.   He has met some one on Salisbury Plain.   It is night; the moon is hidden behind clouds.   Ha! now it comes out.   Now I can see them distinctly.   Dr. Rumsey, don't you hear the blows?   I do.   They seem to beat on my brain.   That man who stands with his back to us carries my stick in his hand.   I know it is mine, for the whole thing is so intensely plain that I can even see the silver tablet on which my name is engraved.   My God! the man also wears my clothes. I would give all that I possess to see his face.   Let us get on the Plain as fast as we can.   I may be able to see the reverse side of the picture from there. Come with me, come at once."

"Poor fellow! matters get worse and worse," thought the doctor. "Well, I must see this thing out."

Aloud he said:

"How soon did this vision come to torment you to-night?"

Awdrey rubbed his eyes.

"At first when I went to my room I was sleepy," he said. "I began to take off my things. Then I saw a globe of light in the further end of the room. At first it was merely light with no picture in the centre. Then faint shadows began to appear, and by slow degrees the perfect and intensely clear picture which I am now looking at became visible. I stared at it quite motionless for a time. I was absorbed by the deepest interest. Then a mad longing to see the face of the man who stands with his back to us, came over me. I walked about the room trying hard to get even a side view of him, but wherever I went he turned so as to keep his face away; wherever I went the face of Frere was the only one I could see. Then in a sort of despair, almost maddened in fact, I rushed from the room.

"Did you not leave the vision behind you?"

"Not I—it went straight in front of me. When I reached your room and opened the door it came in before me. I know now what I must do. I have been always standing more or less to the right of the picture. I must get to the left. I am going to follow it on to the Plain—I am going to trace it to the exact spot where that murder was committed. Will you come with me?"

"Yes, only first you must return to your room, and get into the rest of your clothes. At present you are without a coat."

"Am I? And yet I burn with heat. Well, I'll do what you want. I will do anything which gives me a chance of seeing that man's face."

A few moments later Rumsey and his patient found themselves in the white moonlight of the outer world. Awdrey was now quite silent, but Rumsey noticed that his footsteps faltered once or twice, and that he often paused as if to get his breath. He appeared to be like a man in a frantic hurry; he gazed straight before him, as if he were looking intently at one fixed object.

"It goes before me, and guides me to the spot," he said at last, in a choking voice. He panted more violently than ever. Heavy sighs came from him—these seemed to be wrung from his very heart.

In about ten minutes the men got upon the borders of the Plain. Awdrey then turned abruptly to his left; each moment he walked faster and faster; the doctor had now almost to run to keep up with him. At last they reached the rise of ground. A great clump of alder-trees stood to the left; at the right, a little way off, was a dense belt of undergrowth. On the rising ground itself was short grass and no other vegetation. A little way off, nearly one hundred feet lower down, was a pond. The light of the moon was fully reflected here; across the smooth surface of the pond was a clear path as if of silver. When they reached the brow of this slight elevation, Awdrey stood still.

"There—it was done there," he said, pointing with his finger. "See, the picture does not move any more, but settles down upon the ground. Now we shall see the whole thing. Good God, Rumsey, fancy looking at a murder which was committed five years ago! It is going on there now all over again. There stand the two men life-size. Can't we stop them? Can we do nothing?"

"No, it is only a vision," said the doctor; "but tell me exactly what you see."

"It is too marvellous," said Awdrey. "The men move, and I hear the sound of the blows. It is extraordinary how that fellow keeps his back to me. I can't see his face if I stand here. Come, let us go downhill—if we get near the pond we can look up, and I shall get a view of him in another position."

"Come," said Rumsey. He took Awdrey's arm, and they went down the slope of ground until they almost reached the borders of the pond.

"Now is it any better?" asked the doctor. "Can you see the man's face now?"

"No, he has turned; he still keeps his back to me, the scoundrel. But oh, for God's sake see— he fights harder than ever. Ha! He has thrown Horace Frere to the ground. Now Frere is up—

what a strong chap he is! Now the other man is down. No, he has risen again. Now they both stand and fight, and—Dr. Rumsey, did you see that? The man with his back to us uses his stick, straight in front of him like a bayonet, and—oh, my God!"

Awdrey covered his face with his shaking hands. In a moment he looked up again.

"Can't you see for yourself?" he cried. "Frere is on his back—in my opinion he is dead. What has happened?"

Awdrey swayed from side to side. His excitement was so intense that he would have fallen if Dr. Rumsey had not caught him. The night was a chilly one, but the terrified and stricken man was bathed in perspiration.

"Come, Awdrey, you have told me everything, and it is fully time to return home," said the doctor.

"I vow I won't go back until I see that man's face, Dr. Rumsey. What name did they give him at the trial? Frank—Frank Everett—was he the man convicted of the murder?"

"Yes, of course, you must remember that—he is serving his time now in Portland."

Awdrey faced round suddenly, and looked into the doctor's eyes.

"It is all a mistake then," he said, in a queer sort of whisper. "I swear that before God. I saw Everett once—he was a thickly made man—that fellow is slighter, taller, younger. He carries my stick and wears my clothes. Why in the name of Heaven can't I see his face? What are you saying, doctor?"

"Only that I must take you home, my good fellow. You are my patient, and I cannot permit this excitement any longer."

"But the murder is still going on. Can't you see the whole thing for yourself? That fellow with his back to us is the murderer. He uses his stick as a bayonet. What did I once hear about that? Oh that I could remember! There is a cloud before my mind—oh, God in Heaven, that I could rend it! Do not speak to me for a moment, doctor, I am struggling with a memory."

Awdrey flung himself on the ground—he pressed his hands before his eyes—he looked like a demented man. Suddenly he sprang to his feet.

"I have it," he said with a laugh, which sounded hollow. "If I look in the pond I shall see the man's face. His face must be reflected in it. Stay where you are, doctor, I'll be back with you in a minute. I am getting at it—light is coming—it is all returning to me. He uses his stick as a bayonet, prodding him in the mouth. Old, old—what am I saying?—who told me that long ago? Yes I shall see his face in the pond."

Awdrey ran wildly to the edge of the water. He paused just where the silver light fell full across the dark pond. Rumsey followed him in hot haste. He knew that his patient was in the condition when he might leap into the pond at any moment.

Catching on to an alder-tree, Awdrey now bent forward until he caught the reflection in the water —he slid down on his knees to examine it more carefully.

"Take care, Awdrey, you'll slip in if you are not careful," cried Rumsey.

Awdrey was silent for a moment—his own reflection greeted him—he looked straight down at his own face and figure. Suddenly he rose to his feet: a long shiver ran through his frame. He went up to Rumsey with a queer unsteady laugh.

"I have seen the man's face," he said.

"It was your own face, my dear fellow," said the doctor. "I saw it reflected distinctly in the water."

"I am satisfied," said Awdrey, in a changed and yet steady voice. "We can go home now."

"Well, have you really seen what you wanted to see? Who was the murderer?"

"Frank Everett, who is serving his time in Portland prison. Dr. Rumsey, I believe I have been the victim of the most horrible form of nightmare which ever visited living man. Anyhow it has vanished—the vision has completely disappeared."

"I am glad to hear you say so, Awdrey."

"I do not see it any longer—I know what I wanted to know. Let us go back to the Court."

CHAPTER XVII

"WELL, Het, what do you say to a bit o' news that'll wake you up?" said Farmer Vincent one fine morning in the month of May to his young wife.

Hetty was in her dairy with her sleeves turned up busily skimming cream. She turned as her husband spoke and looked up into his face. He was a roughly built man on a huge scale. He chucked her playfully under the chin.

"There are to be all kinds of doings," he said. "I've just been down to the village and the whole place is agog. What do you say to an election, and who do you think is to be put up for the vacant seat?"

"I don't know much about elections, George," said Hetty, turning again to her cream. "If that's all it won't interest me."

"Ay, but 'tain't all—there's more behind it."

"Well, do speak out and tell the news. I'm going down to see aunt presently."

"I wonder how many days you let pass without being off to see that aunt of yours," said the farmer, frowning perceptibly. "Well, then, the news is this. Squire and Mrs. Awdrey and a lot of company with them came back to the Court this evening. Squire and Madam have been in foreign parts all the winter, and they say that Squire's as well as ever a man was, and he and madam mean to live at the Court in future. Why, you have turned white, lass! What a lot you think of those grand folks!"

"No, I don't, George, not more than anybody ought. Of course I'm fond of Squire, seeing I know him since he was a little kid—and we was always great, me and mine, for holding on to the Family."

"I've nothing to say agin' the Fam'ly," said farmer Vincent, "and for my part," he continued, "I'm glad Squire is coming to live here. I don't hold with absentee landlords, that I don't. There are many things I'll get him to do for me on the farm. I can't move Johnson, the bailiff, one bit, but when Squire's to home 'twill be another matter. Then he's going to stand for Grandcourt. He's quite safe to be returned. So, Het, what with an election and the Fam'ly back again at the Court, there'll be gay doings this summer, or I'm much mistook."

"To be sure there will," said Hetty. She pulled a handkerchief out of her pocket as she spoke and wiped some moisture from her brow.

"You don't look too well, my girl. Now don't you go and overdo things this morning—the weather is powerful hot for the time o' year, and you never can stand heat. I thought it 'ud cheer you up to tell you about Squire, for any one can see with half an eye that you are as proud of him and the Fam'ly as woman can be."

"I'm very glad to hear your news, George," replied Hetty. "Now if you won't keep me any longer I'll make you some plum duff for dinner."

"That's a good girl—you know my weakness."

The man went up to her where she stood, and put one of his great arms round her neck.

"Look at me, Hetty," he said.

"What is it, George?" She raised her full, dark eyes.

He gazed down into their depths, anxiously.

"Are you a bit better, lass?" he asked, a tender intonation in his gruff voice. "Pain in the side any less bad?"

"Yes, George, I feel much better."

"Well, I'm glad of that," he said slowly. "Now you look well at me. Don't you take your eyes off me while I'm a-speaking. I've been counting the days. I mark 'em down on the back of the fowl-house door with a bit of chalk; and it's forty days and more since you gave me the least little peck of a kiss, even. Do you think you could give me one now?"

She raised her lips, slowly. He could not but perceive her unwillingness, and a wave of crimson swept up over his face.

"I don't want that sort," he said, flinging his arm away and moving a step or two back from her. "There, I ain't angry; I ain't no call to be angry;

you were honest with me afore we wed. You said plain as girl could speak, 'I ain't got the least bit of love for you, George,' and I took you at your word; but sometimes, Het, it seems as if it 'ud half kill me, for I love you better every day and every hour."

"I know you're as good a fellow as ever breathed," said Hetty; "and I like you even though I don't love you. I'll try hard to be a good wife to you, George, I will truly."

"You're main pleased about Squire, I take it?"

"I am main pleased."

"'Twere a pity the little chap were took so sudden-like."

"I s'pose so," said Hetty.

"You are a queer girl, Hetty. I never seed a woman less fond o' children than you."

"Well, I ain't got any of my own, you understand," said Hetty.

"I understand." The farmer uttered a huge laugh. "I guess I do," he said. "I wish to God you had a child, Hetty; maybe you'd love it, and love its father for its sake."

With a heavy sigh the man turned and left the dairy.

The moment she found herself alone, Hetty flew to the door and locked it. Then standing in the middle of the spotless room she pressed her two hands wildly to her brow.

"He's coming back," she said aloud; "back to live here; he'll be within a mile of me to-night.

Any day or any hour I may see him. He's coming
back to live. What do folks mean by saying he is
well? If he is well, does he remember? And if he
remembers—oh, my God, I shall go mad if I think
much of that any longer! Squire back again at the
Court and me here, and I knowing what I know,
and Aunt Fanny knowing what she knows! I must
go and speak to aunt to-day. To-night, too, so
soon; he'll be back to-night. My head is giddy
with the thought. What does it all mean? Is he
really well, and does he remember? Oh, this awful
pain in my side! I vowed I'd not take another
drop of the black medicine; but there's nothing
else keeps me steady."

Glancing furtively behind her, although there
was not a soul in sight, Hetty opened a cupboard
in the wall. From a back recess she produced a
small bottle; it was half full of a dark liquid. Taking up a spoon which lay near she poured some
drops into it, and adding a little water, drank it
off. She then put the bottle carefully back into its
place, locked the cupboard, and slipped the key
into her pocket.

"In a minute, dreams will come, and I'll be much
better," she said to herself. "It seems as if I could
bear anything a'most after I'd taken a little of that
black stuff; it's a sight better than gin, and I know
what I'm doing all the time. I'll go and see aunt
the minute I've swallowed my dinner; but now I
must hurry to make the plum duff for George."

She ran briskly off to attend to her numerous

duties. She was now bright and merry; the look of gloom and depression had completely left her face; her eyes shone with a contented and happy light. As she bustled about her kitchen opening and shutting her oven, and filling up the different pots, which were necessary for cooking the dinner, with hot water, her white teeth gleamed, and smiles came and went over her face.

"To think of Aunt Fanny's toothache mixture doing this for me," she said to herself. "Aunt Fanny 'ud put a bit on cotton wool and put it into the hole of her tooth, and the pain 'ud be gone in a jiffy; and now I swallow a few drops, and somehow it touches my heart, and my pain goes. Aunt Fanny wonders where her toothache cure is; she ain't likely to hear from me. Oh, it's quite wonderful how contented it makes me feel!"

Hetty was a good housewife, and there was nothing slatternly nor disorderly about her kitchen.

The dinner, smoking hot and comfortable, was upon the table when Vincent came in at twelve o'clock to partake of it. There was a great piece of bacon and some boiled beans. These were immediately followed by the plum duff. The farmer ate heartily, and Hetty piled up his plate whenever it was empty.

"You scarcely take a pick yourself, little girl," he said, seizing one of her hands as she passed and squeezing it affectionately.

"I ain't hungry, George."

"Excited 'bout Squire, I guess."

"Well, p'raps I am a bit; you don't mind if I go and talk it all over with aunt?"

"That I don't; when you smile at me so cheerful like that there's nought I wouldn't give yer. Now you look here, Griffiths, the steward, is going to get up a sort of display at the Court, and the villagers are going; there is talk of a supper afterward in the barns, but that may or may not be. What do you say to you and me going into the avenue and seeing Squire and Madam drive in. What do you say, Het?"

"Oh, George, I'd like it."

"You would not think of giving a body a kiss for it, eh?"

"Yes, that I would."

She ran behind him, flung her soft arms round his neck, and pressed a kiss against his cheek just above his whiskers.

"That won't do," he said. "I won't take yer for that—I must have it on my lips."

She gave him a shy peck something like a robin. He caught her suddenly in his arms, squeezed her to his heart, and kissed her over and over again.

"I love thee more than words can say," he cried. "I am mad to get your love in return. Will the day ever come, Het?"

"I don't know, George; I'd like to say so to please you, but I can't tell a lie about a thing like that."

"To be sure, you can't," he said, rising as he spoke. "You'd soon be found out."

"I'd like well to love you," she continued, "for

you're good to me; but now I must be off to see Aunt Fanny."

Vincent left the kitchen, and Hetty hurried to her room to dress herself trimly. Ten minutes later she was on her way to the village.

The pretty little place already wore a festive air. Bunting had been hung across the streets, flags were flying gayly from many upper windows. The shop-keepers stood at their doors chatting to one another; several of them nodded to Hetty as she passed by.

"That you, Hetty Vincent?" called out one woman. "You've heard the news, I guess."

"Yes, about Squire and Madam," said Hetty.

"It has come unexpected," said the woman. "We didn't know until this morning that Squire was to be back to-night. Mr. Griffiths got the letter by the first post, and he's been nearly off his head since; there ain't a man in the village though that hasn't turned to help him with a will, and there are to be bonfires and all the rest. They say Squire and Madam are to live at the Court now. Pity the poor child went off so sudden. He were a main fine little chap; pity he ain't there to return home with his father and mother. You look better, Hetty Vincent—not so peaky like. Pain in the side less?"

"Sometimes it is, and sometimes it isn't," answered Hetty; "it's much better to-day. I can't stay talking any longer though, Mrs. Martin, for I want to catch Aunt Fanny."

"Well, you'll find her at home, but as busy as a bee, the whole place is flocking to the inn to learn the latest news. We're a-going up to the Court presently to welcome 'em home. You and your good man will come, too, eh, Hetty?"

"Yes, for sure," answered Hetty. She continued her walk up the village street.

Mrs. Armitage was cooling herself in the porch of the little inn when she saw her niece approaching.

Hetty hurried her steps, and came panting to her side.

"Aunt Fanny, is it true?" she gasped.

"True? Yes, child, it's true," said Mrs. Armitage. "They're coming home. You come along in and stand in the shelter, Hetty. Seems to me you grow thinner and thinner."

"Oh, aunt, never mind about my looks just now; have you heard anything else? How is he?"

Mrs. Armitage looked behind her and lowered her voice.

"They do say that Squire's as well as ever he wor," she remarked. "Why, he's going to stand for Grandcourt. In one way that's as it should be. We always had Awdreys in the House—we like to be represented by our own folk."

"Will any one oppose him?" asked Hetty.

"How am I to say? there's nothing known at present. He is to be nominated to-morrow; and that's what's bringing 'em home in double quick time."

"Are you going to the Court to-night, aunt?"

"I thought I'd run round for an hour just to see the carriage roll by, and get a glimpse of Squire and Madam, but I must hurry back, for there'll be a lot to be done here."

"Shall I come and help you and uncle to-night?"

Mrs. Armitage looked her niece all over.

"That's a good thought," she said, "if your man will spare you."

"Oh, I can ask him; I don't think he'll refuse."

"Well, you're spry enough with your fingers and legs when you like. I can't stay out here talking any more, Het."

Hetty came up close to her aunt, and lowered her voice to a whisper.

"Aunt Fanny," she said, "one word afore you goes in—Do you think it is safe, him coming back like this?"

"Safe," echoed the elder woman in a tone hoarse with a queer mixture of crossness and undefined fear. "Squire's safe enough ef you can keep things to yourself."

"Me?" echoed Hetty. "Do you think I can't hold my tongue?"

"Your tongue may be silent, but there are other ways of letting out a secret. Ef ever there was a tell-tale face yours is one. You're the terror of my life with your aches and your pains, and your startings, as if you saw a shadow behind yer all the time. It's a good thing you don't live in the village. As to Vincent, pore man, he's as blind as a bat; he don't see, or he won't see, what's staring him in the face."

"For God's sake, Aunt Fanny, what do you mean?"

"I mean this, girl. Vincent's wife carries a secret, and she loves one she ought not to love."

"Oh! Aunt Fanny, you rend my heart when you talk like that."

"I won't again," said Mrs. Armitage, "but I had to speak out when you came to-day. It was my opportunity, and I had to take it. Queer stories will be spread ef you ain't very careful. You've nought to do with the Squire, Hetty. Go and see him to-night with the rest of 'em, and then be satisfied. You keep quiet at the farm now he's at the Court; don't you be seen a-talking to him or a-follerin' him about."

"I won't, I won't."

"Well, I thought I'd warn yer—now I must get back to my work."

"One minute first, aunt—you know there ain't a soul I can speak to but you, and I'm near mad with the weight of my secret at times."

"You should take it quiet, girl—you fret o'er much. I really must leave you, Hetty; there's your uncle calling out to me."

"One minute—you must answer my question first."

"Well, well—what a girl you are! I'm glad you ain't my niece. Coming, Armitage. Now, Hetty, be quick. My man's temper ain't what it wor and

I daren't cross 'im. Now what is it you want to say?"

"It's this Aunt Fanny. Ef Mr. Robert is quite well—as well as ever he wor in his life—do you think he remembers?"

"Not he. He'll never remember again. They never do."

"But, aunt, they never get well, either."

"That's true enough."

"And they say he's quite well—as well as ever he was in all his life."

"Well, Hetty I can say no more. We'll see to-night—you and me. You keep alongside of me in the avenue, and when he passes by in the carriage we'll look at him straight in the face and we'll soon know. You noticed, didn't you, how queer his eyes got since that dark night. It'll be fully light when they drive up to the Court, and you and me we'll look at him straight in the face and we'll know the worst then."

"Yes, Aunt Fanny. Yes, I'll keep close to you."

"Do, girl. Now I must be off. You can sit in the porch awhile and rest yourself. Coming, Armitage."

Hetty stayed down at the inn through the remainder of the day.

In the course of the evening Vincent strode in. She was in the humor to be sweet to him, and he was in high spirits at her unwonted words and looks of affection.

The village presented a gayer and gayer spectacle

as the hours went by. High good humor was the order of the day. Squire and Madam were returning. Things must go well in the future.

Griffiths was seen riding up and down altering the plan of the decorations, giving orders in a stentorian voice. At last the time came when the villagers were to assemble, some of them outside their houses, some along the short bit of road which divided the village from the Court, some to line the avenue up to the Court itself.

Hetty and Mrs. Armitage managed to keep together. George Vincent and Armitage preceded them at a little distance. They walked solemnly through the village street, Armitage pleased but anxious to return to the inn, Vincent thinking of Hetty, and vaguely wondering by what subtle means he could get her to love him, Hetty and Mrs. Armitage weighed down by the secret which had taken the sunshine out of both their lives. They made straight for the avenue, and presently stationed themselves just on the brow of a rising slope which commanded a view of the gates on one side and of the Court itself on the other.

Hetty's excitable heart beat faster and faster. Dreadful as her secret was, she was glad, she rejoiced, at the fact that the Squire was coming home. She would soon see him again. To look at him was her pleasure; it was the breath of her highest life; it represented Paradise to her ignorant and unsophisticated mind. Her eyes grew bright as stars. A great deal of her old loveliness returned to her. Vincent, who with Armitage had taken up his position a few steps further down the avenue, kept looking back at her from time to time.

"Why, man," said the landlord of the village inn, with a hoarse laugh, "you're as much in love with that wife of your'n as if you hadn't been wedded for the last five years."

"Ay, I am in love with her," said Vincent. "I've got to win her yet, that's why. Strikes me she looks younger and more spry than I've seen her for many a year, to-night."

"She's mortal fond of Squire and Madam," said the landlord. "She always wor."

"Maybe," replied Vincent, in a thoughtful tone. He looked again at his wife's blooming face; a queer uncomfortable sense of suspicion began slowly to stir in his heart.

The sound of wheels was at last distinctly audible; bonfires were lit on the instant; cheers echoed up from the village. The welcoming wave of sound grew nearer and nearer, each face was wreathed with smiles. Into the avenue, with its background of eager, welcoming faces, dashed the spirited grays, with their open landau.

Awdrey and his wife sat side by side. Other carriages followed, but no one noticed their occupants. All eyes were turned upon Awdrey. He was bending forward in the carriage, his hat was off, he was smiling and bowing; now and then he uttered a cheerful word of greeting. Some of the men, as he passed, darted forward to clasp his outstretched hand. No one who saw him now would have recognized him for the miserable man who had come to the Court a few months back. His youth sat well upon him; his athletic, upright figure, his tanned face, his bright eyes, all spoke of perfect health, of energy both of mind and body. The Squire had come home, and the Squire was himself again. The fact was patent to all.

Margaret, who was also smiling, who also bowed and nodded, and uttered words of welcome, was scarcely glanced at. The Squire was the centre of attraction; he belonged to the people, he was theirs —their king, and he was coming home again.

"Bless 'im, he's as well as ever he wor," shouted a sturdy farmer, turning round and smiling at his own wife as he spoke.

"Welcome, Squire, welcome home! Glad to see yer so spry, Squire. We're main pleased to have yer back again, Squire," shouted hundreds of voices.

Hetty and her aunt, standing side by side, were pushed forward by the smiling, excited throng.

Awdrey's smiles were arrested on his lips, for a flashing instant Hetty's bright eyes looked full into his; he contracted his brows in pain, then once again he repeated his smiling words of welcome. The carriage rolled by.

"Aunt Fanny, he remembers!" whispered Hetty in a low voice.

CHAPTER XVIII

A HASTY supper had been got up in some large barns at the back of the Court. When the Squire's carriage disappeared out of sight, Griffiths rode hastily down to invite the villagers to partake of the hospitality which had been arranged for them. He passed Hetty, was attracted by her blooming face, and gave her a warm invitation.

"Come along, Mrs. Vincent," he said, "we can't do without you. Your husband has promised to stay. I'll see you in the west barn in a few minutes' time."

Vincent came up at this moment and touched Hetty on her shoulder.

"I thought we might as well go in for the whole thing," he said, "and I'm a bit peckish. You'd like to stay, wouldn't you, Het?"

"That I would," she replied. "You'll come too, aunt?" she continued, glancing at Mrs. Armitage.

"No, I can't be spared," replied Mrs. Armitage; "me and Armitage must hurry back to the inn. We've been away too long as it is."

"Oh, George, I promised to help Aunt Fanny to-night," said Hetty, torn by her desire to remain

in the Squire's vicinity and the remembrance of
her promise.

"We'll let you off, Het," said the old uncle, laying his heavy hand on her shoulder. "Go off with
your good man, my girl, and enjoy yourself."

Armitage and his wife hurried down the avenue,
and Hetty and Vincent followed the train of villagers who were going along by the shrubbery in
the direction of the west barn. There were three
great barns in all, and supper had been laid in
each. The west barn was the largest and the most
important, and by the time the Vincents reached
it the building was full from end to end. Hetty
and her husband, with a crowd of other people, remained outside. They all stood laughing and jok-
ing together. The highest good humor was prev-
alent. The Squire's return—the pleasure it gave
the villagers—his personal appearance, the look of
health and vigor which had been so lamentably
absent from him during the past years, and which
now to the delight of every one had so fully returned
—the death of the child—the look on Margaret's
face—were the only topics of the hour. But it was
the subject of the Squire himself to whom the people again and again returned. They were all so
unaffectedly glad to have him back again. Had he
ever looked so well before? What a ring of strength
there was in his voice! And then that tone with
which he spoke to them all, the tone of remembrance, this it was which went straight to the hearts
of the men and women who had known him from

his boyhood. Yes, the Squire was back, a strong man in his prime, and the people of Grandcourt had good reason for rejoicing.

"He'll be as good a Squire as his father before him," said an old man of nearly eighty years, hobbling up close to Hetty as he spoke. "They did whisper that the curse of his house had took 'im, but it can't be true—there ain't no curse on his face, bless 'im. He's good to the heart's core, and strong too and well. He'll be as good a Squire as his father; bless 'im, say I, bless 'im."

"Het, you look as white as a sheet," said Vincent, turning at that moment and catching his wife's eye. "There girl, eat you must. I'll squeeze right into the barn and you come in ahind me. I'm big enough to make way for a little body like you."

Vincent squared his shoulders and strode on in front. After some pushing he and Hetty found themselves inside the barn. The tables which had been laid from one end to the other, were crowded with eager, hungry faces. Griffiths and other servants from the Court were flying here and there, pressing hospitality on every one. Vincent was just preparing to ensconce himself in a vacant corner, and to squeeze room for Hetty close to him, when the door at the other end of the long barn was opened, and Awdrey, Margaret, and some visitors came in.

Immediately all the villagers rose from their seats, and an enthusiastic cheer resounded among the rafters of the old barn. Hetty standing on tiptoe, and straining her neck, could see Awdrey shaking hands right and left. Presently he would come to her, he would take her hand in his. She could also catch a glimpse of Margaret's stately figure, of her pale, high-bred face, of the dark waves of her raven black hair. Once again she looked at the Squire. How handsome he was, how manly, and yet—and yet—something seemed to come up in Hetty's throat and almost to choke her.

"You ain't well, Het," said her husband. He had also risen from his seat, and pushing out, had joined Hetty in the crowd. "The air in this place is too close for you, Hetty. Drat that supper, we'll get into the open air once again."

"No, we won't," answered Hetty. "I must wait to speak to Squire, happen what may."

"Why, it'll be half an hour before he gets as far as here," said Vincent. "Well," he added, looking back regretfully at his plate, which was piled with pie and other good things; "if we must stay I'm for a bit of supper. There's a vacant seat at last; you slip in by me, Het. Ah, that cold pie is just to my taste. What do you say to a tiny morsel, girl?"

"I could not eat, George, it would choke me," said Hetty, "I'm not the least bit hungry. I had tea an hour ago down at the inn. You eat, George, do, George; do go down and have some supper. I'll stand her and wait for Squire and Madam."

"You are daft on Squire and Madam," said the man angrily.

Hetty did not answer. It is to be doubted if she heard him. One fact alone was filling her horizon. She felt quite certain now that the Squire remembered. What then was going to happen? Was he going to be an honorable man? Was he going to use the memory which had returned to him to remove the cruel shame and punishment from another? If so, if indeed so, Hetty herself would be lost. She would be arrested and charged with the awful crime of perjury. The horrors of the law would fall upon her; she would be imprisoned, she would——"

"No matter," she whispered stoutly to herself, "it is not of myself I think now, it is of him. He also will be tried. Public disgrace will cling to his name. The people who love him so will not be able to help him; he would suffer even, even to death: the death of the gallows. He must not tell what he knew. He must not be allowed to be carried away by his generous impulses. She, Hetty, must prevent this. She had guarded his secret for him during the long years when the cloud was over his mind. He must guard it now for himself. Doubtless he would when she had warned him. Could she speak to him to-night? Was it possible?"

"Hetty, how you do stand and stare," said George Vincent; he was munching his pie as he spoke. Hetty had been pressed up against the table where he was eating.

"I'm all right, George," she said, but she spoke

ᴀs if she had not heard the words addressed to her.

"If you're all right, come and have a bit of supper."

"I don't want it. I'm not hungry. Do eat while you can and let me be."

"I'll let you be, but not out of my sight," muttered the man. He helped himself to some more pie, but he was no longer hungry. The jealous fiend which had always lain dormant in his heart from the day when he had married pretty Hetty Armitage and discovered that she had no love to give to him was waking up now into full strength and vigor. What was the matter with Hetty? How queer she looked to-night. She had always been queer after a certain fashion—she had always been different from other girls, but until to-night, Vincent, who had watched her well, had never found anything special to lay hold of. But to-night things were different. There must be a reason for Hetty's undue excitement, for her changing color, for her agitation, for the emotion on her face. Now what was she doing?"

Vincent started from his seat to see his wife moving slowly up the room, borne onward by the pressure of the crowd. Several of the villagers, impatient at the long delay, had struggled up the barn to get a hand-shake from the Squire and his wife. Hetty was carried with the rest out of her husband's sight. Vincent jumped on a bench in order to get a view. He saw Hetty moving for-

ward, he had a good glimpse of her profile, the
color on the cheek nearest to him was vivid as a
damask rose Her whole little figure was alert,
full of determination, of a queer impulsive longing
which the man saw without understanding. Suddenly he saw his wife fall backward against some
of the advancing crowd; she clasped her hands
together, then uttered a shrill, piercing cry.

"Take me out of this for the love of God, Squire,"
she panted.

"Is that young woman Mrs. Vincent?" suddenly
cried another voice. "Then, if so, I've something
to say to her."

It was Mrs. Everett who had spoken. Hetty had
not seen her until this moment. She was walking
up the room accompanied by Awdrey's sisters, Ann
and Dorothy.

"I can't stay—I won't meet her—take me away,
take me away, into the air, Squire," said Hetty.
"Oh, I am suffocating," she continued, "the room
is rising up as if it would choke me."

"Open that door there to your right, Griffiths,"
said Awdrey, in a tone which rose above the tumult.
"Come, Mrs. Vincent, take my arm."

He drew Hetty's hand into his, and led her out
by a side door. The crowd made way for them.
In another instant the excited girl found the cool
evening air blowing on her hot cheeks.

"I am sorry you found the room too close,"
began Awdrey.

"Oh, it was not that, sir, not really. Just wait

a minute, please, Mr. Robert, until I got my l. .th. I did not know that she—that she was coming h re."

"Who do you mean?" asked Awdrey.

"Mrs. Everett. I can't bear her. It was the sight of her, sudden-like, that took the breath from me."

Awdrey did not speak for a moment.

"You are better now," he said then, in a stony tone. "Is your husband here?"

"Yes, but I don't want him."

Hetty, in her excitement, laid both hands on the Squire's arm.

"Mr. Robert, I must see you, and alone," she panted.

Awdrey stepped back instinctively.

"You don't want me to touch you, you don't want to have anything to do with me, and yet—and yet, Mr. Robert, I must see you by yourself. When I can see you alone?"

"I cannot stay with you now," said Awdrey, in a hurried voice. "Come up to the house to-morrow. No, though, I shall have no time to attend to you to-morrow."

"It must be to-morrow, sir. It is life or death; yes, it is life or death."

"Well, to-morrow let it be," said Awdrey, after a pause, "six o'clock in the evening. Don't call at the house, come round to the office. I'll be there and I'll give you a few minutes. Now I see you are better," he continued, "I'll go back to the barn and fetch Vincent."

He turned abruptly. On the threshold of the door by which he had gone out he met Mrs. Everett.

"Where is that young woman?" she demanded.

"You seem to have frightened her," said Awdrey. "You had better not go to her now, she was half-fainting, but I think the fresh air has put her right again."

His face looked cool and composed.

"Fainting or not," said Mrs. Everett, "I must see her, for I have something to say to her. The fact is, I don't mind telling you, Mr. Awdrey, that I accepted your wife's kind invitation more with the hope of meeting that young woman than for any other reason."

Awdrey raised his brows as if in slight surprise.

"I left Mrs. Vincent outside," he repeated.

"Then pray let me pass."

"If you want my wife I'll take you to her," said Vincent's voice at that moment.

"Glad to see you again, Vincent," said Awdrey. He held out his hand to the farmer, who stepped back a pace as if he did not see it.

"Obliged, I'm sure, sir," he said awkwardly. "You'll excuse me now, Squire, I want to get to my wife."

"Is that young woman really your wife?" demanded Mrs. Everett, in an eager voice.

"Yes, ma'am."

"Then I've something very important I wish to say to her."

"I'll find out if she's well enough to see you, ma'am. Hetty is not to say too strong."

The man pushed by, elbowing his way to right and left. Mrs. Everett followed him. He quickly reached the spot where Awdrey had left Hetty. She was no longer there.

"Where is she?" asked Mrs. Everett, in an eager tone.

"I can't tell you, ma'am. She is not here."

"Do you think she has gone home?"

"That's more'n I can say. May I ask what your business is with my wife?"

"Your wife is in possession of a secret which I mean to find out."

Vincent's face flushed an angry red.

"So others think she has a secret," he muttered to himself.

Aloud he said, "May I ask what yer name is, ma'am?"

"My name is Mrs. Everett. I am the mother of the man who was accused of murdering Horace Frere on Salisbury Plain six years ago."

"Ah," said Vincent, "it's a good way back since that 'appened; we've most forgot it now. I'm main sorry for yer, o' course, Mrs. Everett. T'were a black day for yer when your son——"

"My son is innocent, my good sir, and it is my belief that your wife can help me to prove it."

"No, you're on a wrong tack there," said Vincent slowly. "What can Hetty know?"

"Then you won't help me?"

"I say nought about that. The hour is late, and my wife ain't well. You'll excuse me now, but I must foller 'er."

Vincent walked quickly away. He strode with long strides across the grass. After a time he stopped, and looked to right and left of him. There was a rustling sound in a shrub near by. Hetty stole suddenly out of the deep shadow.

"Take me home, George, I've been waiting for you," she said.

"Well, these are queer goings-on," said the man. "There was a lady, Mrs. Everett, and she said— never mind now what she said. Tell me, Het, as you would speak the truth ef you were a-dying, what did yer want with Squire?"

"Nothing. What should I want with him? I was just glad to see him again."

"Why did you turn faint?"

"It was the heat of the room."

"Come on. Take my arm. Let's go out o' this."

The farmer's tone was very fierce. He dragged Hetty's hand through his big arm, and strode away so quickly that she could scarcely keep up with him.

"It hurts my side," she said, at last panting.

"You think nothing hurts but your side," said the man. "There are worse aches than that."

"What do you mean, George? How queer and rough you speak!"

"Maybe I know more'n you think, young woman."

"Know more than I think," she said. "There's nothing more to know."

"Ain't there? P'raps I've found out the reason why your 'eart's been closed to me—p'raps I've got the key to that secret."

"Oh, George, George, you know I'd love you ef I could."

"P'raps I've got the key to that secret," repeated the farmer. "I'm not a bad feller—not bad to look at nor bad to live with—and I gived yer all I got—but never, God above is witness, never from the day I took yer to church, 'ave yer kissed me of your own free will. No, nor ever said a lovin' word to me—the sort of words that come so glib to the lips o' other young wives. You're like one who carries sum'mat at her heart. Maybe I guess to-night."

"But there's nothing to guess," said Hetty. She was trembling, a sick fear took possession of her.

"Ain't there? Why did you make an appointment to meet Squire alone?"

"What in the world do you mean?"

"None o' your soft sawder, now, Hetty. I know what I'm a-talking of. I crep' out of barn t'other way, and I 'eard what you said."

"You heard," said Hetty, with a little scream. Then she suppressed it, and gave a little hysterical laugh. "You're welcome to hear," she continued. "There was nothing in it."

"Worn't there? You seemed mighty eager to have a meetin' with 'im; much more set on it, I take it, than he wor to have a meetin' wi' you.

Gents o' that sort don't care to be reminded o' the follies o' their youth. I seed a big frown coming up between his eyes when you wor so masterful, and when you pressed and pressed to see 'im. Why did yer say t'was life or death? I've got my clue at last, and look you 'ere, you meet Squire at your peril. There, that's my last word. You understand me?"

CHAPTER XIX.

THE next day Vincent got up early. It was his wont to rise betimes. Small as his farm was he managed it well, superintended everything that went on in it, and did, when possible, the greater part of the work himself. He rose now from the side of his sleeping wife, looked for a moment at her fair, flower-like face, clenched his fist at a memory which came over him, and then stole softly out of the room.

The morning was a lovely one, warm for the time of year, balmy with the full promise of spring. The trees were clothed in their tenderest green; there was a faint blue mist near the horizon which would pass into positive heat later on.

Vincent strode along with his hands deep in his pockets. He looked like a man who was struggling under a heavy weight. In truth he was; he was unaccustomed to thought, and he now had plenty of that commodity to worry him. What was the matter with Het? What was her secret? Did Mrs. Everett's queer words mean anything or nothing? Why did Het want to see the Squire? Was it possible that the Squire—? The man dashed out one of his great hands suddenly into space.

"Drat it," he muttered, "ef I thought it I'd kill 'im."

At this moment the sound of footsteps approaching caused him to raise his head; he had drawn up close to a five-barred gate. He saw a woman's bonnet above the hedgerow—a woman dressed in black was coming in his direction—she turned the corner and he recognized Mrs. Everett. He stared at her for a full moment without opening his lips. He felt he did not like her; a queer sensation of possible danger stirred at his heart. What was she doing at this hour? Vincent knew nothing of the ways of women of quality; but surely they had no right to be out at this hour in the morning.

The moment Mrs. Everett saw him she quickened her footsteps. No smile played round her lips, but there was a look of welcome and of gratified longing in her keen, dark eyes.

"I had a presentiment that I should find you," she said. "I wanted to have a talk with you when no one was by. Here you are, and here am I."

"Mornin', ma'am," said Vincent awkwardly.

"Good-morning," answered, Mrs. Everett. "The day is a beautiful one," she continued; "it will be hot by and by."

Vincent did not think it necessary to reply to this.

"I'm due in the five-acre field," he said, after a long pause. "I beg pardon, ma'am, but I must be attending to my dooties."

"If you wish to cross that field," said Mrs.

Everett, "I have not the least objection to accompanying you."

Vincent hesitated. He glanced at the five-barred gate as if he meant to vault over it, then he looked at the lady; she was standing perfectly motionless, her arms hanging straight at her sides; she came a step or two nearer to him.

"Look you 'ere," he said then, suddenly. "I'm a plain body—a man, so to speak, of one idee. There are the men yonder waitin' to fall to with the spring turnips, and 'ere am I waitin' to give 'em orders, and 'ere you are, ma'am, waitin' to say sum'mat. Now I can't attend to the men and to you at the same time, so p'raps you'll speak out, ma'am, and go."

"I quite understand your position," said Mrs. Everett. "I would much rather speak out. I have come here to say something about your wife."

"Ay," said Vincent, folding his arms, "it's mighty queer what you should 'ave to say 'bout Hetty."

"Not at all, for I happen to know something about her."

"And what may that be?"

"I'll tell you if you will give me time to speak. I told you last night who I am—I am Mrs. Everett, the mother of a man who has been falsely accused of murder."

"Falsely!" echoed Vincent, an incredulous expression playing round his lips.

"Yes, falsely. Don't interrupt me, please. Your wife witnessed that murder."

"That's true enough, and it blackened her life, poor girl."

"I'm coming to that part in a minute. Your wife witnessed the murder. She was very young at the time. It was well known that the murdered man wanted to make her his wife. It was supposed, quite falsely, but it was the universal supposition, that my son was also one of her lovers. This latter was not the case. It is just possible, however, that she had another lover—she was a very pretty girl, the sort of girl who would attract men in a station above her own."

Vincent's face grew black as night.

"I have my reason," continued Mrs. Everett, "for supposing it possible that your wife had another lover. There is, at least, not the slightest doubt that the man who killed Mr. Frere did so in a fit of jealousy."

"P'raps so," said Vincent. "It may be so. I loved Het then—I longed to make her my wife then. I'm in her own station—it's best for girls like Het to marry in their own station. She told me that the man who was murdered wanted to make her his wife, but she never loved him, that I will say."

"She may have loved the murderer."

"The man who is suffering penal servitude?" cried Vincent. "Your son, ma'am? Then ef you think so he'd better stay where he is—he'd best stay where 'e is."

"I am not talking of my son, but of the real murderer," said Mrs. Everett slowly.

Vincent stared at her. He thought she was slightly off her head.

"I was in court when your son was tried," he said, at last. "'Twas a plain case. He killed his man—it was brought in manslaughter, worn't it? And he didn't swing for it. I don't know what you mean, ma'am, an' I'd like to be away now at my work."

"I have something more to say, and then I'll go. I met your wife about a year ago. We met on Salisbury Plain."

"Ay, she's fond o'. the Plain, Hetty is."

"I told her then what I now tell you. She fell on her knees in terror—she clasped my dress, and asked me how I had found out. Then she recovered herself, tried to .eat her own words, and left me. Since then she has avoided me. It was the sight of me last night that made your wife turn faint. I repeat that she carries a secret. If that secret were known it might clear my son. I want to find it out. If you will help me and if we succeed, I'll give you a thousand pounds."

"'Taint to be done, ma'am," said Vincent. "Het is nervous, and a bit given to the hysterics, but she knows no more 'bout that murder than all the rest of the world knows; and what's more, I wouldn't take no money to probe at my wife's heart. Good-mornin', ma'am, I must be attending to my turnips."

Vincent vaulted the five-barred gate as he spoke, and walked across the field.

Mrs. Everett watched him until he was out of sight. Then she turned slowly, and went back to the Court. She entered the grounds a little before the breakfast hour. Ann, now Mrs. Henessey, was out in the avenue gathering daffodils, which grew in clumps all along a great border. She raised her head when she saw Mrs. Everett approaching.

"You out?" she cried. "I thought I was the only early bird. Where have you been?"

"For a walk," replied the widow. "The morning is a lovely one, and I was not sleepy." She did not wait to say anything more to Ann, but went into the house.

The breakfast-room at the Court had French windows. The day was so balmy that, early as it was still in the year, these windows stood open. As Mrs. Everett stepped across the threshold, she was greeted by Margaret.

"How pale and tired you look!" said Mrs. Awdrey, in a compassionate voice.

Mrs. Everett glanced round her, she saw that there was no one else present.

"I am sick at heart, Margaret," she said, fixing her sad eyes on her friend's face.

Margaret went up to her, put her slender hand on her shoulder, and kissed her.

"Why won't you rest?" she said; "you never rest; even at night you scarcely sleep; you will kill yourself if you go on as you have been doing of late, and then——"

"Why do you stop, Margaret?" said Mrs. Everett.

"When he comes out you won't be there," said Margaret—tears brimming into her eyes. "I often see the meeting between you and him," she continued. "When he comes out; when it is all over; he won't be old, as men go, and he'll want you. Try and think of the very worst that can happen—his innocence never being proved; even at the worst he'll want you sorely when he is a free man again."

"He won't have me. I shall be dead long, long before then; but I must prove his innocence. I have an indescribable sensation that I am near the truth while I am here, and that is why I came. Margaret, my heart in on fire—the burning of that fire consumes me."

At this moment the Squire entered the room; he looked bright, fresh, alert, and young. He was now a man of extremely rapid movements; he came up to Mrs. Everett and shook hands with her.

"You have your bonnet on," he said.

"Yes, I have been out for a walk," she replied.

"And she has come in dead tired," said Margaret, glancing at her husband. "Please go to your room now, Mrs. Everett," she continued, "and take off your things. We are just going to breakfast, and I shall insist on your taking a good meal."

Mrs. Everett turned toward the door. When she had left the room Margaret approached her husband's side.

"I do believe she is right," she cried suddenly; "I believe her grief will kill her in the end."

"Whose grief, dearest?" asked Awdrey, in an
absent-minded manner.

"Whose grief, Robert? Don't you know? Mrs.
Everett's grief. Can't you see for yourself how
she frets, how she wastes away? Have you no
eyes for her? In your own marvellous resurrection
ought you, ought either of us, to forget one who
suffers so sorely?"

"I never forget," said Awdrey. He spoke
abruptly; he had turned his back on his wife; a
picture which was hanging slightly awry needed
straightening; he went up to it. Ann came in at
the open window.

"What possesses all you women to be out at
cockcrow in this fashion?" said her brother, sub-
mitting to her embrace rather than returning it.

Ann laughed gleefully.

"It's close on nine o'clock," she replied; "here
are some daffodils for you, Margaret"—she laid a
great bunch by Mrs. Awdrey's plate. "You have
quite forgotten your country manners, Robert; in
the old days breakfast was long over at nine
o'clock."

"Well, let us come to table now," said the Squire.

The rest of the party trooped in by degrees.
Mrs. Everett was the last to appear. Awdrey
pulled out a chair near himself; she dropped into
it. He began to attend to her wants; then entered
into conversation with her. He talked well, like
the man of keen intelligence and education he really
was. As he spoke the widow kept watching him

with her bright, restless eyes. He never avoided her glance. His own eyes, steady and calm in their expression, met hers constantly. Toward the end of breakfast the two pairs of eyes seemed to challenge each other. Mrs. Everett's grew fuller than ever of puzzled inquiry; Awdrey's of a queer defiance. In the end she looked away with a sigh. He was stronger than she was; her spirit recognized this fact; it also began to be dimly aware of the truth that he was her enemy.

The Squire rose suddenly from his seat and addressed his wife.

"I've just seen Griffiths pass the window," he said. "I'm going out now; don't expect me to lunch."

CHAPTER XX

ABOUT an hour after her husband had left her, Hetty Vincent awoke. She rubbed her eyes, sat up in bed, and after a moment's reflection began to dress. She was downstairs, bustling about as usual, just as the eight-day clock struck seven. Hetty attended to the household work itself, but there was a maid to help her with the dairy, to milk the cows, and undertake the heavy part of the work. The girl's name was Susan. Hetty and she went into the dairy as usual now and began to perform their morning duties.

There were several cows kept on the farm, and the Vincents largely lived on the dairy produce. Their milk and butter and cream were famous in the district. The great pails of foaming milk were now being brought in by Susan and the man Dan, and the different pans quickly filled.

The morning's milk being set, Hetty began to skim the pans which were ready from the previous night. As she did so she put the cream at once into the churn, and Susan prepared to make the butter.

"Hold a bit, ma'am," she said suddenly, "we never scalded out this churn properly, and the last butter had a queer taste, don't you remember?"

"Of course I do," said Hetty, "how provoking; all that cream is wasted then."

"I don't think so," answered Susan. "If we pour it out at once it won't get the taste. Please hold that basin for me, ma'am, and I'll empty the cream that is in the churn straight into it."

Hetty did so.

Susan set the churn down again on the floor.

"If you'll give me that stuff in the bottle, ma'am," she said, "which you keep in the cupboard, I'll mix some of it with boiling water and wash out the churn, and it'll be as sweet as a nut immediately."

"The water is already boiling in the copper," said Hetty.

The girl went off to fill a large jug with some, and Hetty unlocked the cupboard from which she had taken the bottle of laudanum the night before. The chemical preparation required for sweetening the churn should have stood close to the laudanum bottle. It was not there, and Susan, who was anxious to begin her work, fetched a stepladder and mounting it began to search through the contents of the cupboard.

"I can't find the bottle," she cried, "but lor! ma'am, what is this black stuff? It looks sum'mat like treacle."

"No, it is not; let it alone," said Hetty in alarm.

"I don't want to touch it, I'm sure," replied Susan. "It's got a good big 'poison' marked on it, and I'm awful frightened of that sort o' thing."

"It's toothache cure," said Hetty. "Ef you

swallowed a good lot of it it 'ud kill you, but it's a splendid thing to put on cotton-wool and stuff into your tooth if it aches badly. Just you step down from the ladder, and I'll have a look for the bottle we want, Susan."

The bottle was nowhere to be found in the cupboard but was presently discovered in another corner of the dairy; the morning's work then went on without a hitch.

At his accustomed hour Vincent came in to breakfast. He looked moody and depressed. As he ate he glanced many times at Hetty, but did not vouchsafe a single word to her.

She was in the mood to be agreeable to him and she put on her most fascinating airs for his benefit. Once as she passed his chair she laid her small hand with a caressing movement on his shoulder. The man longed indescribably to seize the little hand and press its owner to his hungry heart, but he restrained himself. Mrs. Everett's words were ringing in his ear: "Your wife holds a secret."

Hetty presently sat down opposite to him. The sunshine was now streaming full into the cheerful farm kitchen, and some of its rays fell across her face. What a lovely face it was; pale, it is true, and somewhat worn, but what pathetic eyes, so dark so velvety; what a dear rosebud mouth, what an arch and yet sad expression!

"She beats every other woman holler," muttered the man to himself. "It's my belief that ef it worn't for that secret she'd love me. Yes, it must be true, she holds a secret, and it's a-killing of her. She ain't what she wor when we married. I'll get that secret out o' her; but not for no thousand pounds, 'andy as it 'ud be."

"Hetty," he said suddenly.

"What in the world is the matter with you, George? You look so moody," said Hetty.

"Well, now, I may as well return the compliment," he replied, "so do you."

"Oh, I'm all right," she answered, with a pert toss of her head. "Maybe, George," she continued, "you're bilious; you ate summat that disagreed wi' you last night."

"Yes, I did," he replied fiercely. "I swallered a powerful lot o' jealousy, and it's bad food and hard to digest."

"Jealousy?" she answered, bridling, and her cheeks growing a deep rose. "Now what should make you jealous?"

"You make me jealous, my girl," he answered.

"I! what in the world did I do?"

"You talked to Squire—you wor mad to see 'im. Het, you've got a secret, and you may as well out wi' it."

The imminence of the danger made Hetty quite cool and almost brave. She uttered a light laugh, and bent forward to help herself to some more butter.

"You must be crazy to have thoughts o' that sort, George," she said. "Ain't I been your wife for five years, and isn't it likely that ef I had a secret you'd have discovered it, sharp feller as you are? No, I was pleased to see Squire. I was always fond o' 'im; and I ain't got no secret except the pain in my side."

She turned very pale as she uttered the last words and pressed her hand to the neighborhood of her heart.

Vincent was at once all tenderness and concern.

"I'm a brute to worry yer, my little gell," he said. "Secret or no secret, you're all I 'as got. It's jest this way, Het, ef you'd love me a bit, I wouldn't mind ef you had fifty secrets, but it's the feelin' that you don't love me, mad as I be about you, that drives me stark, staring wild at times."

"I'll try hard to love you ef you wish it, George," she said.

He left his seat and came toward her. The next moment he had folded her in his arms. She shivered under his embrace, but submitted.

"Now that's better," he said. "Tryin' means succeedin', 'cording to my way o' thinking of it. But you don't look a bit well, Het; you change color too often—red one minute, white the next— you mustn't do no sort o' work this morning. You jest put your feet up this minute on the settle and I'll fetch that novel you're so took up with. You like readin', don't yer, lass?"

"At times I do," said Hetty, "but I ain't in the mood to read to-day, and there's a heap to be done."

"You're not to do it; Susan will manage."

"George, she can't; she's got the dairy."

"Dan shall manage the dairy. He's worth two Susans, and Susan can attend to the housework. Now you lie still where I've put you and read your novel. I'll be in to dinner at twelve o'clock, as usual, and ef you don't look more spry by then I'll go and fetch Dr. Martin, that I will."

"I wouldn't see him for the world," said Hetty in alarm. "Well, I'll stay quiet ef you wish me to."

The rest of the morning passed quickly. Until her husband was quite out of sight Hetty remained on the settle in the cosy kitchen; then she went up to her room, and taking a hat out of the cupboard began to pull it about and to re-arrange the trimming. She put it on once or twice to see if it became her. It was a pretty hat, made of white straw with a broad low brim. It was trimmed simply with a broad band of colored ribbon. On Hetty's charming head it had a rustic effect, and suited her particular form of beauty.

"It don't matter what I wear," she murmured to herself. "'Taint looks I'm a-thinking of now, but I may as well look my best when I go to him. Once he thought me pretty. That awful evening down by the brook when I gathered the forget-me-nots—I saw his thought in his eyes then—he thought well of me then. Maybe he will again this evening. Anyhow I'll wear the hat."

At dinner time Hetty once more resumed the rôle of an invalid, and Vincent was charmed to find her reclining on the settle and pretending to read the yellow-backed novel.

"Here's a brace of young pigeons," he said; "I shot 'em an hour ago. You shall have 'em cooked up tasty for supper. You want fattening and coaxing a bit. Ah, dinner ready; just what I like, corned beef and cabbage. I am hungry and no mistake."

Susan had now left the house to return to her ordinary duties, and the husband and wife were alone. Hetty declared herself much better; in fact, quite well. She drew her chair close to Vincent, and talked to him while he ate.

"Now I call this real cosy," he said. "Ef you try a bit harder you'll soon do the real thing, Het; you'll love me for myself."

"Seems like it," answered Hetty. "George, you don't mind my going down to see aunt this afternoon, do you?"

She brought out her words coolly, but Vincent's suspicions were instantly aroused.

"Turn round and look at me," he said.

She did so bravely.

"You don't go outside the farm to-day, and that's flat," he said. "We won't argufy on that point any more; you stop at 'ome to-day. Ef you're a good girl and try to please me I'll harness the horse to the gig this evening, and take yer for a bit of a drive."

"I'd like that," answered Hetty submissively. She bent down as she spoke to pick up a piece of bread. She knew perfectly well that Vincent would not allow her to keep her appointment with the

Squire. But that appointment must be kept; if in no other way, by guile.

Hetty thought and thought. She was too excited to do little more than pick her food, and Vincent showered attentions and affectionate words upon her. At last he rose from his seat.

"Well, I've 'ad a hearty meal," he cried. "I'll be in again about four o'clock; you might have a cup o' tea ready for me."

"No, I won't," said Hetty; "tea is bad for you; you're up so early, and you're dead for sleep, and it's sleep you ought to have. You come home about four, and I'll give you a glass o' stout."

"Stout?" said the farmer—he was particularly partial to that beverage—"I didn't know there was any stout in the house," he continued.

"Yes," she replied, laughing gayly, "the little cask which we didn't open at Christmas; it's in the pantry, and you shall have a foaming glass when you come in at four; go off now, George, and I'll have it ready for you."

"All right," he said; "why, you're turning into a model wife; quite anxious about me—at least, it seems like it. Well, I'll turn up for my stout, more particular ef you'll give me a kiss along wi' it."

He went away, and Hetty watched him as he crossed the farmyard; her cheeks were flushed, and her heart beat high. She had made up her mind. She would drug the stout.

Vincent was neither a lazy nor a sleepy man; he

worked hard from early morning until late at night, indulging in no excesses of any kind, and preferring tea as a rule to any other beverage; but stout, good stout, such as Hetty had in the little cask, was his one weakness; he did like a big draught of that.

"He shall have a sleep," said Hetty to herself. "It'll do him a power of good. The first time I swallered a few drops of aunt's toothache cure I slept for eight hours without moving. Lor! how bad I felt afore I went off, and how nice and soothed when I awoke. Seemed as if I couldn't be cross for ever so long. George shall sleep while I'm away. I'll put some of the nice black stuff in his stout—the stuff that gives dreams—he'll have a long rest, and I can go and return and he'll never know nothing about it."

She made all her preparations with promptitude and cunning. First, she opened the cask, and threw away the first glass she drew from it. She then tasted the beverage, which turned out, as she expected it would, to be of excellent quality. Hetty saw in imagination her husband draining off one or two glasses. Presently she heard his step in the passage, and ran quickly to the pantry where the stout was kept, concealing the little bottle of laudanum in her pocket. She poured what she thought a small but safe dose into the jug, and then filled it up with stout. Her face was flushed, and her eyes very bright, when she appeared in the kitchen with the jug and glass on a tray. Vincent was hot and dead tired.

"Here you are, little woman," he cried. "Why, if you ain't a sort o' ministering angel, I don't know who is. Well, I'm quite ready for that ere drink o' your'n."

Hetty filled his glass to the brim. It frothed slightly, and looked, as Vincent expressed it, prime. He raised it to his lips, drained it to the dregs, and returned it to her. She filled it again.

"Come, come," he said, smiling, and half-winking at her, and then casting a longing glance at the stout, "ain't two glasses o'er much."

"Not a bit of it," she answered. "You're to go to sleep, you know."

"Well, p'raps I can spare an hour, and I am a bit drowsy."

"You're to lie right down on the settle, and go off to sleep. I'll wake you when it is time."

He drank off another glass.

"You won't run away to that aunt o' your'n while I'm drowsing?" he said.

"No," she replied. "I would not do a shabby sort of trick like that."

He took her hand in his, and a moment later had closed his eyes. Once or twice he opened them to gaze fondly at her, but presently the great, roughly hewn face settled down into repose. Hetty bent over him, laid her cheek against his, and felt his forehead. He never stirred. She then listened to his breathing, which was perfectly quiet and light.

"He's gone off like a baby. That's wonderful stuff in aunt's bottle," muttered Hetty. Finally, she threw a shawl of her own over him, drew down the blind of the nearest window, and went on tiptoe out of the kitchen.

"He'll sleep for hours. I did," she said to herself.

She put the little bottle back into its place in the dairy and moved softly about the house. She was to meet the Squire at six. It was now five o'clock. It would take her the best part of an hour to walk to the Court. She went up to her room, put on her hat, and as she was leaving the house, once again entered the kitchen. Vincent's face was pale now —he was in a dead slumber. She heard his breathing, a little quick and stertorous, but he was always a heavy breather, and she thought nothing about it. She left the house smiling to herself at the clever trick she had played on her husband. She was going to meet the Squire now. Her heart beat with rapture.

CHAPTER XXI.

AWDREY's cure was complete; he had passed right through the doom of his house, and got out on the other side. He was the first man of his race who had ever done that; the others had forgotten as he forgot, and had pined, and dwindled, and slipped and slipped lower and lower down in the scale of life until at last they had dropped over the brink into the Unknown beyond. Awdrey's downward career had been stopped just in time. His recovery had been quite as marvellous as his complaint. When he saw his own face reflected in the pond on Salisbury Plain the cloud had risen from his brain and he remembered what he had done. In that instant his mental sky grew clear and light. He himself had murdered Horace Frere; he had not done it intentionally, but he had done it; another man was suffering in his stead; he himself was the murderer. He knew this absolutely, completely, clearly, but at first he felt no mental pain of any sort. A natural instinct made him desirous to keep his knowledge to himself, but his conscience sat light within him, and did not speak at all. He was now anxious to conceal his emotions from the doctor; his mind had completely recovered its balance, and he found

this possible. Rumsey was as fully astonished at
the cure as he had been at the disease; he accompanied Awdrey back to London next day, and told
Margaret what a marvellous thing had occurred.
Awdrey remembered all about his son; he was full
of grief for his loss; he was kind and loving to his
wife; he was no longer morose; no longer sullen
and apathetic; in short, his mental and physical
parts were once again wide awake; but the strange
and almost inexplicable thing in his cure was that
his moral part still completely slumbered. This
fact undoubtedly did much to establish his mental
and physical health, giving him time to recover his
lost ground.

Rumsey did not profess to understand the case,
but now that Awdrey had quite come back from the
borderland of insanity, he advised that ordinary
remedies should immediately be resorted to; he told
Margaret that in a few months her husband would
be as fully and completely able to attend to the duties of life as any other man of his day and station.
He did not believe, he said, that the strange attack
through which Awdrey had passed was ever likely
to return to him! Margaret and her husband shut
up their house in town, and went abroad; they
spent the winter on the continent, and day by day
Awdrey's condition, both physical and mental,
became more satisfactory. He slept well, he ate
well; soon he began to devour books and news-
papers; to absorb himself in the events of the day;
to take a keen interest in politics; the member for

Grandcourt died, and Awdrey put up for the constituency. He was obliged to return suddenly to England on this account, and to Margaret's delight elected to come back at once to live at the Court. The whole thing was arranged quickly. Awdrey was to be nominated as the new candidate for Grandcourt; he was to have, too, his rightful position as the Squire on his own property. Friends from all round the country rejoiced in his recovery, as they had sincerely mourned over his strange and inexplicable illness. He was welcomed with rejoicing, and came back something as a king would to take possession of his kingdom.

On the night therefore, that he returned to the Court, the higher part of his being began to stir uneasily within him. He had quite agreed to Margaret's desire to invite Mrs. Everett to meet them on their return, but he read a certain expression in the widow's sad eyes, and a certain look on Hetty's face, which stirred into active remorse the conscience which had suffered more severely than anything else in the ordeal through which he had lived. It was now awake within him, and its voice was very poignant and keen; its notes were clear, sharp, and unremitting.

In his excellent physical and mental health his first impulse was to defy the voice of conscience, and to live down the deed he had committed. His first wish was to hide its knowledge from all the world, and to go down to his own grave in the course of time with his secret unconfessed. He did

not believe it possible, at least at first, that the
moral voice within could not be easily silenced;
but even on the first night of his awakening he was
conscious of a change in himself. The sense of
satisfaction, of complete enjoyment in life and all
its surroundings which had hitherto done so much
for his recovery, was now absent; he was conscious,
intensely conscious, of his own hypocrisy, and he
began vehemently to hate and detest himself. All
the same, his wish was to hide the thing, to allow
Mrs. Everett to go down to the grave with a broken
heart—to allow Everett to drink the cup of suffering
and dishonor to the dregs.

Awdrey slept little during the first night of his
return home. In the morning he arose to the full
fact that he must either carry a terrible secret to
his grave, or must confess all and bear the punishment which was now awarded to another. His
strong determination on that first morning was to
keep his secret. He went downstairs, putting a
full guard upon himself. Margaret saw nothing
amiss with him—his face was full of alertness, keenness, interest in life, interest in his fellow-creatures.
Only Mrs. Everett, at breakfast that morning, without understanding it, read the defiance, the veiled
meaning in his eyes. He went away presently,
and spent the day in going about his property, seeing his constituents, and arranging the different
steps he must take to insure his return at the head
of the poll. As he went from house to house, however, the new knowledge which he now possessed

of himself kept following him. On all hands he was being welcomed and rejoiced over, but he knew in his heart of hearts he was a hypocrite of the basest and lowest type. He was allowing another man to suffer in his stead. That was the cruellest stab of all; it was that which harassed him, for it was contrary to all the traditions of his house and name. His mental health was now so perfect that he was able to see with a wonderfully clear perception what would happen to himself if he refused to listen to the voice of conscience. In the past, while the cloud was over his brain, he had undergone terrible mental and physical deterioration; he would now undergo moral deterioration. The time might come when conscience would cease to trouble him, but then, as far as his soul was concerned, he would be lost. He knew all this, and hated himself profoundly, nevertheless his determination grew stronger and stronger to guard his secret at all hazards. The possibility that the truth might out, notwithstanding all his efforts to conceal it, had not occurred to him, to add to his anxieties.

The day, a lovely one in late spring, had been one long triumph. Awdrey was assured that his election was a foregone conclusion. He tried to think of himself in the House; he was aware of the keenness and freshness of his own intellect; he thought it quite possible that his name might be a power in the future government of England. He fully intended to take his rightful position. For

generations men of his name and family had sat in
the House and done good work there—men of his
name and family had also fought for their country
both on land and sea. Yes, it was his bounden
duty now to live for the honor of the old name;
to throw up the sponge now, to admit all now
would be madness—the worst folly of which a man
could be capable. It was his duty to think of Margaret, to think of his property, his tenants, all that
was involved in his own life.

Everett and Mrs. Everett would assuredly suffer;
but what of that if many others were saved from
suffering? Yes, it was his bounden duty to live
now for the honor of the old name; he had also
his descendants to think of. True his child was
gone, but other children would in all probability
yet be his—he must think of them. Yes, the
future lay before him; he must carry the burden
of that awful secret, and he would carry it so close-
ly pressed to his innermost heart that no one should
guess by look, word, manner, by a gloomy eye, by
an unsmiling lip, that its weight was on him. He
would be gay, he would be brave, he would banish
grief, he would try to banish remorse, he would
live his life as best he could.

"I must pay the cost some day," he muttered to
himself. "I put off the payment, and that is best.
There is a tribunal, at the bar of which I shall
doubtless receive full sentence; but that is all in
the future; I accept the penalty; I will reap the
wages by and by. Yes, I'll keep my secret to the

death. The girl, Hetty, knows about it, but she must be silenced."

Awdrey rode quickly home in the sweet freshness of the lovely spring evening. He remembered that he was to meet Hetty; the meeting would be difficult and also of some importance, but he would be guarded, he would manage to silence her, to quiet her evident fears. Hetty was a guileless, affectionate, and pretty girl; she had been wonderfully true to him; he must be good to her, for she had suffered for his sake. It would be best to make an excuse to send Hetty and her husband to Canada; Vincent, who was a poor man, would doubtless be glad to emigrate with good prospects. Yes, they must go; it would be unpleasant meeting Hetty, knowing what she knew. Mrs. Everett must also not again be his guest; her presence irritated him, he disliked meeting her eyes; and yet he knew that while she was in the house he dared not shirk their glance; her presence and the knowledge that her pain was killing her made the sharp voice within him speak more loudly than he could quite bear. Yes, Mrs. Everett must go, and Hetty must go, and—what was this memory which made him draw up his horse abruptly?—his lost walking-stick. Ridiculous that such a trifle should worry a man all through his life; how it had haunted him all during the six years when the cloud was over his brain. Even now the memory of it came up again to torment him. He had murdered his man with that stick; the whole thing was the purest accident, but that did not greatly matter, for the man had died; the ferrule of Awdrey's stick had entered his brain, causing instant death.

"Afterward I hid it away in the underwood," thought Awdrey. "I wonder where it is now— doubtless still there—but some day that part of the underwood may be cut down and the stick may be found. It might tell tales, I must find it."

He jogged his horse, and rode slowly home under the arching trees of the long avenue. He had a good view of the long, low, rambling house there—how sweet it looked, how homelike! But for this secret what a happy man he would be to-night. Ah, who was that standing at his office door? He started and hastened his horse's steps. Hetty Vincent was already there waiting for him.

"I must speak to her at once," he said to himself. "I hope no one will see her; it would never do for the people to think she was coming after me. This will be a disagreeable interview and must be got over quickly."

The Squire rode round the part of the avenue which led directly past the front of the long house. His wife, sisters, and Mrs. Everett were all seated near the large window. They were drinking tea and talking. Margaret's elbow rested upon the window-ledge. She wore a silk dress of the softest gray. Her lovely face showed in full profile. Suddenly she heard the sound of his horse's steps and turned round to greet him.

"There you are; we are waiting for you," she called out.

"Come in, Robert, and have a cup," called out Dorothy, putting her head out of the window.

Dorothy was his favorite sister. Under other circumstances he would have sprung from his horse, given it to the charge of a groom who stood near, and joined his wife and friends. Now he called back in a clear, incisive voice:

"I have to attend to some business at my office, and will be in presently. Here, Davies, take my horse."

The man hurried forward and Awdrey strode round to the side entrance where his office was.

Hetty, looking flushed and pretty in her rustic hat with a bunch of cowslips pinned into the front of her jacket, stood waiting for him.

Awdrey took a key out of his pocket. The office had no direct communication with the house, but was always entered from outside. He unlocked the door and motioned Hetty to precede him into the room. She did so, he entered after her, locked the door, and put the key into his pocket. The next thing he did was to look at the windows. There were three large windows to the office, and they all faced on to a grass lawn outside. Any one passing by could have distinctly seen the occupants of the room.

Awdrey went and deliberately pulled down one of the blinds.

"Come over here," he said to Hetty. "Take

this chair." He took another himself at a little
distance from her. So seated his face was in
shadow, but the full light of the westering sun fell
across hers. It lit up her bright eyes until they
shone like jewels, and gave a bronze hue to her
dark hair. The flush on her cheeks was of the
damask of the rose; her brow and the rest of her
face was milky white.

Long ago, as a young man, Awdrey had ad-
mired Hetty's real beauty, but no thought other
than that of simple admiration had entered his
brain. His was not the nature to be really attracted by a woman below himself in station.
Now, however, his pulse beat a little faster than
its wont as he glanced at her. He remembered with
a swift, poignant sense of regret all that she had
done for him and suffered for him. He could see
traces of the trouble through which she had lived
in her face; that trouble and her present anxiety
gave a piquancy to her beauty which differentiated
it widely from the ordinary beauty of the rustic
village girl. As he watched her he forgot for a
moment what she had come to speak to him about.
Then he remembered it, and he drew himself
together, but a pang shot through his heart. He
thought of the small deceit which he was guilty of
in drawing down the blind and placing himself and
his auditor where no one from the outside could
observe them.

"You want to speak to me," he said abruptly.
"What about?"

"You must know, Mr. Robert," began Hetty. Her coral lips trembled, she looked like some one who would break down into hysterical weeping at any moment.

"This must be put a stop to," Awdrey bestowed another swift glance upon her, and took her measure. "I cannot pretend ignorance," he said, "but please try not to lose your self-control."

Hetty gulped down a great sob; the tears in her eyes were not allowed to fall.

"Then you remember?" she said.

Awdrey nodded.

"You remember everything, Mr. Robert?"

Awdrey nodded again.

"But you forgot at the time, sir."

Awdrey stood up; he put his hands behind him.

"I forgot absolutely," he said. "I suffered from the doom of my house. A cloud fell on me, and I knew no more than a babe unborn."

"I guessed that, sir; I was certain of it. That was why I took your part."

Awdrey waited until she was silent. Then he continued in a monotonous, strained tone.

"I have found my memory again. Four or five months ago at the beginning of this winter I came here. I visited the spot where the murder was committed, and owing to a chain of remarkable circumstances, which I need not repeat to you, the memory of my deed came back to me."

"You killed him, sir, because he provoked you," said Hetty.

"You were present and you saw everything?"

"I was, sir, I saw everything. You killed him because he provoked you."

"I killed him through an accident. I did so in self-defence."

"Yes, sir."

Hetty also stood up. She sighed deeply.

"The knowledge of it has nearly killed me," she said at last, sinking back again into her seat.

"I am not surprised at that," said the Squire. "You did what you did out of consideration for me, and I suppose I ought to be deeply indebted to you"—he paused and looked fixedly at her—"all the same," he continued, "I fully believe it would have been much better had you not sworn falsely in court—had you not given wrong evidence."

"Did you think I'd let you swing for it?" said the girl with flashing eyes.

"I should probably not have swung for it, as you express it. You could have proved that the assault was unprovoked, and that I did what I did in self-defence. I wish you had not concealed the truth at the time."

"Sir, is that all the thanks you give me? You do not know what this has been to me. Aunt Fanny and I——"

"Does your aunt, Mrs. Armitage, know the truth?"

"I had to tell Aunt Fanny or I'd have gone mad, sir. She and me, we swore on the Bible that we

would never tell mortal man or woman what I
saw done. You're as safe with Aunt Fanny and
me, Mr. Robert, as if no one in all the world knew.
You were one of the Family—that was enough for
aunt—and you was to me——" she paused, colored,
and looked down. Then she continued abruptly,
"Mr. Everett was nothing, nothing to me, nothing
to aunt. He was a stranger, not one of our own
people. Aunt Fanny kept me up to it, and I didn't
make one single mistake in court, and not a soul in
all the world guesses."

"One person suspects," said Awdrey.

"You mean Mrs. Everett, sir. Yes, Mrs. Everett
is a dreadful woman. She frightens me. She
seems to read right through my heart."

The Squire did not reply. He began to pace up
and down in the part of the room which was lying
in shadow. Hetty watched him with eyes which
seemed to devour him—his upright figure was
slightly bent, his bowed head had lost its look of
youth and alertness. He found that conscience
could be troublesome to the point of agony. If it
spoke like this often and for long could he endure
the frightful strain? There was a way in which
he could silence it. There was a path of thorns
which his feet might tread. Could they take it?
That path would lead to the complete martyrdom,
the absolute ruin of his own life. But life, after
all, was short, and there was a beyond. Margaret
—what would Margaret feel? How would she bear
the awful shock. He knew then, a flash of thought

convinced him, that he must never tell Margaret the truth if he wished to keep this ghastly thing to himself, for Margaret would rather go through the martyrdom which it all meant, and set his conscience and her own free.

Awdrey looked again at Hetty. She was ghastly pale, her eyes were almost wild with fear—she seemed to be reading some of his thoughts. All of a sudden her outward calm gave way, she left her seat and fell on her knees—her voice rose in sobs.

"I know what you're thinking of," she cried. "You think you'll tell—you think you'll save him and save her, but for God's sake——"

"Do not say that," interrupted Awdrey.

"Then for the devil's sake—for any sake, for my sake, for your own, for Mrs. Awdrey's, don't do it, Squire, don't do it."

"Don't do——" began Awdrey. "What did you think I was going to do?"

"Oh, you frightened me so awfully when you looked like that—I thought you were making up your mind. Squire, don't tell what you know—don't tell what I've done. I'll be locked up and you'll be locked up, and Mrs. Awdrey's heart will be broke, and we'll all be disgraced forever, and, Squire, maybe they'll hang you. Think of one of the family coming to that. Oh, sir, you've no right to tell now. You'll have to think of me now, if you'll think of nothing else. I've kept your secret for close on six years, and if they knew what

I had done they would lock me up, and I couldn't
stand it. You daren't confess now—for my sake,
sir."

"Get up, Mrs. Vincent," said Awdrey. "I can't
talk over matters with you while you kneel to me.
You've done a good deal for me, and I'm bound to
consider your position. Now, I'm going to tell
you something which perhaps you will scarcely
understand. I remembered the act of which I was
guilty several months ago, but until last night my
conscience did not trouble me about it. It is now
speaking to me, and speaking loudly. It is impossible for me to tell you at present whether I
shall have strength of mind to follow it and do the
right—yes, the right, the only right thing to do,
or to reject its counsels and lead a life of deceit
and hypocrisy. Both paths will be difficult to
follow, but one leads to life, the highest life, and
the other to death, the lowest death. It is quite
possible that I may choose the lowest course. If
I do, you, Hetty Vincent, will know the truth
about me. To the outside world I shall appear to
be a good man, for whatever my sufferings, I shall
endeavor to help my people, and to set them an
outward example of morality. I shall apparently
live for them, and will think no trouble too great
to promote their best interests. Only you, Hetty,
will know me for what I am—a liar—a man who
has committed murder, and then concealed his
crime—a hypocrite. You will know that much as
I am thought of in the county here among my

own people, I am allowing an innocent man to wear out his life in penal servitude because I have not the courage to confess my deed. You will also know that I am breaking the heart of this man's mother."

"The knowledge won't matter to me, Squire. I'd rather you were happy and all the rest of the world miserable. I'd far, far rather."

"Do you think that I shall be happy?"

"I don't know," cried Hetty. "Perhaps you'll forget after a bit, and that voice inside you won't speak so loud. It used to trouble me once, but now—now it has grown dull."

"It will never cease to speak. I know myself too well to have any doubt on that point, but all the same I may take the downward course. I can't say. Conscience has only just begun to trouble me. I may obey its dictates, or I may deliberately lead the life of a hypocrite. If I choose the latter, can you stand the test?"

"I have stood it for five years."

"But I have not been at home—the Court has been shut up—an absentee landlord is not always to the front in his people's thoughts. In the future, things will be different. Look at me for a moment, Hetty Vincent. You are not well—your cheeks are hollow and your eyes are too bright. Mrs. Everett is persuaded that you carry a secret. If she thinks so, others may think the same. Your aunt also knows."

"Aunt is different from me," said Hetty. "She

didn't see it done. It don't wear her like it wears me. But I think, sir, now that you have come back, and I am quite certain that I know your true mind, and when I know, too, that you are carrying the burden as well as me, and that we two,"—she paused, her voice broke—"I think, sir," she added, "that it won't wear me so much in the future."

"You must on no account be tried. If I resolve to keep the secret of my guilt from all the rest of the world, you must leave the country."

"Me leave the country!" cried Hetty—her face became ghastly pale, her eyes brimmed again with tears. "Then you would indeed kill me," she said, with a moan—"to leave you—Mr. Robert, you must guess why I have done all this."

"Hush," he said in a harsh tone. He approached the window, where the blind was drawn up. He saw, or fancied he saw—Mrs. Everett's dark figure passing by in the distance. He retreated quickly into the shaded part of the room.

"I cannot afford to misunderstand your words," he said, after a pause, " but listen to me, Hetty, you must never allude to that subject again. If I keep this thing to myself I can only do it on condition that you and your husband leave the country. I have not fully made up my mind yet. Nothing can be settled to-night. You had better not stay any longer."

Hetty rose totteringly and approached the door. Awdrey took the key from his pocket, and unlocked it for her. As he did so he asked her a question.

"You saw everything? You saw the deed done?"

"Yes, sir, I saw the stick in your hand, and——"

"That is the point I am coming to," said the Squire. "What did I do with the stick?"

"You pushed it into the midst of some underwood, sir, about twenty feet from the spot where——" She could not finish her sentence.

"Yes," said Awdrey slowly. "I remember that. Has the stick ever been found?"

"No, Mr. Robert, that couldn't be."

"Why do you say that? The underwood may be cut down at any moment. The stick has my name on it. It may come to light."

"It can't, sir—'tain't there. Aunt Fanny and me, we thought o' that, and we went the night after the murder, and took the stick out from where you had put it, and weighted it with stones, and threw it into the deep pond close by. You need not fear that, Mr. Robert."

Awdrey did not answer. His eyes narrowed to a line of satisfaction, and a cunning expression came into them, altogether foreign to his face.

He softly opened the door, and Hetty passed out, then he locked it again.

He was alone with his conscience. He fell on his knees and covered his face.

"God, Thy judgments are terrible," he groaned.

CHAPTER XXII.

There was a short cut at the back of the office which would take Hetty on to the high road without passing round by the front of the house. It so happened that no one saw her when she arrived, and no one also saw her go. When she reached the road she stopped still to give vent to a deep sigh of satisfaction. Things were not right, but they were better than she had dared hope. Of course the Squire remembered—he could not have looked at her as he had done the night before, if memory had not fully come back to him. He remembered —he told her so, but she was also nearly certain that he would not confess to the world at large the crime of which he was guilty.

"I'll keep him to that," thought Hetty. "He may think nought o' himself—it's in his race not to think o' theirselves—but he'd think o' his wife and p'raps he'd think a bit o' me. There's Mrs. Everett and there's her son, and they both suffer and suffer bad, but then agen there's Mrs. Awdrey and there's me—there's two on us agen two," continued Hetty, rapidly thinking out the case, and ranging the pros and cons in due order in her mind, "yes, there's two agen two," she repeated,

"Mrs. Everett and her son are suffering now—then it 'ud be Mrs. Awdrey and me—and surely Mrs. Awdrey is nearer to Squire, and maybe I'm a bit nearer to Squire than the other two. Yes, it is but fair that he should keep the secret to himself."

The sun had long set and twilight had fallen over the land. Hetty had to walk uphill to reach the Gables, the name of her husband's farm. It would therefore take her longer to return home than it did to come to the Court. She was anxious to get back as quickly as possible. It would never do for Vincent to find out that she had deceived him. If he slept soundly, as she fully expected he would, there was not the least fear of her secret being discovered. Susan never entered the house after four in the afternoon. The men who worked in the fields would return to the yard to put away their tools, but they would have nothing to do in connection with the house itself—thus Vincent would be left undisturbed during the hours of refreshment and restoration which Hetty hoped he was enjoying.

"Yes, I did well," she murmured to herself, quickening her steps as the thought came to her. "I've seen Squire and there's nought to be dreaded for a bit, anyway. The more he thinks o' it the less he'll like to see himself in the prisoner's dock and me and Mrs. Awdrey and aunt as witnesses agen 'im—and knowing, too, that me, and, perhaps, aunt, too, will be put in the dock in our turn. He's bound to think o' us, for we thought o' him —he won't like to get us into a hole, and he's safe

not to do it. Yes, things look straight enough for
a bit, anyway. I'm glad I saw Squire—he looked
splendid, too, stronger than I ever see 'im. He
don't care one bit for me, and I—his eyes flashed
so angry when I nearly let out—yes, I quite let out.
He said, 'I can't affect to misunderstand you.'
Ah, he knows at last, he knows the truth. I'm
glad he knows the truth. There's a fire inside o'
me, and it burns and burns—it's love for him—all
my life it has consumed within me. There's
nought I wouldn't do for 'im. Shame, I'd take it
light for his sake—it rested me fine to see 'im, and
to take a real good look at 'im. Queer, ain't it,
that I should care so much for a man what never
give me a thought, but what is, is, and can't be
helped. Poor Vincent, he worships the ground I
walk on, and yet he's nought to me; he never can
be anything while Squire lives. I wonder if Squire
thought me pretty to-night. I wonder if he noticed
the wild flowers in the bosom of my jacket—I
wonder. I'm glad I've a secret with 'im; he must
see me sometimes, and he must talk on it; and
then he'll notice that I'm pretty—prettier than
most girls. Oh, my heart, how it beats!"

Hetty was struggling up the hill, panting as she
went. The pain in her side got worse, owing to
the exercise. She had presently to stop to take
breath.

"He said sum'mat 'bout going away," she murmured to herself; "he wants me and Vincent to
leave the country, but we won't go. No, I draw

the line there. He thinks I'll split on 'im. I!
Little he knows me. I must manage to show him
that I can hold my secret, so as no one in all the
world suspects. Oh, good God, I wish the pain in
my side did not keep on so constant. I'll take
some of the black stuff when I get in; it always
soothes me; the pain will go soon after I take it,
and I'll sleep like a top to-night. Poor George,
what a sleep he's havin'; he'll be lively, and in the
best o' humors when he wakes; you always are
when you've taken that black stuff. Now, I must
hurry on, it's getting late."

She made another effort, and reached the summit
of the hill.

From there the ground sloped away until it
reached the Gables Farm. Hetty now put wing to
her feet and began to run, but the pain in her side
stopped her again, and she was obliged to proceed
more slowly. She reached home just when it was
dark; the place was absolutely silent. Susan, who
did not sleep in the house, had gone away; the men
had evidently come into the yard, put their tools
by, and gone off to their respective homes.

"That's good," thought Hetty. "Vincent's still
asleep—I'm safe. Now, if I hurry up he'll find
the place lighted and cheerful, and everything nice,
and his supper laid out for him, and he'll never
guess, never, never."

She unlatched the gate which led into the great
yard; the fowls began to rustle on their perches,
and the house dog, Rover, came softly up to her,

and rubbed his head against her knee; she patted him abstractedly and hurried on to the house.

She had a latchkey with which she opened the side door; she let herself in, and shut it behind her. The place was still and dark.

Hetty knew her way well; she stole softly along the dark passage, and opened the kitchen door. The fire smouldered low in the range, and in the surrounding darkness seemed to greet her, something like an angry eye. When she entered the room, she did not know why she shivered.

"He's sound asleep," she murmured to herself; "that lovely black stuff ha' done 'im a power o' good. I'll have a dose soon myself, for my heart beats so 'ard, and the pain in my side is that bad."

She approached the fireplace, opened the door of the range, and stirred the smouldering coals into the semblance of a blaze. By this light, which was very fitful and quickly expired, she directed her steps to a shelf, where a candlestick and candle and matches were placed. She struck a match, and lit the candle. With the candle in her hand she then, softly and on tiptoe, approached the settle where her husband lay. She did not want to wake him yet, and held the candle in such a way that the light should not fall on his face. As far as she could tell he had not stirred since she left him, two or three hours ago; he was lying on his back, his arms were stretched out at full length at each side, his lips were slightly open—as well as she could

see, his face was pale, though he was as a rule a
florid man.

"He's sleepin' beautiful," thought Hetty,
"everything has been splendid. I'll run upstairs
now and take off my hat and jacket and make myself look as trim as I can, for he do like, poor
George do, to see me look pretty. Then I'll come
down and lay the supper on the table, and then
when everything is ready I think I'll wake him.
He fell asleep soon after four, and it's a good bit
after eight now. I slept much longer than four
hours after my first dose of the nice black stuff,
but I think I'll wake 'im when supper is ready.
It'll be real fun when he sees the hour and knows
how long he 'as slept."

Holding her candle in her hand Hetty left the
kitchen and proceeded to light the different lamps
which stood about in the passages. She then went
to her own nice bedroom and lit a pair of candles
which were placed on each side of her dressing
glass. Having done this, she drew down the blinds
and shut the windows. She then carefully removed
her hat, took the cowslips out of the bosom of her
dress, kissed them, and put them in water.

"Squire looked at 'em," she said to herself.
"He didn't touch 'em, no, but he looked at 'em,
and then he looked at me and I saw in his eyes
that he knew I were pretty. I was glad then.
Seemed as if it were worth living just for Squire to
know that I were really pretty."

She placed the flowers in a jug of water, folded

up her jacket and gloves, and put them away with her hat in the cupboard in the wall. She then, with the candle still in her hand, went downstairs.

The kitchen felt chilly, and Hetty shivered as she entered it. All of a sudden a great feeling of weakness seemed to tremble through her slight frame; her heart fluttered too, seeming to bob up and down within her. Then it quieted down again, but the constant wearing pain grew worse and ached so perceptibly that she had to catch her breath now and then.

"I'll be all right when I can have a good dose," she thought. She went to the window, farthest from the one near which Vincent was lying, and drew down the blind; then going to the coal cellar she brought out some firewood and large knobs of coal. She fed the range and the fire soon crackled and roared. Hetty stood close to it, and warmed her hands by the blaze.

"What a noise it do make," she said to herself. "It ought to wake him; it would if he worn't sleepin' so sound from that lovely black stuff. Well, he can keep on for a bit longer, for he were dead tired, poor man. I'll get his supper afore I wake 'im."

She went out to the scullery, turned on the tap and filled the kettle with fresh cold water. She set it on the stove to boil, and then taking a coarse white cloth from a drawer laid it on the centre table. She took out plates, knives and forks and glasses for two, put them in their places, laid a

dish of cold bacon opposite Vincent's plate, and
some bread and a large square of cheese opposite
her own. Having done this, she looked at the
sleeping man. He was certainly quiet; she could
not even hear him breathing. As a rule he was a
stertorous breather, and when first they were married Hetty could scarcely sleep with his snoring.

"He don't snore to-night—he's resting wonderful," she said to herself. "Now, I just know what
I'll do—he mayn't care when he wakes for nothing
but cold stuff—I'll boil some fresh eggs for his supper, and I'll make some cocoa. I'll have a nice jug
of milk cocoa and a plate of eggs all ready by the
time he wakes."

She fetched a saucepan, some milk, and half-a-
dozen new-laid eggs. Soon the cocoa was made
and poured into a big jug, the eggs just done to a
turn were put upon a plate; they were brown eggs,
something the color of a deep nut.

"I could fancy one myself," thought Hetty; "I
ain't eat nothing to speak of for hours. Oh, I do
wish the pain in my side 'ud get better."

She pressed her hand to the region of her heart
and looked around her. The farm kitchen was
now the picture of comfort—the fire blazed merrily.
Hetty had lit a large paraffin lamp and placed it in
the centre of the table; it lit up the cosy room, even
the beams and rafters glistened in the strong light;
shadows from the fire leaped up and reflected themselves on the sleeper's face.

"He's very white and very still," thought Hetty;

"maybe he has slept long enough. I think I'll wake him now, for supper's ready."

Then came a scratching at the window outside, and the fretful howl of a dog.

"There's Rover; what's the matter with him? I wish he wouldn't howl like that," thought the wife. "I hate dogs that howl. Maybe I had best let 'im in."

She ran to the kitchen door, flew down the passage, and opened the door which led into the yard.

"Rover, stop that noise and come along in," she called.

The great dog shuffled up to her and thrust his head into her hand. She brought him into the kitchen. The moment she did so he sat down on his haunches, threw up his head, and began to howl again.

"Nonsense, Rover, stop that noise," she said. She struck him a blow on his forehead, he cowered, looked at her sorrowfully, and then tried to lick her hand. She brought him to the fire; he came unwillingly, slinking down at last with his back to the still figure on the settle.

"Queer, what's the matter with him?" thought Hetty. "They say, folks do, that dogs see things we don't; some folks say they see sperrits. Aunt would be in a fuss if Rover went on like that. Dear, I am turning nervous; fancy minding the howl of a dog. It's true my nerves ain't what they wor. Well, cocoa will spoil, and eggs will spoil, and time has come for me to wake Vincent. What a laugh we'll have together when I tell 'im of his long sleep."

She approached the sofa now, but her steps dragged themselves as she went up to it and bent down over her husband and called his name.

"George!" she said. "George!" He never moved. She went a little nearer, calling him louder.

"George, George, wake up!" she said. "Wake, George, you've slept for over four hours. Supper is ready, George—cocoa and eggs, your favorite supper. Wake! George, wake!"

The dog howled by the fire.

"Rover, I'll turn you out if you make that noise again," said Hetty. She went on her knees now by the sleeping man, and shook him. His head moved when she did so and she thought he was about to open his eyes, but when she took her hands away there was not a motion, not a sound.

"What is it?" she said to herself. For the first time a very perceptible fear crept into her heart. She bent low and listened for the breathing.

"He do breathe gentle," she murmured. "I can scarcely hear; do I hear at all. I think I'll fetch a candle."

In shaking the farmer she had managed to dislodge one of his hands, which had fallen forward over the edge of the settle. She took it up, then she let it fall with a slight scream; it was cold, icy cold!

"Good God! Oh, God in heaven! what is it?" muttered the wife.

'The real significance of the thing had not yet flashed upon her bewildered brain, but a sick fear was creeping over her. She went for the candle, and bringing it back, held it close to the ashen face. It was not only white, it was gray. The lips were faintly open, but not a breath proceeded from them. The figure was already stiff in the icy embrace of death.

Hetty had seen death before; its aspect was too unmistakable for her not to recognize it again. She fell suddenly forward, putting out the candle as she did so. Her face, almost as white as the face of the dead man, was pressed against his breast. For a brief few moments she was unconscious.

CHAPTER XXIII.

THE twilight darkened into night, but Awdrey still remained in the office. After a time he groped for a box of matches, found one, struck a match, took a pair of heavy silver candlesticks from a cupboard in the wall, lit the candles which were in them, and then put them on his office table. The room was a large one, and the light of the two candles seemed only to make the darkness visible. Awdrey went to the table, seated himself in the old chair which his father and his grandfather had occupied before him, and began mechanically to arrange some papers, and put a pile of other things in order. His nature was naturally full of system; from his childhood up he had hated untidiness of all sorts. While he was so engaged there came a knock at the office door. He rose, went across the room, and opened it; a footman stood without.

"Mrs. Awdrey has sent me to ask you, sir, if you are ready for dinner."

"Tell your mistress that I am not coming in to dinner," replied Awdrey. "Ask her not to wait for me; I am particularly busy, and will have something later."

The man, with an immovable countenance, turned

away. Awdrey once more locked the office door. He now drew down the remaining blinds to the other two windows, and began to pace up and down the long room. The powers of good and evil were at this moment fighting for his soul—he knew it; there was a tremendous conflict raging within him; it seemed to tear his life in two; beads of perspiration stood on his brow. He knew that either the God who made him or the devil would have won the victory before he left that room.

"I must make my decision once for all," he said to himself. "I am wide awake; my whole intellectual nature is full of vigor; I have no excuse whatever; the matter must be finally settled now. If I follow the devil——" he shrank as the words formed themselves out of his brain; he had naturally the utmost loathing for evil in any form, his nature was meant to be upright; at school he had been one of the good boys; one of the boys to whom low vices, dishonorable actions of any kind, were simply impossible; he had had his weaknesses, for who has not?—but these weaknesses were all more or less akin to the virtues.

"If I choose the devil!" he repeated. Once again he faltered, trembling violently; he had come to the part of the room where his father's old desk was situated, he leaned up against it and gazed gloomily out into the darkness which confronted him.

"I know exactly what will happen if I follow the downward path," he said again. "I must force myself to think wrong right, and right wrong. There is no possible way for me to live this life of deception except by deceiving myself. Must I decide to-night?"

He staggered into the chair which his father used to occupy. His father had been a man full of rectitude; the doom of the house had never overtaken him; he had been a man with an almost too severe and lofty code of honor. Awdrey remembered all about his father as he sat in that chair. He sprang again to his feet.

"There is no use in putting off the hour, for the hour has come," he thought. "This is the state of the case. God and the devil are with me to-night. I cannot lie in the presence of such awful, such potent Forces. I must face the thing as it is. This is what has happened to me. I, who would not willingly in my sober senses, hurt the smallest insect that crawls on the earth, once, nearly six years ago, in a sudden moment of passion killed a man. He attacked me, and I defended myself. I killed him in self-defence. I no more meant to kill him than I mean to commit murder to-night. Notwithstanding that fact I did it. Doubtless the action came over me as a tremendous shock—immediately after the deed the doom of my house fell on me, and I forgot all about what I myself had done—for five years the memory of it never returned to me. Now I know all about it. At the present moment another man is suffering in my stead. Now if I follow the devil I shall be a brute and a scoundrel;

the other man will go on suffering, and his mother, whose heart is already broken, may die before he recovers his liberty. Thus I shall practically kill two lives. No one will know—no one will guess that I am leading a shadowed life. I feel strong enough now to cover up the deed, to hide away the remorse. I feel not the least doubt that I shall be outwardly successful—the respect of my fellow-men will follow me—the love of many will be given to me. By and by I may have children, and they will love me as I loved my father, and Margaret will look up to me and consult me as my mother looked up to and consulted my father, and my honor will be considered above reproach. My people too will rejoice to have me back with them. I can serve them if I am returned for this constituency—in short, I can live a worthy and respected life. The devil will have his way, but no one will guess that it is the devil's way—I shall seem to live the life of an angel."

Awdrey paused here in his own thought.

"I feel as if the devil were laughing at me," he said, speaking half aloud, and looking again into the darkness of the room—"he knows that his hour will come—by and by my span of life will run out —eventually I shall reach the long end of the long way. But until that time, day by day, and hour by hour, I shall live the life of the hypocrite. Like a whited sepulchre shall I be truly, for I shall carry hell here. By and by I shall have to answer for all at a Higher Tribunal, and meanwhile I shall carry hell here." He pressed his hand to his breast—his face was ghastly. "Shall I follow the devil? Suppose I do not, what then?"

There came another tap at the office door. Awdrey went across the room and opened it. He started and uttered a smothered oath, for Margaret stood on the threshold.

"Go away now, Maggie, I can't see you; I am very much engaged," he said.

Instead of obeying him she stepped across the threshold.

"But you have no one with you," she said, looking into the darkness of the room. "What are you doing, Robert, all by yourself? You look very white and tired. We have finished dinner—my uncle has come over from Cuthbertstown, and would like to see you—they all think it strange your being away. What is the matter? Won't you return with me to the house?"

"I cannot yet. I am particularly engaged."

"But what about? Uncle James will be much disappointed if he does not see you."

"I'll come to him presently when I have thought out a problem."

Margaret turned herself now in such a position that she could see her husband's face. Something in his eyes seemed to speak straight to her sympathies,—she put her arms round his neck.

"Don't think any more now, my darling," she said. "Remember, though you are so well, that you were once very ill. You have had no dinner,

it is not right for you to starve yourself and tire
yourself. Come home with me, Robert, come
home!"

"Not yet," he replied. "There is a knot which
I must untie. I am thinking a very grave problem
out. I shall have no rest, no peace, until I have
made up my mind."

"What can be the matter?" inquired Margaret.
"Can I help you in any way?"

"No, my dearest," he answered very tenderly,
"except by leaving me."

"Is it anything to do with accounts?" she asked.
She glanced at the table with its pile of letters and
papers. "If so, I could really render you assistance; I used to keep accounts for Uncle James in
the old days. Two brains are better than one.
Let me help you."

"It is a mental problem, Maggie; it relates to
morals."

"Oh, dear me, Robert, you are quite mysterious,"
she said with a ghost of a smile; but then she met
his eyes and the trouble in them startled her.

"I wish I could help you," she said. "Do let
me."

"You cannot," he replied harshly, for the look
in her face added to his tortures. "I shall come
to a conclusion presently. When I come to it I
will return to the house."

"Then we are not to wait up for you? It is getting quite late, long past nine o'clock."

"Do not wait up for me; leave the side door on

the latch; I'll come in presently when I have made up my mind on this important matter."

She approached the door unwillingly; when she reached the threshold she turned and faced him.

"I cannot but see that you are worried about something," she said. "I know, Robert, that you will have strength to do what is right. I cannot imagine what your worry can be, but a moral problem with you must mean the victory of right over wrong."

"Maggie, you drive me mad," he called after her, but his voice was hoarse, and it did not reach her ears. She closed the door, and he heard her retreating footsteps on the gravel outside. He locked the door once more.

"There spoke God and my good angel," he murmured to himself. "Help me, Powers of Evil, if I am to follow you; give me strength to walk the path of the lowest."

These words had scarcely risen in the form of an awful prayer when once again he heard his wife's voice at the door. She was tapping and calling to him at the same time. He opened the door.

"Well?" he said.

"I am sorry to disturb you," she replied, "but you really must put off all your reflections for the time being. Who do you think has just arrived?"

"Who?" he asked in a listless voice.

"Your old friend and mine, Dr. Rumsey."

"Rumsey!" replied Awdrey, "he would be a strong advocate on your side, Maggie."

" On my side ? " she queried.

" I cannot explain myself. I think I'll see Rum-sey. It would be possible for me to put a question to him which I could not put to you—ask him to come to me."

" He shall come at once," she answered, " I am heartily glad that he is here."

So he turned back and went to the house—she ran up the front steps—Rumsey was in the hall.

" My hearty congratulations," he said, coming up to her. " Your letter contained such good news that I could not forbear hurrying down to Grand-court to take a peep at my strange patient; I always call Awdrey my strange patient. Is it true that he is now quite well ? "

" Half an hour ago I should have said yes," replied Margaret; " but——"

" Any recurrence of the old symptoms ? " asked the doctor.

" No, nothing of that sort. Perhaps the excitement has been too much for him. Come into the library, will you ? "

She entered as she spoke, the doctor following her.

" I wrote to you when I was abroad," continued Margaret, " telling you the simple fact that my husband's state of health had gone from better to better. He recovered tone of mind and body in the most rapid degree. This morning I considered him a man of perfect physical health and of keen brilliant intellect. You know during the five years when the cloud was over his brain he refused to read, and lost grip of all passing events. There is no subject now of general interest that he cannot talk about—all matters of public concern arouse his keenest sympathies. To-day he has been nominated to stand for his constituency, vacant by he death of our late member. I have no doubt that he will represent us in the House when Parliament next sits."

"Or perhaps before this one rises," said the doctor. "Well, Mrs. Awdrey, all this sounds most encouraging, but your 'but' leads to something not so satisfactory, does it not?"

"That is so; at the present moment I do not like his state. He was out and about all day, but instead of returning home to dinner went straight to his office, where he now is. As far as I can see, he is doing no special work, but he will not come into the house. He tells me that he is facing a problem which he also says is a moral one. He refuses to leave the office until he has come to a satisfactory conclusion."

"Come, he is overdoing it," said the doctor.

"I think so. I told him just now that you had arrived; he asked me to bring you to him; will you come?"

"With pleasure."

"Can you do without a meal until you have seen him?"

"Certainly; take me to him at once."

Mrs. Awdrey left the house, and took Dr. Rumsey round by the side walk which led to the office. The door was now slightly ajar; Margaret entered the doctor following behind her.

"Well, my friend," said Dr. Rumsey, in his cheerful voice, "it is good to see you back in your old place again. Your wife's letter was so satisfactory that I could not resist the temptation of coming to see you for myself."

"I am in perfect health," replied Awdrey. "Sit down, won't you, Rumsey? Margaret, my dear, do you mind leaving us?"

"No, Robert," she answered. "I trust to Dr. Rumsey to bring you back to your senses."

"She does not know what she is saying," muttered Awdrey. He followed his wife to the door, and when she went out turned the key in the lock.

"It is a strange thing," he said, the moment he found himself alone with his guest, "that you, Rumsey, should be here at this moment. You were with me during the hour of my keenest and most terrible physical and mental degradation; you have now come to see me through the hour of my moral degradation—or victory."

"Your moral degradation or victory?" said the doctor; "what does this mean?"

"It simply means this, Dr. Rumsey; I am the unhappy possessor of a secret."

"Ah!"

"Yes—a secret. Were this secret known my wife's heart would be broken, and this honorable

house of which I am the last descendant would go
to complete shipwreck. I don't talk of myself in
the matter."

"Do you mean to confide in me?" asked the
doctor, after a pause.

"I cannot; for the simple reason, that if I told
you everything you would be bound as a man and
a gentleman to take steps to insure the downfall
which I dread."

"Are you certain that you are not suffering from
delusion?"

"No, doctor, I wish I were."

"You certainly look sane enough," said the doctor, examining his patient with one of his penetrating glances. "You must allow me to congratu-
late you. If I had not seen you with my own eyes
I could never have believed in such a reformation.
You are bronzed; your frame has widened; you
have not a scrap of superfluous flesh about you.
Let me feel your arm; my dear sir, your muscle is
to be envied."

"I was famed for my athletic power long ago,"
said Awdrey, with a grim smile. "But now,
doctor, to facts. You have come here; it is
possible for me to take you into my confidence to
a certain extent. Will you allow me to state my
case?"

"As you intend only to state it partially it
will be difficult for me to advise you," said the
doctor.

"Still, will you listen?"

"I'll listen."

"Well, the fact is this," said Awdrey, rising, "either God or the devil take possession of me to-night."

"Come, come," said Rumsey, "you are exaggerating the state of the case."

" I am not. I am going through the most desperate fight that ever assailed a man. I may get out on the side of good, but at the present moment I must state frankly that all my inclinations tend to getting out of this struggle on the side which will put me into the Devil's hands."

"Come," said the doctor again, "if that is so there can be no doubt with regard to your position. You must close with right even though it is a struggle. You confess to possessing a secret; that secret is the cause of your misery; there is a right and a wrong to it?"

"Undoubtedly; a very great right and a very grave wrong."

"Then, Awdrey, do not hesitate; be man enough to do the right."

Awdrey turned white.

"You are the second person who has come here to-night and advised me on the side of God," he said.

"Out with your trouble, man, and relieve your mind."

"When I relieve my mind," said Awdrey, "my wife's heart will break, and our house will be ruined."

"What about you?"

"I shall go under."

"I doubt very much if your doing right would ever break a heart like your wife's," said Rumsey, "but doing wrong would undoubtedly crush her spirit."

"There you are again—will no one take the Devil's part? Dr. Rumsey, I firmly believe that it is much owing to your influence that I am now in my sane mind. I believe that it is owing to you that the doom of my house has been lifted from my brain. When I think of the path which you now advocate, I could curse the day when you brought me back to health and sanity. A very little influence on the other side, a mere letting me alone, and I should now either be a madman or in my grave; then I would have carried my secret to the bitter end. As it is——"

There was a noise heard outside—the sound made by a faltering footstep. The brush of a woman's dress was distinctly audible against the door; this was followed by a timid knock.

"Who is disturbing us now?" said Awdrey, with irritation.

"I'll open the door and see," said the doctor.

He crossed the room as he spoke and opened the door. An untidily dressed girl with a ghastly white face stood without. When the door was opened she peered anxiously into the room.

"Is Mr. Awdrey in?—yes, I see him. I must speak to him at once."

She staggered across the threshold.

"I must see you alone, Squire," she said—"quite alone and at once."

"This has to do with the matter under consideration," said the Squire. "Come in, Hetty; sit down. Rumsey, you had best leave us."

CHAPTER XXIV

A REAL faint, or suspension of the heart's action, is never a long affair. When Hetty fell in an unconscious state against the body of her dead husband she quickly recovered herself. Her intellect was keen enough, and she knew exactly what had happened. The nice black stuff which gave such pleasant dreams had killed Vincent. She had therefore killed him. Yes, he was stone dead—she had seen death once or twice before, and could not possibly mistake it. She had seen her mother die long ago, and had stood by the deathbed of more than one neighbor. The cold, the stiffness, the gray-white appearance, all told her beyond the possibilty of doubt that life was not only extinct, but had been extinct for at least a couple of hours. Her husband was dead. When she had given him that fatal dose he had been in the full vigor of youth and health—now he was dead. She had never loved him in life; although he had been an affectionate husband to her, but at this moment she shed a few tears for him. Not many, for they were completely swallowed up in the fear and terror which grew greater and greater each moment within her. He was dead, and she had killed him. Long ago she had concealed the knowledge of a murder because she loved the man who had committed it. Now she had committed murder herself—not intention· ally, no, no. No more had she intended to kill Vin- cent than Awdrey when he was out that night had intended to take the life of Horace Frere. But Frere was dead and now Vincent was dead, and Hetty would be tried for the crime. No, surely they could not try her—they could not possibly bring it home to her. How could a little thing like she was be supposed to take the life of a big man? She had never meant to injure him, too—she had only meant to give him a good sleep, to rest him thoroughly—to deceive him, of course—to do a thing which she knew if he were aware of would break his heart; but to take his life, no, nothing was further from her thoughts. Nevertheless the deed was done.

Oh, it was horrible, horrible—she hated being so close to the dead body. It was no longer Vincent, the man who would have protected her at the risk of his life, it was a hideous dead body. She would get away from it—she would creep up close to Rover. No wonder Rover hated the room; per- haps he saw the spirit of her husband. Oh, how frightened she was! What was the matter with her side?—why did her heart beat so strangely, gallop- ing one, two, three, then pausing, then one, two, three again?—and the pain, the sick, awful pain. Yes, she knew—she was sick to death with terror.

She got up presently from where she had been

kneeling by her dead husband's side and staggered across to the fireplace. She tried wildly to think, but she found herself incapable of reasoning. Shivering violently, she approached the table, poured out a cup of the cocoa which was still hot, and managed to drink it off. The warm liquid revived her, and she felt a shade better and more capable of thought. Her one instinct now was to save herself. Vincent was dead—no one in all the world could bring him back to life, but, if possible, Hetty would so act that not a soul in all the country should suspect her. How could she make things safe? If it were known, known everywhere, that she was away from him when he died, then of course she would be safe. Yes, this fact must be known. Once she had saved the Squire, now the Squire must save her. It must be known everywhere that she had sought an interview with him—that at the time when Vincent died she was in the Squire's presence, shut up in the office with him, the door locked—she and the Squire alone together. This secret, which she would have fought to the death to keep to herself an hour ago, must now be blazoned abroad to a criticising world. The lesser danger to the Squire must be completely swallowed up in the greater danger to herself. She must hurry to him at once and get him to tell what he knew. Ah, yes, if he did this she would be safe—she remembered the right word at last, for she had heard the neighbors speak of it when it a celebrated trial was going on in Salisbury—she must prove an alibi—then it would be known that she had been absent from home when her husband died.

The imminence of the danger made her at last feel quiet and steady. She took up the lighted candle and went into the dairy—she unlocked the cupboard in the wall and took out the bottle of laudanum. Returning to the kitchen she emptied the contents of the bottle into the range and then threw the bottle itself also into the heart of the fire —she watched it as it slowly melted under the influence of the hot fire—the laudanum itself was also licked up by the hungry flames. That tell-tale and awful evidence of her guilt was at least removed. She forgot all about Susan having seen the liquid in the morning—she knew nothing about the evidence which would be brought to light at a coroner's inquest—about the facts which a doctor would be sure to give. Nothing but the bare reality remained prominently before her excited brain. Vincent was dead—she had killed him by an overdose of laudanum which she had given him in all innocence to make him sleep—but yet, yet in her heart of hearts, she knew that her motive would not bear explanation.

"Squire will save me," she said to herself—"if it's proved that I were with Squire I am safe. I'll go to him now—I'll tell 'im all at once. It's late, very late, and it's dark outside, but I'll go."

Hetty left the room, leaving the dog behind her— he uttered a frightful howl when she did so and

followed her as far as the door—she shut and locked
the door—he scratched at it to try and release himself, but Hetty took no notice—she was cruel as regarded the dumb beast's fear in her own agony and
terror.

She ran upstairs to her room, put on her hat and
jacket, and went out. Stumbling and trembling,
she went along the road until she reached the summit of the hill which led straight down in a gentle
slope toward Grandcourt. She was glad the ground
sloped downward, for it was important that she
should quicken her footsteps in order to see the
Squire with as little delay as possible. She was
quite oblivious of the lapse of time since her last
visit, and hoped he might still be in the office. She
resolved to try the office first. If he were not there
she would go on to the house—find him she must;
nothing should keep her from his presence to-
night.

She presently reached Grandcourt, entered the
grounds by a side entrance and pursued her way
through the darkness. The sky overhead was
cloudy, neither moon nor stars were visible. Faltering and falling she pressed forward, and by and
by reached the neighborhood of the office. She
saw a light burning dimly behind the closed blinds
—her heart beat with a sense of thankfulness—she
staggered up to the door, brushing her dress against
the door as she did so—she put up her hand and
knocked feebly. The next instant the door was
opened to her—a man, a total stranger, confronted

her, but behind him she saw Awdrey. She tottered into the room.

The comparative light and warmth within, after the darkness and chilly damp of the spring evening, made her head reel, and her eyes at first could take in no object distinctly. She was conscious of uttering excited words, then she heard the door shut behind her. She looked round—she was alone with the Squire. She staggered up to him, and fell on her knees.

"You must save me as I saved you long ago," she panted.

"What is it? Get up. What do you mean?" said Awdrey.

"I mean, Squire—oh! I mean I wanted to come to you to-day, but Vincent,"—her voice faltered— "Vincent were mad wi' jealousy. He thought that I ought not to see you, Squire; he had got summat in his brain, and it made him mad. He thought that, perhaps, long ago, Squire, I loved you—long ago. I'm not afeared to say anything to-night, the truth will out to-night—I loved you long ago, I love you still; yes, yes, with all my heart, with all my heart. You never cared nothin' for me, I know that well. You never did me a wrong in thought or in deed, I know that well also; but to me you were as a god, and I loved you, I love you still, and Vincent, my husband, he must have seen it in my face; but you did me no wrong—never, in word or in deed—only loved you—and I love you still."

"You must be mad, girl," said Awdrey. "Why

have you come here to tell me that? Get up at
once; your words and your actions distress me
much. Get up, Hetty; try to compose yourself."

"What I have come to say had best be said kneeling," replied Hetty; "it eases the awful pain in
my side to kneel. Let me be, Squire; let me
kneel up against your father's desk. Ah! that's
better. It is my heart—I think it's broke; anyhow,
it beats awful, and the pain is awful."

"If you have come for any other reason than to
say the words you have just said, say them and go,"
replied Awdrey.

Hetty glanced up at him. His face was hard,
she thought it looked cruel, she shivered from head
to foot. Was it for this man she had sacrificed her
life? Then the awful significance of her errand
came over her, and she proceeded to speak.

"Vincent saw the truth in my face," she continued. "Anyhow, he was mad wi' jealousy, and
he said that I worn't to come and see yer. He
heard me speak to yer last night, he heard me say
it's a matter o' life and death and he wor mad. He
said I worn't to come; but I wor mad too, mad to
come, and I thought I'd get over him by guile. I
put summat in his stout, and he drank it—summat,
I don't know the name, but I had took it myself
and it always made me a sight better, and I gave
it to 'im in his stout and he drank it, and then he
slept. He lay down on the settle in the kitchen,
and he went off into a dead sleep. When he slept
real sound I stole away and I come to you. I saw

you this evening and you spoke to me and I spoke
to you, and I begged of you to keep our secret, and
I thought perhaps you would, and I come away
feelin' better. I went back 'ome, and the place
were quiet, and I got into the kitchen. Vincent
was lying on the settle sound asleep. I thought
nought o' his sleepin', only to be glad, for I knew
he'd never have missed me. I made his supper for
him, and built up the fire, and I lit the lamps in
the house, and I took off my outdoor things. The
dog howled, but I didn't take no notice. Presently
I went up to Vincent, and I shook 'im—I shook 'im
'ard, but he didn't wake. I took his hand in mine,
it wor cold as ice; I listened for his breath, there
wor none. Squire," said Hetty, rising now to her
feet, "my man wor dead; Squire, I have killed 'im,
just the same as you killed the man on Salisbury
Plain six years ago. My husband is dead, and I
have killed him. Squire, you must save me as I
saved you."

"How?" asked Awdrey. His voice had completely altered now. In the presence of the real
tragedy all the hardness had left it. He sank into
a chair near Hetty's side, he even took one of her
trembling hands in his.

"How am I to help you, you poor soul?" he said
again.

"You must prove an alibi—that's the word. You
must say 'Hetty wor wi' me, she couldn't have
killed her man,' you must say that; you must tell
all the world that you and me was together here,"

"I'll do better than that," said Awdrey suddenly.

"What do you mean?" Hetty started back and gazed at him with a queer mixture of hope and terror in her face. "Better—but there ain't no better," she cried. "Ef you don't tell the simple truth I'll be hanged; hanged by the neck until I die—I, who saved you at the risk of my own soul nearly six years gone."

"I'll not let you be hanged," said Awdrey, rising. "Get up, Hetty; do not kneel to me. You don't quite know what you have done for me to-night. Sit on that chair—compose yourself—try to be calm. Hetty, you just came in the nick of time. God and the devil were fighting for my soul. In spite of all the devil's efforts God was getting the better of it, and I—I didn't want him to get the best. I wanted the devil to help me, and, Hetty, I even prayed to him that he might come and help me. When I saw you coming into the room I thought at first that my prayer was answered. I seemed to see the devil on your face. Now I see differently—your presence has lifted a great cloud from before my mind—I see distinctly, almost as distinctly as if I were in hell itself, the awful consequences which must arise-from wrong-doing. Hetty, I have made up my mind; you, of all people, have been the most powerful advocate on the side of God to-night. We will both do the right, child—we will confess the simple truth."

"No, Squire, no; they'll kill me, they'll kill me, if you don't help me in the only way you can help me—you are stronger than me, Squire—don't lead me to my death."

"They won't kill you, but you must tell the whole truth as I will tell the truth. It can be proved that you gave the poison to your husband with no intent to kill—that matter can be arranged promptly. Come with me, Hetty, now—let us come together. If you falter I'll strengthen you; if I falter you'll strengthen me. We will go together at once and tell—tell what you saw and what I did nearly six years ago."

"What you did on Salisbury Plain?" she asked.

"Yes, the time I killed that man."

"Never, never," she answered; she fell flat on her face on the floor.

Awdrey went to her and tried to raise her up.

"Come," he said, "I have looked into the very heart of evil, and I cannot go on with it—whatever the consequence we must both tell the truth—and we will do it together; come at once."

"You don't know what will happen to you," said Hetty. She shivered as she lay prone before him.

"No matter—nothing could happen so bad as shutting away the face of God. I'll tell all, and you must tell all. No more lies for either of us. We will save our souls even if our bodies die."

"The pain—the pain in my side," moaned Hetty.

"It will be better after we have gone through what is before us. Come, I'll take your hand."

She gave it timidly; the Squire's fingers closed over it.

"Where are we to go?" she asked. "Where are you taking me?"

"Come with me. I'll speak. Presently it will be your turn—after they know all, all the worst, it will be your turn to speak."

"Who are to know all, Squire?"

"My wife, my sisters, Mrs. Everett, my friends."

"Oh, God, God, why was I ever born!" moaned Hetty.

"You'll feel better afterward," said Awdrey. "Try and remember that in the awful struggle and ordeal of the next few minutes your soul and mine will be born again—they will be saved—saved from the power of evil. Be brave, Hetty. You told me to-night that you loved me—prove the greatness of your love by helping me to save my own soul and yours."

"I wonder if this is true," said Hetty. "You seem to lift me out of myself." She spoke in a sort of dull wonder.

"It is true—it is right—it is the only thing; come at once."

She did not say any more, nor make the least resistance. They left the office together. They trod softly on the gravel path which led to the main entrance of the old house. They both entered the hall side by side. Hetty looked pale and untidy; her hair fell partly down her back; there were undried tears on her cheeks; her eyes had a wild and startled gleam in them; the Squire was also deadly pale, but he was quiet and composed. The fierce struggle which had nearly rent his soul in two was completely over at that moment. In the calm there was also peace, and the peace had settled on his face.

Mrs. Henessey was standing in the wide entrance hall. She started when she saw her brother; then she glanced at Hetty, then she looked again at the Squire.

"Why, Robert!" she said, "Robert!"

There was an expression about Hetty's face and about Awdrey's face which silenced and frightened her.

"What is it?" she said in a low voice, "what is wrong?"

"Where are the others?" asked the Squire. "I want to see them all immediately."

"They are in the front drawing-room—Margaret, Dr. Rumsey, Dorothy, my husband and Dorothy's, and Margaret's uncle, Mr. Cuthbert."

"I am glad he is there; we shall want a magistrate," said Awdrey.

"A magistrate! What is the matter?"

"You will know in a moment, Anne. Did you say Rumsey was in the drawing-room?"

"Yes; they are all there. Margaret is playing the "Moonlight Sonata"—you hear it, don't you through the closed doors—she played so mournfully that I ran away—I hate music that affects me to tears."

Awdrey bent down and said a word to Hetty; then he looked at his sister.

"I am going into the drawing-room, and Hetty Vincent will come with me," he said.

"I used to know you as Hetty Armitage," said Anne. "How are you, Hetty?"

"She is not well," answered Awdrey for her, "but she will tell you presently. Come into the drawing-room, too, Anne; I should like you to be present."

"I cannot understand this," said Anne. She ran on first and opened the great folding-doors—she entered the big room, her face ablaze with excitement and wonder—behind her came Awdrey holding Hetty's hand. There was an expression on the Squire's face which arrested the attention of every one present. Mr. Cuthbert, who had not seen him since his return home, rose eagerly from the deep arm-chair into which he had sunk, intending to give him a hearty welcome, but when he had advanced in the Squire's direction a step or two, he paused —he seemed to see by a sort of intuition that the moment for ordinary civilities was not then. Margaret left her seat by the piano and came almost into the centre of the room. Her husband's eyes seemed to motion her back—her uncle went up to her and put his hand on her shoulder; he did not know what he expected, nor did Margaret, but each one in the room felt with an electric thrill of sympathy that a revelation of no ordinary nature was about to be made.

Still holding Hetty's hand, Awdrey came into the great space in front of the fireplace; he was about to speak when Rumsey came suddenly forward.

"One moment," he said. "This young woman is very ill; will some one fetch brandy?" He took Hetty's slight wrist between his finger and thumb, and felt the fluttering pulse.

Anne rushed away to get the brandy. The doctor mixed a small dose, and made Hetty swallow it. The stimulant brought back a faint color to her cheeks, and her eyes looked less dull and dazed.

"I have come into this room to-night with Hetty Vincent, who used to be Hetty Armitage, to make a very remarkable statement," said Awdrey.

Rumsey backed a few steps. He thought to himself: "We shall get now to the mystery. He has made up his mind on the side of the good—brave fellow! What can all this mean? What is the matter with that pretty girl? She looks as if she were dying. What can be the connection between them?"

"What can be the connection between them?" was also the thought running in the minds of every other spectator. Margaret shared it, as her uncle's hand rested a little heavier moment by moment on her slight shoulder. Squire Cuthbert was swearing heavily under his breath. The sisters and their husbands stood in the background, prepared for any "denouement"—all was quietness and expectancy. Mrs. Everett, who up to the present instant had taken no part in the extraordinary scene, hurried now to the front.

"Squire," she said, "I don't know what you are going to say, but I can guess. In advance, however, I thank you from my heart; a premonition seizes me that the moment of my son's release is at hand. You have got this young woman to reveal her secret?"

"Her secret is mine," said Awdrey.

Squire Cuthbert swore aloud.

"Just wait one moment before you say anything," said Awdrey, fixing his eyes on him. "The thing is not what you imagine. I can tell the truth in half-a-dozen words. Mrs. Everett, you are right— you see the man before you who killed Horace Frere on Salisbury Plain. Your son is innocent."

"My God! You did this?" said Mrs. Everett.

"Robert, what are you saying?" cried Margaret.

"Robert!" echoed Anne.

"Dear brother, you must be mad!" exclaimed Dorothy.

"No, I am sane—I am sure I was mad for a time, but now I am quite sane to-night. I killed Horace Frere on Salisbury Plain. Hetty Vincent saw the murder committed; she hid her knowledge for my sake. Immediately after I committed the deed the doom of my house fell upon me, and I forgot what I myself had done. For five years I had no memory of my own act. Rumsey, when I saw my face reflected in the pond, six months ago, the knowledge of the truth returned to me. I remembered what

I had done. I remembered, and I was not sorry, and I resolved to hide the truth to the death; my conscience, the thing which makes the difference between man and beast, never awoke within me—I was happy and I kept well. But yesterday—yesterday when I came home and saw my people and saw Hetty here, and noticed the look of suffering on your face, Mrs. Everett, the voice of God began to make itself heard. From that moment until now my soul and the powers of evil have been fighting against the powers of good. I was coward enough to think that I might hide the truth and suffer, and live the life of a hypocrite." The Squire's voice, which had been quite quiet and composed, faltered now for the first time. "It could not be done," he added. "I found I could not close with the devil."

At this moment a strange thing happened. Awdrey's wife rushed up to him, she flung her arms round his neck, and laid her head on his breast.

"Thank God!" she murmured. "Nothing matters, for you have saved your soul alive."

Awdrey pushed back his wife's hair, and kissed her on her forehead.

"But this is a most remarkable thing," said Mr. Cuthbert, finding his tongue, and coming forward. "You, Awdrey—you, my niece's husband, come quietly into this room and tell us with the utmost coolness that you are a murderer. I cannot believe it—you must be mad."

"No, I am perfectly sane. Hetty Vincent can

prove the truth of my words. I am a murderer, but not by intent. I never meant to kill Frere; nevertheless, I am a murderer, for I have taken a man's life."

"You tell me this?" said Squire Cuthbert. "You tell me that you have suffered another man to suffer in your stead for close on six years."

"Unknowingly, Squire Cuthbert. There was a blank over my memory."

"I can testify to that," said Rumsey, now coming forward. "The whole story is so astounding, so unprecedented, that I am not the least surprised at your all being unable to make a just estimate of the true circumstances at the present moment. Nevertheless, Awdrey tells the simple truth. I have watched him as my patient for years. I have given his case my greatest attention. I consider it one of the most curious psychological studies which has occurred in the whole of my wide experience. Awdrey killed Horace Frere, and forgot all about it. The deed was doubtless done in a moment of strong irritation."

"He was provoked to it," said Hetty, speaking for the first time.

"It will be necessary that you put all that down in writing," said Rumsey, giving her a quick glance. "Squire, I begin to see a ghost of daylight. It is possible that you may be saved from the serious consequences of your own act, if it can be proved before a jury that you committed the terrible deed as a means of self-protection."

"It was for that," said Hetty again. "I can tell exactly what I saw."

The excited people who were listening to this narrative now began to move about and talk eagerly and rapidly. Rumsey alone altogether kept his head. He saw how ill Hetty was, and how all-important her story would be if there was any chance of saving Awdrey. It must be put in writing without delay.

"Come and sit here," he said, taking the girl's hand and leading her to a chair. All the others shrank away from her, but Mrs. Everett, whose eyes were blazing with a curious combination of passionate anger and wild, exultant joy, came close up to her for a moment.

"Little hypocrite—little spy!" she hissed. Don't forget that you have committed perjury. Your sentence will be a severe one."

"Hush," said Rumsey, "is this a moment—?" A look in his eyes silenced the widow—she shrank away near one of the windows to relieve her overcharged feelings in a burst of tears.

"Sit here and tell me exactly what you saw," said Rumsey to Hetty. "Mr. Cuthbert, you are doubtless a magistrate?"

"Bless my stars, I don't know what I am at the present moment," said the worthy Squire, mopping his crimson brow.

"Try to retain your self-control—remember how much hangs on it. This young woman is very ill —it will be all important that we get her deposition before——" Rumsey paused; Hetty's eyes were fixed on his face, her lips moved faintly.

"You may save the Squire after all if you tell the simple truth," said Rumsey kindly, bending toward her and speaking in a low voice. "Try and tell the simple truth. I know you are feeling ill, but you will be better afterward. Will you tell me exactly what happened? I shall put it down in writing. You will then sign your own deposition."

"I'll tell the truth," said Hetty—"is it the case that if I tell just the truth I may save Squire?"

"It is his only chance. Now begin."

The others crowded round when Hetty began to speak; all but Mrs. Everett, who still sat in the window, her face buried in her handkerchief.

Hetty began her tale falteringly, often trembling and often pausing, but Rumsey managed to keep her to the point. By and by the whole queer story was taken down and was then formally signed and sworn to. Rumsey finally folded up the paper and gave it to Squire Cuthbert to keep.

"I have a strong hope that we may clear Awdrey," he said. "The case is a clear one of manslaughter which took place in self-defence. Mrs. Vincent's deposition is most important, for it not only shows that Awdrey committed the unfortunate deed under the strongest provocation, but explains exactly why Frere should have had such animosity to the Squire. Now, Mrs. Vincent, you have rendered a very valuable service, and as you are ill we cannot expect you to do anything further to-night."

Here Rumsey looked full at Margaret.

"I think this young woman far too unwell to leave the house," he said—"can you have a room prepared for her here?"

"Certainly," said Margaret; she went up to Hetty and laid one of her hands on her shoulder.

"Before Hetty leaves the room, there is something to be said on her own account," said the Squire.

He then related in a few words the tragedy which had taken place at the Gable Farm. While he was speaking, Hetty suddenly staggered to her feet and faced them.

"If what I have told to-night will really save you, Squire, then nothing else matters," she said; "I'm not afeared now, for ef I 'ave saved you at last, nothing matters,"—her face grew ghastly white, she tumbled in a heap to the floor.

The doctor, Margaret, and the Squire rushed to her assistance, but when they raised her up she was dead.

"Heart disease," said Rumsey, afterward, "accelerated by shock."

·   ·   ·   ·   ·   ·   ·

A few more words can finish this strange story. At the Squire's own request, Mr. Cuthbert took the necessary steps for his arrest, and Rumsey hurried to town to get the interference of the Home Secretary in the case of Everett, who was suffering for Awdrey's supposed crime in Portland prison. The doctor had a long interview with one of the officials at the Home Office, and disclosed all the queer circumstances of the case. Everett, according to the Queen's Prerogative, received in due course a free pardon for the crime he had never committed, and was restored to his mother and his friends once again.

Awdrey's trial took place almost immediately afterward at Salisbury. The trial was never forgotten in that part of the country, and was the one topic of conversation for several days in the length and breadth of England. So remarkable and strange a case had never before been propounded for the benefit of the jury, but it was evident that the very learned Judge who conducted the trial was from the first on the side of the prisoner.

Hetty's all-important deposition made a great sensation; her evidence was corroborated by Mrs. Armitage, and when Rumsey appeared as a witness he abundantly proved that Awdrey had completely forgotten the deed of which he had been guilty. His thrilling description of his patient's strange case was listened to with breathless attention by a crowded court. The trial lasted for two days, during which the anxiety of all Awdrey's friends can be better imagined than described. At the end of the trial, the jury returned a verdict of "Not Guilty." In short, his strange case had been abundantly proved: he had done what he did without intent to kill and simply as a means of self-defence.

On the evening of his return to Grandcourt, he

and Margaret stood in the porch together side by side. It was a moonlight night, and the whole beautiful place was brightly illuminated.

"Robert," said the wife, "you have lived through it all—you will now take a fresh lease of life."

He shook his head.

"It is true that I have gone through the fire and been saved," he said, "but there is a shadow over me—I can never be the man I might have been."

"You can be a thousand times better," she replied with flashing eyes, "for you have learned now the bitter and awful lesson of how a man may fall, rise again, and in the end conquer."

THE END.

www.ingramcontent.com/pod-product-compliance
Lightning Source LLC
Chambersburg PA
CBHW031937130726
47905CB00008BA/2506